MW01515718

Hold on Tight

ANJELICA GRACE

Never give up on your dreams!

♡ Anjelica Grace

Copyright © 2019 Anjelica Grace

All Rights Reserved

In accordance with the U.S. Copyright Act of 1976, the scanning, uploading, and electronic sharing of any part of this work without permission of the author is unlawful piracy and theft of the author's intellectual property.

This story or any portion thereof may not be reproduced or used in any manner whatsoever without the

expressed written permission of the author except for brief quotations used in a book review.

This short story is a work of fiction. The names, characters, places, and incidents are products of the writer's

imagination or have been used fictitiously and are not to be construed as real. Any resemblance to actual persons, living or dead, events, locales, or organizations is entirely coincidental.

The use of actors, artists, movies, TV shows, and song titles/lyrics throughout this book are done so for Storytelling purposes and should in no way be seen as advertisement. Trademark names are used in an editorial fashion with no intention of infringement of the respective owner's trademark.

This short story is intended for adults only. Contains sexual content and language that may offend some. Suggested reading audience is 18 years or older

This book is dedicated to anyone who has ever had a dream of accomplishing more. If I can do it, so can you.

To my parents: Mom, Dad, and Brian, if it weren't for the support, encouragement, and love you have always given me, I never would've followed through and made my own dreams come true. You three have made all of this, and everything I do in life, possible, and there will never be enough words to share my gratitude and love for you.

And to my best friends: Sami and Em, I'd be a lost person in this world if it weren't for you two. And I most definitely wouldn't be where I am now. Thank you for accepting and loving crazy me, for me. And for supporting me, and my dreams, even when I've felt like giving up on them.

"Whatever the mind of man can conceive and believe, it can achieve." - Napoleon Hill

One

Chase

The ground comes hard and fast as my body meets it with a bone-rattling thud. A cloud of dust flies up, and the vibration of the steps from our 1,700-pound bull, Thunder, shakes around me. Some of our ranch hands jump in front of me, ushering Thunder away, while I pick myself up and dust myself off, removing my hat and swiping away the streak of sweat lining my forehead.

I've been home for twenty-four hours, I'm leaving again in twelve, and I need to keep busting ass so I'm ready to ride this weekend. Thunder is our best bull here on the ranch, which makes him my best to practice on so I finish on top in Arizona.

"You good, Boss?" Kip, one of my hands, asks. He's a good kid. He's taken on a lot of responsibilities here since we hired him. He helps Allie keep everything running smoothly with the ranch while I'm on the road.

"I'm good. Thanks." He gives me a short nod and walks back toward the fence, jawing with a couple of the other guys, each of them laughing and joking around, until my Pipsqueak comes out, climbing her way onto the fence. Her presence effectively ends the guys' joking around, but each man on the fence and beside it says hello and starts to talk to her instead.

"What are you doing out here, Ava?" I ask, and approach the fence, using the first rail to press up to her height since she's sitting on it, and kiss her cheek.

"Can I ride with you today?" Her wide, chocolate brown eyes, that remind me so much of her mother's, light up when the words come out.

"I don't know if I'll have time today, I have to get a few more practice rides in, then do my chores, and go over work stuff before I leave again tomorrow."

"Oh," she says, her eyes dropping down to her belly, "okay. Maybe next time you come home."

I look around to each of the men who work for us, then back to my little girl. "Maybe..." I pause, trying to find a solution so I don't disappoint my little girl, "Maybe you can help me with some of my chores in the barn later, so I have a little more time to ride with you today?"

She looks up with the biggest grin I've ever seen and nods her head rapidly. I hook an arm around her small body, making sure she doesn't fall from the rail, and smile back. "So that's a yes, then?"

"Yes!" she shouts.

"I need to finish a couple more practice rides first. Are you going to stay out here or go back in with your mom and sister?"

"Can I stay?"

I take in a deep breath and nod once. "But you need to be off the fence while I'm riding. Stay a few feet back, right? I can't risk you getting hurt."

"'Kay, I'll get down. I promise."

She is still the most precocious child I have ever met. It only gets more obvious with each year she adds to her life. She's seen what can happen in here when a rider falls

2

or a bull or bronc get out of hand, she understands the dangers, and refuses to break the rules we've set forth for her and her baby sister.

"I'll keep an eye on her," Kip says, swinging the gate open.

"I appreciate that. She's the most precious cargo there is."

"Yes, sir. She'll be safe while you focus on riding."

I know she will. I know I can count on him, and every other man out here, to keep my girls safe while I'm riding, here and abroad.

I kiss Ava's rosy cheek and drop back down to the ground. "Bring out Loki, next. I don't want to overdo it with Thunder."

A few of the guys jog out of the practice pen and go to get Loki ready, while Kip and a few other hands lead Thunder through the chutes and back to the holding pen.

"Loki is my favorite," Ava chirps out.

"Is that so?"

"It is. He's silly and so fast." She looks to make sure the chute gate is shut then hops off the fence and walks over to me, her little boots kicking up dust with each step. "Nobody can ride him."

I squat down to her level, tugging on one of the braids hanging over her shoulder, and grin. "I can ride him, Pip. You'll see."

She throws her arms around my neck and gives me a big hug, whispering, "Duh. You're the best."

Wrapping her tight, I hug her back. "Thank you."

Two and a half years ago, when I failed to defend my title, Allie swore she and the girls would support me—no matter what—until I got the title back. And they have. Ava most of all. She's taken such an interest in riding—our horses, not our bulls—and helping out around the ranch. She watches video with me. She knows all our bulls, and all the best bulls on the circuit. She's become my little coach and cheerleader. Her mom and sister have supported me, too. But they've also been more vocal about me being gone lately.

"Welcome."

She pulls back and looks up when Loki thunders his way into the chute, riled up and wild already. He's thrashing against the chute, snorting and grunting. He's one of our younger bulls, and big. He isn't quite the size Thunder is, though. But Ava had it right when she said he's fast. And he is silly, at least in the eyes of a nine-year-old. He will buck and turn on a dime. He's wild. He's good.

He's dangerous. I know she was also right when she said nobody has ridden him, yet. Many of the guys have tried, and they've sent me video of their attempts. Rather, other guys have sent me video of their pals getting their asses thrown off.

"See, he's silly." Ava gives me one last quick hug then walks out behind the fence, as she's supposed to do when a bull is near, and climbs up onto a stack of hay bales so she can watch over the seven-foot fence around the pen.

Before I get ready to climb into the chute and mount Loki, I glance toward the house, spotting Allie on the porch looking at Ava.

"You stay right there, Pipsqueak," I call over to her, loud enough that Allie knows I'm watching over Ava, even while I train, "don't run off, okay?"

"I won't!"

Allie must've heard that, too, because when I look back to the house again, she's disappeared and the screen door is swinging shut.

I let out a steady breath, putting thoughts of Allie, the girls, and the house behind me and focus on Loki, on getting positioned over him, on the ride at hand.

Training should always be taken as seriously as competition, otherwise mistakes will be made.

Allie

I'm glad he's spending time with one of our girls while he's home, but we have another who looks like she's about to cry from where she's slumped down onto the couch.

"What's wrong, Aubrey Jane?" I ask, walking over to sit beside her.

"I want to be with Daddy." She crosses her arms over her chest and her bottom lip pouts out as tears well in her eyes. "And Ava won't play with me."

"Why won't Ava play with you?" I guide her hair behind her ear.

"She wants to watch Daddy. And ride her horse." Her bottom lip sticks out farther and she kicks her legs forward, letting them land back against the couch with tiny thuds.

"You don't want to watch, too?"

Aubrey shakes her head and whispers, "They scare me."

Where one of our daughters is fearless, just like her father, the other is more cautious and knows exactly what she is, and isn't, comfortable with.

"They are pretty big, and scary, but Daddy can handle them; he's really good at riding bulls. And he would never, ever let one touch you or Ava."

She looks up at me with her big blue eyes, made even bluer from the tears forming. She's not a big fan of our livestock, thanks to a little accident she saw last year. Chase was gone, and one of our guys got bucked pretty hard and got hurt. It wasn't terrible. Chase takes that kind of abuse riding professionally very regularly, but to a five-year-old, it was terrifying. Ever since then, she's been afraid of them. The bulls, the broncs, everything that isn't one of our family horses.

"Promise?" Her voice is so small, timid.

"I promise. Your daddy will protect you forever. So will I." I wipe the tears from her eyes, and kiss her forehead. "What do you say I go out and watch him with you and Ava? Then maybe we can all go for a ride on our horses together?"

Aubrey gives it thought, and nods her head up and down slowly, then hops off the couch to go put her boots on and grab her doll. Once she's ready, we go out together, crossing the distance between the pen Chase is practicing in and our front door.

When we reach Ava seated up on the bales, I help Aubrey climb up beside her. I'm about to go take my spot on the fence, where I've always stood to watch him, when Aubrey reaches out for my arm and shakes her head.

"Okay, I'll sit with you two."

I climb up beside our girls, pulling Aubrey into my lap, watching Chase try to mount Loki.

"Has he ridden him yet, Ava?"

She shakes her head no and giggles. "Loki's being so silly, he won't let Daddy get on him."

Hold on Tight

Of course he won't. This is probably the one bull we have I shouldn't have brought Aubrey out to watch. Loki is the one our guy was riding when he got hurt, and that's not lost on Aubrey. She looks up at me, clutching her doll tight.

"Daddy is going to be okay," I say, as smoothly and reassuringly as I can.

Chase curses from the chutes and then looks our way—to see if Ava heard, I'm sure—and finds us here, too.

A wide grin fills his face and he hops down after saying something to Kip and the guys, ambling over to us.

"If it isn't my three girls," he says easily, bracing his arms on the bales of hay we're perched on. "What are you two doing out here?"

"Aubrey wanted to see you, but she was afraid to come alone, ya know because of—" I drop off, nodding my head toward Loki.

"Ah," he reaches for her boot-covered toe and gives a little squeeze. "Does Loki scare you, Monkey?"

Aubrey nods her head, but stays quiet otherwise.

"He's not going to hurt you, I promise. I will never let anything hurt you, or Ava." Chase glances up at me briefly before looking back to Aubrey in my lap. "You, Ava, and Mommy will always be safe. And Loki is just having fun. He's silly. Right, Pip?"

Ava nods and answers with another giggle, "Right, Daddy!"

"You better get back over there, Cowboy," I say to my husband, smirking. "Your bull looks like he's starting to settle, and you're going to miss your window if you're gabbing with us girls."

"You're right, Darlin'." He winks at me then holds his hands out for a high five from the girls, and then from

7

me. When our hands connect, he slips his fingers between mine, giving it a little squeeze, just like we've done since we were younger when I'd go with him to every rodeo. I give his hand a squeeze back, too, smiling at him.

That one move, the simple connection of our fingers, says so much. It's our silent *I love you*. My silent *be careful*. And it's his *I made it, I'm okay* gesture when he gets off the bulls, too.

Chase slowly lets go of our grip and looks at me a second longer, communicating once more that he felt it too. He felt the familiarity, the ease, the connection that at times feels lost with him gone so often. Then he turns to walk back to the chute.

His jeans are worn and dirty, and his chaps cover his legs, but his ass—that tight, jean-clad ass—is on full display. He's still the sexiest man I've ever seen. As he climbs up the rails, so he can prepare to mount Loki, his ass flexes and I have to do everything I can to keep my mouth shut, and my thoughts to myself. Our girls don't need to hear them.

When he reaches the top of the chute, before he lowers himself to Loki's back, he glances at me…and laughs.

He laughs. He did that just for me.

There is no point in trying to hide my ogling, he knows I'm going to do it. He knows I've always done it. And he knows I always will.

I let out a little chuckle of my own at being caught. This familiarity with each other's routine, the lightness with which it comes back to us, is everything.

Ava's curious voice interrupts my thoughts, "Whatcha laughing at?"

While Chase lowers himself completely and gets set, I look back at Ava and smile, answering, "Just your daddy and me. I love to watch him, too."

I hold on to Aubrey a little tighter when Chase is ready, feeling her little body go rigid in my arms as they release the gate and Loki crashes out like a bat out of hell.

I glance quickly at Ava, smiling at how she's up on her feet on the hay now, bouncing on her toes while Chase rides. She's me, when I was a little girl. I turn my attention back to the spectacle in front of us, hearing Kip call out each passing second Chase stays up.

Chase almost loses it around six seconds, and Aubrey gasps, but he catches himself and rights his positioning atop Loki, making his eight and staying up longer.

He's showing off.

It's not often all three of us watch him ride, and I know he wants to show us how good he is, and also show Aubrey he's absolutely fine.

After about twelve seconds, he loosens his grip, preparing to dismount then drops off. He moves out of the way, so Loki doesn't charge, and waits the beast out until he's guided back into the chutes so he can make his way back to the holding pen.

Ava cheers loudly beside us and shouts, "You did it, Daddy! Yessss!" Before I can stop her, she hops off the hay and runs toward the pen, scampering up the fence to get closer to Chase. Aubrey follows suit, sliding out of my lap and down to the ground, and joins Ava. Aubrey very slowly climbs the fence, taking care with each step up, so she can greet Chase too.

And me? I take the moment to watch them.

Chase heads over to them both, with a proud grin in place, and steps onto the first plank.

"You did it!" Ava excitedly says to him.

"I did, didn't I?" Chase taps Ava's nose and then looks at Aubrey. "See, Monkey, it's okay."

He inconspicuously moves his arms to the top of the fence, flanking each of our girls, making sure they don't fall.

This is the side of my husband I love the most. He's a sexy bull rider always, but when he's being a dad to both our girls, I couldn't be more attracted to him or love him anymore if I tried. He's just not around much for me to see this side of him anymore.

This is the Chase I've been trying hard to have another baby with for two and a half years now.

While he talks to the girls, I lower myself from the hay and make my way to the fence, climbing up where I can keep a reach on each of the girls from this side, too.

"Nice ride," I say, settling my feet, moving each of my arms around the girls and over his.

"Thanks," he says, pulling his left arm out from beneath mine and holding his hand up, waiting for me to high-five him. He clasps our fingers together again, not letting go this time.

"How many more rides are you planning?"

He looks between the girls and me, then toward all the guys waiting for his instructions. "Ya know, I was going to try for another one or two, but I owe Ava a ride, and I don't think I can top what I just did to Loki."

I nod slightly, rubbing my thumb over his hand still in my grasp. "Aubrey and I were thinking we'd ride with you."

"In that case…" Chase looks toward his crew, calling out, "We're calling it a day, guys. I have a riding date with my girls that's more important to get to."

Two

Chase

I pick up Ava's towel from her floor and take it into the girls' connecting bathroom, hanging it on the back of her door. After, I turn and watch her sleep for a few moments. Her blankets and stuffed animals surround her, forming a cocoon of warmth and security around her sleeping form. She clings to her little stuffed horse, the one I bought for her when she was still a baby, and snores quietly.

I switch off her bedroom light and walk through the girls' shared bathroom, peeking in on Aubrey in her room. Where Ava is still, and wrapped around her stuffed animal in the center of her bed, Aubrey is my little wild child. Her arms and legs are fully stretched out, turning her into a sleeping star, almost hanging off the bed. She has kicked all her covers off and her favorite stuffed monkey is on the floor beside her bed.

Even in their sleep, our girls are so different from each other. Something I fail to stop and notice, but most importantly appreciate, when they're awake.

Then again, it's not often I get to take this much time to watch them anymore. I'm gone a lot. I know that. I know I'm missing out. I can see it. I can feel it when I lift them up when I get home and they're each a little bigger.

I miss this. Nightly tuck ins and checking on them before I turn in.

I miss them. Their bickering and laughs, and all of their hugs and love.

I miss my wife. The only woman I've ever loved, the one who gets me, and puts up with all of this.

But I can't stop now. Not yet. This year is my year. I'm currently number one in the standings, and if I keep it up, if I continue to travel and rack up wins and money, I will finish the year as the World Champion. It will all have finally paid off, figuratively and literally.

After I adjust Aubrey in her bed, righting her blankets and her tiny body so she doesn't fall, I kiss her head and walk out. As I pass through the door, I shut her overhead light off but make sure her nightlight is still shining in its place so she doesn't wake up scared, then walk down our dark hallway to my and Allie's room.

"They're both down and out," I say, crossing the threshold and closing the door behind me. Allie is already in bed with a book perched in her lap.

"You exhausted them with that ride and chores after," she replies, looking up from the words in front of her.

"They exhausted me, too." I chuckle and strip out of my T-shirt and jeans, wincing when I lift my shirt over my head.

"How bad is it?" she asks, setting her book aside.

"It's strained, nothing more." I crawl into bed beside her and sit back against our headboard, leaving one leg hanging off the bed and stretching the other out down the mattress.

"Don't play that game with me, Chase," she says, moving to her knees and facing me, placing her delicate fingers over my arm. "I'm not a doctor, I'm not another rider…" She gently presses in, searching out the root of my discomfort.

"Back side." I hold my arm away from my body, just enough for her to slide her hand over my right triceps. "It really isn't bad. Riding today worked it a little more than I thought it would is all."

"Not if, but when and how bad, right?"

"Right, and it's not bad, I promise." We both know the reality of my job is I'm just as likely to get seriously hurt as I am to win. Well, actually, getting hurt is probably a higher probability than winning. Therefore, we don't talk in ifs, but when and how bad. Muscle strains are common and minor, not even worth talking about—unless it's your wife asking.

"Maybe you should take the weekend off?" she asks, right before pressing a kiss to my arm. Her lips are soft and it's the type of kiss meant to soothe and heal, not get a reaction.

"I can't, Allie, you know that. I'm on top, this is a big weekend, it would give me more padding in the standings."

She sighs, and her warm breath radiates over my arm before she kisses it again. "One event won't drop you down, Chase. I miss you. The girls miss you. You can take a couple days, let your arm heal up more, then get back at it next week. Just two days. Two extra days at home."

"I wish it were that simple." I do, I wish I could be here with my girls all the time. But rodeo, riding, that's the job I chose—and just like any other job—I can't stay home just to stay home. Especially not when I'm sitting at number one.

"I know. I just wish it could be, just this once. We need you, baby. I need you. This bed is way too big without you in it beside me."

She's the strongest woman I know, but I can hear it in her voice: the pain, the sorrow, the stress. It makes the constant ache deep in my chest grow a little worse.

"I need you, too. Always. To talk to, to support me, to give me a high five before all my rides… And shitty motel beds just aren't the same as being here, holding you tight. They never will be," I say, honestly. I pull my other leg up onto the bed and turn to her, moving my hand up to her jaw and drawing her in, kissing her lips, smoothing my tongue over the bottom one. "That need runs deep in my body, too. I don't get enough of you."

I kiss her again and pull her over me.

"Your arm," she says, and kisses me back.

"It's fine, just sore. And it won't stop me from loving you."

She exhales softly and slumps her shoulders forward, dropping her head to my chest. "I need you in that way, too. But not tonight. We can't tonight." She raises her eyes to mine, and I see it. The words she didn't say, but she meant.

She's not crying.

Not this time.

Not anymore.

After two and a half years, one miscarriage, and too many periods that have come and dashed our hopes away, she doesn't cry anymore. She's not pregnant, now—still.

"Okay, baby." I give her as big of an understanding smile as I can muster and swallow hard. "What if I just hold you tonight?"

"I need that more than anything."

We both adjust and reposition so I can still hold her close, keeping her to me with my arm secured around her body and my hand on her hip. She lays her head on my shoulder with her body pressed in close to my side, and her hand immediately goes to my chest, rubbing slow circles right over my heart.

While I hold her, I can't help but think of our life. About the girls. About the baby we lost last year. Or the early days, when Allie was at every rodeo with me and we were both young and naïve to the ways of adult life.

Things were simple then. And the pain of losing a child and failing month after month to make another was nothing I would have ever even started to think of. I wouldn't have been able to grasp them at all.

I also didn't know the absolute love and joy being a father would give me, either.

Time is a double-edged sword. Who knew it could be such a blessing, and a curse? Speeding up and slowing down on its own whim, stealing precious moments before I can cherish them, or happening so slowly and vividly I can cement them in my memory forever.

"I liked having you watching me, today." It's an abrupt change of topic, I know. But I want her to know it meant something to me. It was a moment in time I'll cherish forever. Seeing Allie and Aubrey come out, having all of my girls right there, that's what gave me the gumption to stay on Loki. They're my strength. All three of them.

"I liked watching you," she replies in her soft, sleepy voice. "It's like we slipped right back into the old days. Pre-ride rituals, our unspoken words…"

I chuckle and squeeze her hip gently. "I was just thinking about the old days. They're what you being out there reminded me of, too."

"Things were so simple then, weren't they?" Her fingers are drawing lazy hearts along my chest while she speaks now.

"They were, but I wouldn't change what we have now. Not our ranch, not our marriage, and especially not our girls."

"I wouldn't either, Chase. I really wouldn't. I just wish…" Her voice trails off and she keeps drawing, not finishing her thought, but I don't need her to, either.

"I wish for a lot of things, Darlin'. The biggest being that I could be with you all more, or you could be with me, too." She didn't say that's what she wished for, but she would have. I know her. I know how her mind works.

"Having the girls out on the circuit constantly is no life for them, baby. Aubrey would be miserable. And they would have to give up the activities at home they love. We always swore we wouldn't force them; not like I was forced."

"You're right, but what if you all came to one with me this year?"

Allie raises her head and looks at me. "Which one were you thinking?"

"Come to Cheyenne. They have the carnival, concerts, it's just as much about the family and fun as it is the riding."

"The Daddy of 'em All?"

I nod my head and grin. "The Daddy of 'em All…"

Allie

I haven't been to a Cheyenne Frontier Days in years. It's close enough. The girls would absolutely love it. Ava could do all the rodeo stuff with her daddy, meet some of the riders she only sees or hears about online or on TV, and watch some of the women ride.

And my sweet Aubrey would love the carnival, and some of the less rodeo-driven, kid-oriented activities. Plus, it would be seven to ten days with my husband. We haven't had that much time with him since last December.

"We're in," I say to him, returning his smile with one of my own. "Do you have a room of your own, or do I need to pull strings in the morning?"

His fingers slip beneath my tank top and slowly rub my back. "I was supposed to share with Cody."

Cody. Our girls will be thrilled at getting to see him again. He's been Chase's best friend since they were kids, and he took me in as an honorary little sister when we met.

"Tell Uncle Cody we are getting our own room, but we will try to keep it close to his, if possible. The girls are going to go crazy seeing him."

Chase's laugh fills the room and his chest rises and falls heavily beneath my head with it. "You got it. He'll be happy to see you all, too."

I don't say it, but he better be. He used to live here, about thirty minutes down the road, until he up and left to follow some skank to Texas. That lasted about a year and a half before she was caught in bed with someone

17

else on the circuit. She was a buckle bunny, and he wasn't winning as much as she thought he should be. She broke his heart.

Since then, he's stayed in Texas, away from his family—us—chasing that damned dream on his own. The same one my husband is after. The one that constantly keeps good men away from the women and children who love them.

Chase rolls just the slightest bit more toward me and wraps both his arms around me, nuzzling into the top of my head.

"Good," I respond, then kiss his throat and snuggle into him, breathing him in deep, clinging to his warmth, his scent, and how good and safe this feels now, because I know he will be gone again tomorrow

Three

Allie

Peanut butter, jelly, honey, and bread line the counter in front of me. The girls and I have a full day out and about. Ava has a dentist appointment and riding. Aubrey has gymnastics, and I want to keep them out of the house as long as possible. They need the day away. I need it, too.

"Mommy," Ava saunters over, "can I have strawberry jelly?" She hops up onto the stool beside the counter and sits to watch me.

"It's already out. Will you help me make yours? We're running behind."

She nods. "Knife, please," she says matter-of-factly, as she reaches for the bread. I wait for her to get her slices out and then I grab two for Aubrey's sandwich, spreading her peanut butter first then passing the knife and jar toward Ava.

"Please be careful. Go slow with the knife."

"Duhhhh. I know the rules."

Nine going on nineteen, that's my daughter. I swear. I watch her carefully scoop the peanut butter out on the knife and then spread it over the bread, adding more than I would've given her. Then she grabs the squeezable jelly and tips it over her bread.

"Ew!" she shouts, then looks up with wide eyes. "Why is the jelly gross?"

I laugh and shake my head. "Give me, you didn't shake it first."

She passes the jelly over and I close the lid, shaking it so the liquid isn't settled at the top anymore, then hand it back. "Now try it."

She takes the jelly back and flips it over, lining the center of her bread with a wide strip. "Can I have a new knife?"

I shake my head. "No, use the same knife, it's okay. We don't need to dirty another one."

With great determination, she spreads the jelly over her peanut butter and bread, making sure every inch has a light layer over it, then she very carefully slides off the stool and carries the knife to the sink, dropping it in with a clang.

"Did Aubrey get her shoes on?" I ask, as I spread honey over Aubrey's sandwich instead of jelly. My girls wouldn't have the same favorite sandwich, they're such polar opposites of each other.

"I think so. She was buckling them." Ava grabs two baggies out of the drawer and carries them over to me. "Can we take some chips?"

"Go grab two bags out of the pantry. You know what kind your sister likes."

While Ava grabs the bags, I grab two small Gatorades for them and get everything put into an insulated lunch tote.

"Can I watch Daddy tonight?" she asks, dropping their chips inside.

Chase has his final ride at the rodeo tonight, and we've been able to catch a few over the internet and a crappy feed over the past few days. "Maybe. We'll see later, okay?"

She nods her head, the hard-set look on her face identical to Chase's when he's trying to figure something

20

out, so he can get what he wants. I know she wants to see him. She misses him. And watching is how she stays close while he's away. But I really can't guarantee she'll be able to watch tonight. For one, I don't know if we'll be home, and for another, we may not be able to bring the feed up.

"Do you think he'll win?"

"He and Uncle Cody are both doing really well. And they're really close in points. So I think if Daddy doesn't win, Uncle Cody will. Unless they both fall off tonight."

"Daddy won't fall. He's the best." She is Chase's biggest fan. As far as she's concerned, he hung the moon, the stars, and then he threw in the sun for good measure, too. But she isn't wrong. He's undoubtedly riding better this year than he ever has. I just wish it didn't come at the cost of time with us.

"He is the best, you're right." I smile at her. "We'll try to watch tonight, Ava. I promise we will try, if we can. But first, we need to go. Can you get Aubrey for me?"

"Yep." She walks out of the kitchen, and then I hear her shout, "Oh! My hat! Aubrey, time to go!"

I hear her pattering footsteps get farther away in a hurry, and then I hear Aubrey's smaller steps coming toward me.

"Hi, angel face," I greet her.

"Hi, Mommy face," she says back, showing off her toothless grin that makes my heart melt a little every time I see it.

"Are you ready for gymnastics?"

She lifts her T-shirt in response, letting me see her favorite purple leo that Chase bought her when school ended this year. "My baby has hers on, too." She holds up her favorite doll that also has a leo on.

21

"You're both so cute," I say, planting a kiss on top of her head. "We will leave as soon as Ava comes back, she is getting her hat. Why don't you go out to the car, and take this for me?" I hand her the tote with their lunches and watch her set out for the garage.

Ava's hurried footsteps ring down the hall again and she appears with a proud smile. "I almost forgot my lucky hat!"

It matches Chase's almost identically, and she refuses to ride without it. Both our girls have their ways of keeping their daddy close while he's gone. And they're both going to be on full display at their practices and lessons all day.

It's been a long day. I'm so ready to head home, get dinner going, and relax with a book and a glass of wine. But we have to get through this last practice, first. Ava is sitting beside me on the barely padded bench with her head resting on my shoulder, and my phone in her hands. She's not watching videos, or playing games. Not even a little. She's pulling up the PRCA standings and checking to make sure Chase is still sitting at number one.

"Baby," I say lightheartedly, "the results won't change any until after they ride tonight. He's still going to be in first."

She looks up at me with heavy eyes and sun-kissed cheeks and nods. "You're right. He's still the best." She closes out my phone and hands it back to me, not asking for more time or games. She's still holding out hope that screen time tonight will include watching him. Instead, she points over to Aubrey working on the mini balance beam. "Look, she's doing it!"

I look to where she's pointing and watch Aubrey jumping off the beam before landing perfectly, steadily, back on the same beam beneath her. "She is." I grin wide and continue to watch Aubrey. She's excelling in a way neither Chase, nor I, expected her to her. And she loves it.

"Do you think I could do that?" It's not at all something I would've expected Ava to ask, but I'm not upset she did.

"I think if you practiced at it, you could do anything you want to do." I look down at her when Aubrey runs back to the end of the line behind her small class. "Do you want to try gymnastics, Ava?"

She returns my look, scrunching her nose up, and shaking her head no. "No way! I want to keep riding. I was just wondering." She's so sure of her answer, she almost sounds shocked I would ask such a thing.

"Okay," I murmur into the crown of her head. "If you want to try something else though, you can. Anytime you want. Okay? Daddy and I both want you to do what you want to. Only you."

"'Kay. But I'll never stop riding. I love it."

She settles her head back against my arm and we continue to watch Aubrey. When it's her turn again, I pull my phone back out and capture a video of her jumps and landings, her spinning and stopping, all with precise steps on the beam. Her smile grows wider with each successful turn. She is truly in her element, and she loves it. She keeps practicing on the mini beam for a while, and then they move over to the floor and work on other basic skills. She's mastering them quickly. I couldn't be prouder if I tried.

But, it also makes me sad. Chase is missing out on some truly spectacular moments with our girls this summer. He's not getting to see her here in person. He can't give her hugs and high fives when she finishes, and shower her in praise and love. I hate he's missing it all.

For Aubrey.

For Chase.

For Ava, too. Because she's got her own triumphs to celebrate, and more than with Aubrey, she is seeking Chase's approval. She wants to ride the big rides and events, just like him. And he's not around to watch her grow and learn, to be a part of the journey she's already committed them both to.

By the time we're finally home for the night, both the girls are exhausted, in desperate need of showers, and Ava is dying to watch Chase. While they get cleaned up, I do some of the chores that are our responsibility out in the barn, and then I send the videos I got of the girls today to him with a text.

Allie: Hey! The girls had great days at their practices. Enjoy watching these later. Be safe riding. Mind your arm. And give 'em hell tonight, Cowboy. We miss and love you more than you can imagine. Talk to you later.

I won't hear back from him, not until late tonight, or tomorrow sometime. So I pocket my phone and finish what I need to, then head in to try to set up the computer and TV for the girls to watch him. This is how it goes. He's been gone for three days now, and I'm not sure when we'll get to see him again. So I'll do what I can to at least let the girls see him on the screen.

Chase

There's something about the hot, muggy air that makes the smell of everything so much more noticeable today. The fried goods being sold for rodeo goers, the smell of manure from all the livestock, the staleness of the tent surrounding me while I get my shit on and ready to ride, mixed with the stench of blood and sweat from all the riders who have taken their turns today already. It's the unmistakable scent of home. My second home—or maybe my first—but not my permanent.

My forever home is wherever my wife is. Fuck, do I miss her. I read her text again and hit play with a smile, watching Aubrey wearing the purple leo I got her, owning the beam and mats. Then I swipe over to Ava up on the horse at the training grounds, wearing her hat. The same damn one I'll be wearing when I ride tonight. My girls, all three of them, are amazing. I can't wait to hear all about everything they've been doing, but that has to wait. I need to get focused on the here, and now; I've got a ride coming up.

I silence my phone and lock it in my mini locker, then run through my mental checklist one last time, making sure I've got everything I need.

Chaps.

Glove.

Protective vest.

Hat.

And my rope. Every last bit of it is as much a part of me as the heart beating in my chest. As the gold band that has never, and will never, leave my finger. I kiss over my ring silently, closing my eyes and thinking of Allie one last time, then pull out the tape and wrap it over, securing my ring in place so I can't risk anything yanking it, or my finger, off.

It's my ritual. The thing I do before every ride to keep Allie with me. I don't even think she knows I do it, but a ride just wouldn't be the same, I wouldn't feel as comfortable or as confident, if I didn't.

With my rope over my shoulder I step out of the tent and into the hot evening air. It's fresher than the tent, but still holds all the smells of the rodeo around me. I make my way over to the arena, passing the other riders in various states of preparation, conversation, or reflection. The crowd in the stands is good tonight. They're loud, even though this is a smaller rodeo. It's the perfect night to go out there and make my final ride for this event.

I walk up to the chutes, catching the end of the team roping event, watching the winners of the round take their victory lap.

"There you are," Cody's voice booms out.

I look up and make my way over to him beside the second chute they're loading the bulls into for the round.

"Here I am," I remark, settling beside him and raising my foot to the rail in front of me. "You're the third rider?"

"That I am," he says, smirking. "Drew the baby I wanted for tonight, too."

"Are we talking bulls or women now?" I ask, glancing his way.

"Yes, sir."

I chuckle and shake my head at him. "I know who you drew for the ride, which woman is going back to the hotel on your arm?"

"Pretty blonde up there," he angles his head toward the stands, giving the nod to a blonde girl and her friend, drawing out their smiles and waves.

"Only you, man. Only you." I tip my hat to them and clap a hand over his shoulder. "Good luck with that."

"I don't need luck, brother," he retorts. "You know that. These rides are mine. All of them."

The cocky bastard. The way he's been riding this rodeo, I don't doubt that for a second. We've been jockeying for first in the average since night one ended.

"We'll see about that, asshole." Just because I think he may have a shot at beating me tonight doesn't mean I have to tell him.

Cody laughs and turns back toward me. "You're just jealous I'm getting the girls and the buckle this weekend."

"You can take the girls," I answer, rubbing my fingers over my taped wedding band. "I've already got the woman of my dreams, you know that."

I watch Trevor McKinnon nod from where he's perched over his bull in the chute, indicating to the guys on the ground he's ready for them to release the gate. He drew a crazy one tonight. His first second or two out of the gate are good, but then the bull turns in on him and he loses his grip, sliding on its back before he's sent flying. I cringe when he lands.

"That's going to leave a mark," Cody pipes up beside me.

"No shit." We're all used to it. Most rides come with their own aches and pains after, but the adrenaline, the rush—add in the money we can make—and the glory that comes with being the best... It's all worth it. Hell, it's more than worth the knocks.

"Speaking of having the woman of your dreams." He taps his knuckles over the rail in front of us. "How are Allie and the girls?"

I'm not sure what the best way to answer is. They're healthy, they're home and safe. The girls are happy. But Allie hasn't sounded very happy lately. Even if her texts would seem to say otherwise. I know better. It makes me feel like shit.

I sigh, "Honestly?"

He gives a little nod as we make our way toward where he'll be getting ready in the chute.

"This season is taking its toll on Allie. She sounds tired every time I talk to her. Even when I'm home, her smile doesn't quite reach her eyes every time. She wants me home more. And with every passing month that it's another no, her spirits fall a little more. So do mine."

"It'll happen when it's meant to," he says half-heartedly. His attention is already on the ride ahead of him, so I don't even bother answering. At this point, I don't know that I believe him, anyway.

They load his bull, and the fourth, into the chutes once the next ride starts, and Cody starts to mentally prepare. His focus shifts to the bull he's lowering himself on, and so does mine. I help him get set, adjusting the rope, giving the bull a nudge so Cody has room to sink his legs down between the bull and the wall of the chute. I watch him wrap his hand beneath the rope, adjust his grip, and steady himself when the bull bucks up, anxious to get out already.

"Eight seconds," I shout over the ruckus of the chute and cowboys around us, helping him prepare. "Eight and you might beat me." I pat his back hard and step back, watching Cody give his nod. The gate pulls open and he's out, riding his ass off.

The clock ticks on, each passing second is one closer to the eight he needs. As my best friend, I want him to make his ride. As his competitor, I need his score to be low. The purse here isn't the absolute best, but it's still pretty hefty in size, and it'll still add to my overall total for the year. I need as much of a padding going into finals at the end of the year as I can get. I want the title all but wrapped up by then.

The buzzer sounds and he works himself off the bull and behind a fighter, letting them usher the massive animal back through the trail of chutes and out of the arena before he hobbles over toward me.

"I pulled an ass muscle, dammit" he complains, with a triumphant smile on his face.

"Serves you right." I laugh and shake his hand. "That was one hell of a ride, you fucker. You couldn't just fall and let me take this, could you?"

He laughs loudly and flips me off, pulling his hat from his head and moving his hand through his hair. "Nah, I want to make your ass work for it."

He would. And I'm glad. I don't want it given to me, even if it's by him.

We watch the rest of the riders this round, until it's my turn to get ready. I climb onto the plank and tap Nitro, my bull, with my heel, watching his reaction, gauging how he's going to be while I climb on top of him. He doesn't react too extremely, so I lower myself down, straddling the mass of muscles that are his back and flanks. I hand my rope to Cody where he's standing to help me, and he pulls it tight, giving me a chance to slide my hands up and down the rope, heating the sticky rosin on it, making it better for my grip so I don't lose it during my ride.

Adrenaline is coursing through me now, making my hands shake just slightly, not enough for anyone else to notice it, but enough for me to know I'm ready. My body is preparing for the fight or flight feeling—and it's always fight in me. It's been trained to respond that way for years.

I steel myself against the nerves and slip my hand into the hold, positioning it just where I want it, before Cody loosens the slack one final time, so I can take it and wrap it for my final grip. It feels good. It feels right, and I take a deep breath before I move my body into position, just over my hand, up around Nitro's shoulders with my chest forward and head tucked, focusing on Nitro's spine. I tune everything out now, except for the massive body beneath me, the position of my hand, and the hard pat Cody sends to my back. Eight seconds. He'll be saying it to me, just like I did to him.

With one final breath I nod my head, indicating I'm ready to ride. And just like that, the gate is pulled open and we're off.

Nitro is a monster of a bull. He thrashes beneath me, going one way and then turning back on me a split second later, bucking high. My time is getting close, but I can feel my grip slipping, my legs sliding on his sides, and then he hurls himself into the air, and what little grip I had left is gone. My hand comes free and I'm flying off of him in grand fashion.

I drop my arms down, preparing for impact, and land solidly—picking my head up first to spot Nitro as fast as I can, so he doesn't catch me off guard if he rushes me, and then pushing myself to my feet. The fighters already have Nitro moving back toward the gate and holding area where the pens are by the time I'm upright. I bend to pick up my hat and rope, noting instantly my arm is more fucked up now. Pain radiates up the back of it, and the muscle knots up instantly with my reach.

The pain's easy to forget about when I hear my score announced. In my haze of holding on for dear life, I must've missed the buzzer, but I made my ride. Eighty-two is a fuckton better than the zero I was expecting, but it's not enough to beat Cody tonight. It also means he may well take the average, too.

Shit.

I perch my hat back on my head, gritting my back teeth together when the pain amps up in my arm again.

"Hell of a ride, brother!" Cody says, slapping a hand to my back when I clear the gate. He walks beside me down the stretch of gravel, dirt, and patches of grass leading away from the arena. "I didn't think you were going to last. It looked like he had your number.

"Hell, even I didn't know I lasted. I missed the buzzer."

"You hit it right as he went airborne, right before he sent your ass flying. He had you on the ropes the whole time. And yet you still wouldn't go down. This really may be your year. Finally."

"It won't be enough to beat you this go, though." I adjust the rope over my shoulder with my bad arm and flinch, but ignore it as best I can and go on talking, "Enjoy the feeling of being on top while you are, next rodeo's mine."

"Your arm?" he asks. It's not the smart-ass response I expected him to reply with. Also, not what I wanted him to say, either. Cody knows I've been riding hurt. But for him to say something, he knows it's not just a tweak this time either, I don't need that.

"What do you mean, my arm?" I try to play it off, I need to. I don't have time to be hurt, or to explain myself.

"The way you're holding it. The look on your face. You've always got an ugly mug, but you'd scare your own children with look you're wearing now."

I laugh out, tucking my arm closer to my side and nod my head. It's the only affirmation he's going to get. I respond vocally with, "Fuck you. We both know I'm the better looking one out of the two of us."

"Keep dreaming," he retorts easily. "Doc's back there looking at Mitch now. Grab a bag of ice, suck it up, then meet me back out here. Yeah?"

"Christ, you're more demanding than Allie." I stop and look him over. "I'll be back in a few. And speaking of my wife…not a word to her about this. Okay?"

He throws his arms up defensively. "Like I've got a death wish. She'd have me by the balls for not forcing you to take a weekend off. I'll let you tell her you still haven't healed."

"Good." I smirk. "She'd maybe let you keep them, though, she's set on you having kids one day that she can spoil."

I leave him standing there with a slacked jaw and go back toward the medical tent to get some ice and talk to Doc about my arm.

Four

Allie

C hase has been gone for over a week again, now. The weather has been unbearably hot, and the girls are one meltdown each away from making me snap. Ava insists we livestream every single one of Chase's rides, still, and Aubrey asks me daily when her daddy will be home.

Aubrey refuses to watch him this week, afraid she will see him get hurt more, and Ava refuses to do anything with her sister while their daddy is on the computer. The fights that come nearly daily during a rodeo are getting out of hand.

One child acts as though she doesn't need him here because she's his biggest cheerleader one minute, and then the next; she wants him home more than anything because she wants to be just like him one day. And he has to be here to teach her all about riding.

The other, depending on the day, acts like he is the only parent she has. And I get it. She's six and she loves her dad. She misses him. She misses stories. She wants and needs to feel safe. And Mommy just isn't the same. I really get it. But I can't make Chase come home. I can't give Aubrey her daddy just because she wants him. Just like I can't make Chase show up so Ava can enter her first rodeo and have him be there for her, because right now, that's what she wants more than anything in the world.

It's too much.

When we last said goodbye to him, the morning after we decided the girls and I would go to Cheyenne too, I thought we would see him home between events. We watched his final ride on Sunday, and I thought he'd be home Monday. But Cody and another of their buddies invited him to a camp in Texas. It's a camp to help young riders learn, but I can't help but wonder why he chose strangers' children over his own.

I can't help but be angry that again, when I need him home, when I need a break, he is nowhere to be found. I love the man more than life, and I would never ask him to give up his dream, but I need him, too.

Then again...this isn't the first time he's pulled a Houdini after I've told him I'm not pregnant. Not at all. The first time was about three months after my miscarriage. My doctor had given us the green light, and Chase was determined. We both were.

We didn't want to replace the baby we lost. Not in the least. But I think we both got a sense of how much love we still have to give, and it made that feeling so real. It made the planning and dreaming our favorite way to pass the time on the phone. Then it was gone. And we were left with so much love to give, and so much grief over what we lost, we didn't know up from down. So trying again, as soon as we could, was how we were going to honor our lost baby. It was how we would cope with what we no longer had. If we focused our energy on what could still be, we wouldn't have to acknowledge what might have been.

I still think of our little boy or girl every day. When I'm all alone at night, when Ava and Aubrey are sleeping in their room and Chase is on the road, I frequently break down. I mourn the child I was carrying, who was a part of me and Chase, and the life we would have had as a family of five. I feel anger and resentment that I was alone when it happened. He was off chasing a title I don't give a shit if he ever wins again. Because while I love he's a cowboy—because it's a part of him—it's not why I love him. I love my Cowboy because of the man his is—was—is, depending on whether he's home and present, or on the road and distracted.

On the nights I'm alone, I feel guilt I couldn't keep my baby safe for forty weeks. I feel a hole, wide and raw, in my heart that was supposed to be where I stored all the love for our baby. Another space will open up if I ever conceive again, but that hole, it will never be filled.

So we tried, as soon as the doctor said it was safe to, and Chase was sure—he was positive—we would be successful. Until the day came when I told him, without any doubt, it was not to be. He ended our call almost immediately after, and the next day he let me know he wouldn't be home before the next rodeo; he and Cody were going to rent a truck and drive to the next city. He needed some time to process.

That was the first time he stayed away after I told him it still wasn't our time to grow our family. He's done it a handful of times since. With every "not this month" that has come since the miscarriage, I know he has felt more and more like a failure. He's not one. But he feels that way. We've been tested, each of us, and they don't have any concrete, identifiable reasons why I can't get pregnant. It just hasn't happened.

It's put a strain on us, nearly as much as his constantly being gone has. Two and a half years ago, we made a plan—one more season to take the title—we'd have a baby, and our life would be set. But one more season turned to three; with constant travel, rides, missed birthdays and events, which has taken its toll.

"Mama," Ava says quietly, poking her head into our home office. "Is Daddy calling tonight?"

I push back in the chair and hold my arm out to her, inviting her to come sit in my lap. "Where's your sister?"

"Playing with her stupid Barbies," she says with an attitude unlike anything I've ever heard from her as she sits in my lap.

"Ava Anne!" I scold her. "Drop the tone, and you know how I feel about that word when you're talking about your sister."

She settles into my lap and nods. "I'm sorry. She was saying things about Daddy and it hurt my feelings."

"What was she saying?"

"She said that Daddy was a meanie, just like me." She looks at the picture of all of us on the desk, fighting tears back. "He's not a meanie and neither am I."

"No, you aren't," I say, kissing the side of her head. "Why did Aubrey call you and Daddy meanies?"

"Because I said when he comes home, he's going to teach me to ride, and we can go to rodeos together so I don't miss him anymore."

Dammit, Chase. This is why we need you home.

"Oh, baby," I sigh out. "You can't go to rodeos with him. Not without me and Aubrey being with you, too."

"I can too!" she screams, and gets off my lap, hurrying away from me. "He's my daddy! I can go if I want to!"

"Ava Anne," I say sternly. "That is enough. You aren't going anywhere. Daddy will be home soon, and he's going to try to call tonight. He will tell you the same thing."

She bolts out of the office, crying and stomping down the hall, until I hear her bedroom door slam shut.

"You better call tonight, Chase. The girls need to hear your voice. And I do, too," I say out loud—to no one in particular—and scan our office, looking at the picture frames hanging from our walls. Each picture carries a memory with it. Most highlight his rodeo achievements, others bring back some of our special memories as a family that have come fewer and farther between over the past couple years.

No rodeo, no title, no amount of money in the world is worth this feeling. It can't be. Not when you have two little girls at home who need you.

Chase

I settle into my bed in our hotel room and adjust the ice pack on my arm, then reach for my phone. It's been a long, long week. Even just helping kids, showing them how to ride, I've managed to aggravate my injury further. The bruising is deep, and the muscle is constantly aching. That's part of why I didn't go home this time. I couldn't hide this until the bruise dissipates. Allie would just fuss and worry. It's not something either of us needs right now.

While it's been a blast being able to teach the kids, to pass on the same knowledge I've gained, and see the passion they all have to become big-time riders, I really do miss my girls.

I haven't talked to any of them in two days; times have been off and when they're free, I'm not. And when I am, they're not. But hopefully, God willing, that will change now.

Before I open my messages, I stare at the background on my phone for a few moments. Allie is holding Aubrey in her lap, while Ava wraps her arms around Allie's shoulders and neck from behind. They've all got huge smiles on their faces, and look happy as can be. I remember the day I took the photo. It was last Christmas and we had just finished opening presents. The girls were thrilled over everything they got and Allie and I had spent the night before doing some celebrating of our own, so she still had that extra glow to her. Of course a couple weeks later she told me, again, we still weren't expecting. I've started to get used to that.

With a sigh I open my messages and send one to my wife.

Chase: Hey Darlin'. I'm in. Can you talk tonight?

I wait a few minutes, checking the time and trying to remember if she said they had something going on tonight, when finally, my phone pings with her reply.

Allie: Hi. We can. The girls need it. It was a bad day here.

Chase: I'm calling now. We can talk just the two of us when I'm done with the girls…

I go into my apps and open up my video chat, dialing Allie, smiling immediately as she accepts and her face comes into full view.

"Aren't you a sight for sore eyes," I say.

"Hi, Cowboy." She smiles, but it doesn't quite reach her eyes again. "Let me call the girls in here real fast. They're going to be so excited to see you."

I nod my head and just take in her features, chuckling a little to myself when she shouts for our daughters. We both wait in silence until their little voices get closer and closer.

"Girls, someone's on the phone and wants to see and talk to you."

"Daddy? Is it Daddy?" I hear my Pipsqueak ask.

"Me first! Me first!" my Monkey says in return.

"No, me first! I'm older," Ava snaps back at her.

Aubrey starts to respond when Allie interrupts them, "Enough! Or neither of you talk to him and you go to bed right now!"

I'm a little taken aback by her tone. I've never heard her so hard on them. Judging by the silence her words are met with, the girls are shocked, too.

I want to diffuse this before it goes any further, so I jump into the conversation and say, "Why don't I talk to all three of you at once? I can call again once you set the computer up? Would that be better?"

Allie looks at the phone with tired eyes and nods her head. "Give me two minutes then we'll be ready for you, Chase."

The call disconnects before I can even answer. Allie has never, in all the time I've known her, been this way.

It worries me.

And I will get to the bottom of it.

But first, I need her to call back. It's been, taking a peek at the time, fifteen minutes already. What's going on?

Just as I'm getting ready to dial Allie's phone, I get an incoming video call. It doesn't even finish ringing the first time before I accept, watching the screen come to life with their faces filling it. They're sitting at the desk in the office, and Allie is in the chair with the girls on either side of her.

"There's my girls!" I say, noting the looks on each of their faces, trying to stay upbeat for them. "How are you?"

"Hi, Daddy," Ava says, first.

Aubrey waves her little hand and says more quietly than I'm used to, "Hi, Daddy."

Allie pulls her into her lap then adds a strained, "Hey."

"What are you all up to tonight?"

"Getting ready for bed," Ava says sullenly. Aubrey nods her head and adds, "We're in trouble."

"You're in trouble, what did you do?" I ask, adjusting the wrap holding my ice pack in place and shifting my phone's angle so I see their faces better.

"Like I said earlier, it's been a bad day here. How bad is your arm?" Allie asks, dropping the topic of the girls' behavior before we really even begin.

"I landed wrong showing the kids what to do earlier, it's no big deal, Darlin'." I try to make light of it. She's already upset enough. So are the girls. I shrug my shoulder to add to the notion that I'm fine.

Even from hundreds of miles away, the tension in the air is suffocating me. None of them are smiling, Allie looks pissed-off and exhausted, the girls look like they've been crying, and there's nothing I can do about any of it from here.

"Take ibuprofen for the swelling and pain, keep icing it, and take it easy tomorrow, Chase," Allie says, almost robotically, repeating a variation of the same instructions she's given me hundreds of times before. Only this time, unlike any other, she sounds annoyed as she's saying it.

"Why don't you all tell me what's going on? Maybe I can help, buy the girls a little more time up before they have to go to bed."

40

That gets my girls to smile wide and nod, but it does nothing to improve the scowl on my wife's face.

"What's been happening today, girls?" I ask, looking between each of them as best as I can, given our connection.

"We've been fighting all day," Ava whispers.

"And talking back to Mommy," Aubrey interjects.

"You both know better than that," I say sternly. "Apologize to each other and your mom right now."

Both the girls say sorry to each other, and then to Allie.

"You girls need to help Mommy, not make things harder on her. Do you hear me?" A stifled sound leaves Allie's stock-still body. Was she snorting?

The girls nod their heads and I watch Allie.

"Good, I bet she will let you stay up a little later then. But you should go brush your teeth and get your jammies on, right now. I love you both. I'll call again tomorrow so we can talk about more fun things. Okay?"

They answer in unison, "Okay. Love you." Aubrey slides off Allie's lap and she and Ava walk away, leaving me and Allie to talk.

"You can't do that, Chase," Allie scolds, and repositions the computer in front of her as she scoots closer.

"I can't do what?"

"Call in and think telling them to behave is going to fix things. You don't think I tried?" She shakes her head, then rests it on her hands.

"Sometimes they just need me to remind them, too," I say, a little defensively.

"No, Chase, sometimes they need you here, period." She looks up at the camera from her hands and sighs. "Their attitudes are because they miss you. Their fights

41

today have been over spending time with you when you get home."

I don't know what to say. The set of her shoulders, the tone of her voice, it all screams she's had enough. But my strong wife doesn't give up.

"Talk to me, Allie. I'm here right now."

She shakes her head again, almost as if she's denying what I'm saying. "It's fine. Just a bad day here. But I need to go tell the girls, that even though Daddy said they could stay up later, they can't. Because they can't. There has to be a punishment for their behavior. It's the only way I can keep control when you aren't here."

"You're right. I'm sorry. I was just trying to help..." This is not how I expected tonight's call to go, and right now, I'm wishing I wouldn't have called at all. Instead of a happy conversation with my wife and kids, it's been scolding and tension.

"It's fine. But I really do need to go. I've got to get the girls straightened out and into bed. Maybe we can try this again tomorrow night. Hopefully, tomorrow will be a better day."

"Yeah, I hope so. I love you, Allie."

"I love you, too, Chase."

Allie disconnects the call and I toss my phone down onto the bed beside me. How did everything go so wrong, so fast?

Five

Allie

The days have started to run together. The monotony enough to make one blur into the next, into the next. The girls have relaxed their fighting and attitudes, a little, since I overruled Chase and followed through on their early bedtime punishments last week. But it's starting to pick back up again. After he finished his camp, he was off to the next rodeo. A five-day event that has left him battered, bruised—but still sitting at number one in the world—and away from home for a grand total of sixteen days now.

Sixteen.

It's the longest we've ever been apart. He was only home for thirty-six hours after a four-day stretch away before that. I haven't spent quality time with my husband in close to a month now. He's been away for three weeks, essentially, with a very small window where we actually spent time awake together.

He has been home for one point five days out of the last twenty-two.

It's a staggering number to me. I know he's been gone, but to put it into days and weeks, it leaves a tightness and ache in my chest akin to what I imagine would be the feel of a very large bull sitting on top of it.

If he makes it home, like he said he would, the girls and I will get five days with him before he has to leave for another rodeo again. That rodeo should only be a few days away before he comes home and we pack up for Cheyenne.

Aubrey runs into the house, her dark pigtails flapping against her head, her white and pink tank top covered in dirt, and she comes to a halt in front of me.

"Mommy!" she shouts, unnecessarily.

"Aubrey!" I say back, just as enthusiastically.

"Daddy comes tonight!" She does a little happy jump and throws her hands into the air.

I reach out and tighten one of her pigtails, nodding my head and grinning, "Yes, he comes home tonight."

She starts spinning in fast circles in front of me, saying in a singsong voice "Yay, yay, yay, Daddy's coming home."

She spins away from me and out of the room like a little tornado, still singing her made-up song as she disappears down the hall.

Ava was just as happy this morning, only instead of singing and spinning, she spoke words a mile a minute, telling me everything she wants to do with Chase while he's here. Starting, of course, with getting out on their horses so she can show him how well she's doing with her riding.

In fact, that's what she's out doing right now. She begged me all morning to let Kip keep an eye on her while she rides Lightning. After a solid hour of telling her to wait until later, I took her out, helped her get Lightning saddled and ready, then asked Kip if he could hang out in the pen with her for a while, so she could practice before her daddy gets home.

It's something Chase should be here to see, but in his absence, she's determined to be the best she can be just for him. She wants his approval as much as she wants to learn for herself, if not more.

I step out to the porch and watch her ride around the pen. Kip is standing close by, guiding her, giving her basic directions. He's been good for the girls. He's young, but he's smart and kind. And he's a hard worker. Ruben, one of our other guys, walks up and calls Kip over. I can see him signaling to Ava to stop, then saying something I can't make out to her as he walks to the fence to talk to our employee.

What happens next happens in a blink. One moment Ava's seated on a still Lightning, the next, she's nudging her horse, urging him on, pushing a limit she shouldn't be.

Then, time slows down, and I'm watching her in slow motion as she pushes too hard to get to the barrel Kip has set up for her. Lightning turns hard, perfectly, aside from the fact it's not a pro rider on his back, it's my little girl. And she's leaning too far into the turn.

"Ava!" I shout, jumping off the porch and setting out at a dead sprint toward the pen. Kip turns toward Ava when I shout, taking off toward her just as she loses her balance and falls hard off her horse.

My heart lodges in my throat when I see her hit her head on the edge of the barrel, and I push myself to run faster, squeezing through the narrow opening of the pen when Ruben opens it for me, allowing me easier access to my daughter.

Kip reaches her first, sliding to a halt next to her still body and dropping to his knees. He doesn't move her, not right away.

"Kip, Kip is she okay?" I clear the last ten or so yards in no time and drop beside them, putting my hands to her body, to her head. I pull away when she whines out, and my fingers are covered in blood.

45

"I'm so sorry, Mrs. Canton. Oh God. I'm so sorry." Kip is panicking now. He's seen plenty of grown men fall off horses and bulls, but never a nine-year-old he was looking after. He sees the blood on my fingers and his face pales. He was responsible for watching her, and he feels at fault for this, I can sense it in the way he keeps apologizing. But he *was* watching her. Just like I would have done. Like Chase would have.

An odd calmness settles over me in reaction to his frantic tone and movements. She needs me to be okay right now. I will be for her. It's like second nature. "Kip, it's okay. But I need you to scoot back so I can check on her."

He does as I asked and slides back, leaving me room to move around to the side Ava's head is facing. Her eyes are wide with fear, and she tries to move, crying out.

"Mommy, it hurts. My head hurts."

I bend forward, looking at the cut and welt along her head, just above her temple. "I know, baby. I know. Does anything else hurt?" I start to pull my tank top off while she talks, pressing the cotton material over her head to tamper the bleeding. Leaving me in a tight-fitting camisole beneath it.

"Kip, I need you to call 9-1-1, okay?" He doesn't answer me, only nods his head. That's when Ruben walks up. "I'm on the phone with them now, Mrs. Canton. The operator wants to know if Ava is conscious."

"My head hurts, Mommy." Her words answer Ruben for me, and he relays that to the dispatcher. Ava tries to move and I press my other hand to her shoulder.

"Stay still, Ava Anne." I rub her arm and continue, "We need to make sure you're okay before you can move."

I look up at Kip and then Ruben, who is still on the phone, and Kip looks like he's going to faint.

"Kip, I need you to go and get Lightning settled in his stall, please, we don't want to lose him. Ruben can help me with Ava if it's needed. We'll be okay here."

He nods, wide-eyed and pushes to his feet, going to grab Lightning to get him put away. Ruben stays on the line with the dispatchers, keeping a small distance between him and us to not crowd Ava.

"I want Daddy," she cries, lifting her hand up to mine, holding it over her head.

"I'll call him, just as soon as the ambulance gets here."

"Ambulance?" She starts crying harder. I'm certain she's okay, but she fell from her horse and hit her head, I can't take any risks. Not with her. What if she hurt her neck, too?

"Yeah, an ambulance. You get to ride in an ambulance, and I bet they'll even turn the sirens on for you, if you want them to."

"Where's Daddy?" I think the shock of falling is wearing off now, and the pain and fear of what happened is starting to set in.

"I'm going to call him once we get you taken care of. I promise. He'll be home soon."

The ambulance finally pulls into our property, the sirens alerting us to their nearness. Ruben ends his call with the dispatcher when he sees them and then he goes to flag them down.

"You're okay, Ava. I promise, baby."

In all the commotion, from watching Ava take off, to her fall, I didn't stop to think about Aubrey. Not until I look toward where the ambulance will be pulling in and she's coming outside of the house, clinging to her stuffed animal and watching.

Ruben spots her, too, and walks over to lift her up into his arms. Clearing her of any possible danger while the ambulance drives up to the pen. He guides them, bringing Aubrey with him.

The paramedics enter the pen and make their way to us. They carry a neck brace, and backboard, moving with deliberate strides.

"Ma'am," the man says, and kneels beside me. "Who do we have here?"

He slides his gloved hand over mine, removing the tank top from Ava's head and taking a look at the gash there, replacing my shirt with gauze from his kit.

"This is Ava," I answer. "She's nine. No allergies to medicines, no health concerns you need to know about, either."

"Hi, Ava," he says softly, giving me a silent acknowledging nod before continuing, "I'm Paul, this is my friend, Reed, she's going to help me roll you onto your back and put a big brace around your neck, okay?"

Ava whimpers out a meek approval and searches for me with her eyes. "I'm here, baby. You're doing so good."

Ruben walks up with Aubrey, who immediately starts to get frantic in his arms. "Aubrey Jane, I need you to stay with Mr. Ruben. He's going to drive you in Mommy's car behind us when we leave. But you have to be my big girl while I'm with your sister."

Ruben gives me a tight smile and nods his head. "I'll go in and get your keys, Mrs. Canton. Do you need anything else?"

"My purse, please. And my cell phone. It's all on the kitchen counter."

"Yes, ma'am," he answers easily, and takes off toward the house with Aubrey.

I focus my attention back on Ava, just as Paul and Reed roll her to her back. She's got blood rolling down her cheek and eyes, but she looks okay otherwise. That's a good sign.

"Ma'am," Paul says. "We're going to take her to Edgewater Hospital. They'll handle any other transfer needs if they arise."

"Okay, thank you."

Paul and Reed work seamlessly to lift Ava and get her to the ambulance, where Ruben is waiting for me with my phone and purse.

"We'll be right behind you, Mrs. Canton."

"Thank you, Ruben." As soon as his back is to me, I swipe up on my phone and dial Chase. I tap my foot impatiently, waiting for him to answer. Once his voice comes through, I don't even give him time to say more than hello before I'm telling him, "Ava had an accident riding Lightning. We're on the way to the hospital now. Edgewater."

Chase

Panic. Sheer panic. That's all I feel after Allie's quick, frantic call. My little girl fell off her horse and she's hurt bad enough to go to the hospital. I floor my truck, going ten, fifteen, twenty over the speed limit, watching for cops, and praying with everything I have.

Please let me get there quickly.
Please let her be okay.
Please let this be a bad dream.

Allie didn't give me much; she was in a hurry to get into the ambulance with Ava. I heard the paramedics telling her they were ready to go, so I couldn't ask questions. I'm going strictly based on what she said. Ava fell off Lightning. They're going to Edgewater Hospital.

Interstate signs, exit signs, they all blur as I pass by in a blaze. An hour. That's roughly how long it will take me to get to my girls. To my Pipsqueak.

Please, God, just let her be okay.

My thoughts are racing, and the longer I'm thinking, the more questions start coming to mind. Where was Allie? Was Ava riding by herself? How did she fall? What was she doing? Was she being safe? How could this happen?

I have no answers to any of my questions. That angers me as much as the fact I wasn't there. I didn't keep my daughter safe. I swore to Allie, if we let Ava start riding, she'd be safe. I would guarantee she was always safe.

Anger. Guilt. Frustration. Fear. Panic. They're all circling and mixing in my mind. There is a knot the size of Texas in my throat, keeping me from swallowing. My stomach hurts. I want to blame someone. But who?

It's been forty minutes since Allie called. Surely, they're at the hospital by now. They have to have answers.

Why hasn't she called me?

The only reason she wouldn't have called yet is Ava is hurt really bad. She's trying to be strong for our daughters.

Shit.

Aubrey. Where's she? Is she okay? Did she see? Is she afraid?

Not knowing anything is torture. I need answers. I need to be at the fucking hospital already.

My hold on my steering wheel gets tighter. My knuckles ache and go white with my grip. Why hasn't Allie called me yet, dammit!

Please just let my little girl be okay.

Forty more miles until my exit. I can push the speed a little more, I need to get there. But getting pulled over going this fast would take more time away from my little girl. What the fuck do I—

My phone ringing pulls me out of my head and I reach to my passenger seat, grabbing the phone and answering without checking to see who it even is.

"Darlin'?"

"Chase—" Relief is all I feel hearing her calm voice. But is it too calm? I interrupt her before she can get another word out.

"Allie, what's going on? Is she okay? Please tell me she's okay. What happened?"

"Slow down," she says in a soft, quiet voice. "She's okay. They're going to run some tests soon."

"Tests? For what? You have to tell me what's going on." I know my tone sounds angry, but Christ, I'm terrified and she's not giving me any fucking answers.

"Chase," she says a little more forcefully. "She is okay. I need you to slow down. I don't want you dying in a car accident trying to get here. Slow down. Please. And I will tell you what's going on. She's okay."

I release my hold on my wheel a little and take a breath. "Baby, please just tell me..." I manage to get the words out in a calmer voice. And I let up on the gas pedal minutely.

"I'll explain what happened with Lightning when you get here," she says. "It's really the least important part. For right now, they suspect she has a concussion, she hit her head pretty hard and they suspect she lost consciousness briefly." Allie stops momentarily and I

51

listen to her answering a question asked by someone at the hospital. "Sorry, insurance question. Where was I?"

"How did she lose consciousness?"

"She hit her head, she was going around a barrel, too fast, and she fell off him on the turn. She hit her head on the edge of the barrel."

"Fuck," I hiss out and close my eyes, picturing my first baby falling like a rag doll off her horse and hitting a barrel. "Is she awake now? Is she in pain?"

"She's awake, and asking for her daddy. She hurts. Her head, mostly. She's nauseated, and her neck is hurting, too. They want to run some tests, make sure she didn't crack her skull or break anything. That's what we're waiting for now."

"I'll be there as soon as I can. I'm about thirty-five miles out. It'll be quick."

"She'll be glad to have you here. I'm going to let you go so you can drive safely. Don't push the speed, Chase. She really is okay. And we need you to get here the same way." I hear her answering Ava next, telling her I'm coming, and it only makes me want to drive faster.

"Allie, wait!" I shout a little louder than necessary, but I don't want her to hang up just yet.

"I'm still here," she answers.

"Aubrey, where's Aubrey? Is she okay?"

Allie sighs out. "She's in the waiting room with Ruben, he followed in my car with her. She's scared, Chase. You know her fears. This time it was her sister who got hurt…"

The pinch I feel in my heart with those words is acute. "I know her fears. I'll be there soon. For all three of you. I'm almost there."

As soon as our call is ended, I floor it. To hell with the risks. My girls need me and I'll be there for them soon.

Six

Allie

I know my husband. And I know when it comes to the girls, or me, and him thinking something may be wrong or one of us needs him for something serious, he will move heaven and hell to get here as fast as he can. So I also know speed limits, traffic lights, and his own safety won't matter to him at all until he gets here.

"Mommy," Ava says quietly, squinting up at me, "when will Daddy be here?"

I bend over her bed and kiss her forehead, minding the knot and bruise that are already starting to form around her temple. "He's going to be here really soon. Maybe fifteen more minutes."

She nods and closes her eyes again. The lights are dimmed, but they're still too bright for her. And the noises of the ER are too loud. She's overstimulated and scared. She's come close to throwing up, but they gave her something for the nausea and it seems to be easing up now. She's the bravest girl I know, though. She didn't cry when they put the IV in her arm. When the doctor was examining her, she flinched and grimaced in pain, but she wouldn't let anyone see how bad it hurt.

She is her father's daughter. It's something I both love and loathe in this situation. I don't want her to hide what she's feeling, because we need to know. But I also love how she's so resilient and determined.

One of the nurses comes in to check on Ava and tells me there's one more form I need to sign. The nurse says she's going to check Ava's vitals, and she'll sit with her for a few minutes over her break so I can take care of the paperwork.

"Sweet Girl," I kiss Ava's head one more time. "I'm going to go sign one last paper and check on your sister really fast, and then I will be right back, okay?"

"'Kay."

I leave her in the nurse's hands and step out of the small room and over to the nurses' station, asking for the form I need, so I can fill it out, and then go check on Aubrey. I go over the paperwork, sign my consent, and head toward the waiting room where Ruben is sitting with Aubrey.

"Hey, you two," I say as cheerfully and lightheartedly as I can when I approach them. Aubrey is sitting in Ruben's lap, playing on his phone, and she looks like she's been crying.

Aubrey looks up at me and her bottom lip pouts out. "Is Ava okay?"

"She will be," I say, with a nod and smile. "Are you okay, baby girl?"

Aubrey shakes her head no and tears start slipping from her eyes again. Oh, my sweet, precious girl.

"Come here. Let me hold you for a couple of minutes."

Aubrey hands Ruben his phone and slides from his lap, stepping into my arms and wrapping her small, shaking ones around my neck as tightly as she possibly can, and then starts crying in earnest.

"Shhh…Shhhhh… I've got you. It's okay. Ava's okay," I try to soothe her. I glance up at Ruben where he's sitting and say appreciatively, "Thank you for staying, sitting here with her. Ava's so sensitive to light and noise I didn't want to bring Aubrey back just yet. Not when Ava needs my full attention."

"It's my pleasure, ma'am," he responds with his smooth, easygoing voice. "She was showing me her favorite game. I know you have screen time rules, but…it was the only way I could get her to calm down."

I stand upright, holding Aubrey in my arms, feeling her legs wrap around me and her head rest on my shoulder, tears soaking through my shirt. "No, you've been great. Screen time isn't even a thought today. I just need both the girls content."

He gives a slight nod and smile. "How is Ava?"

"Concussion for sure. They fear she may have a cracked her skull, and they want to make sure her neck and spine are okay. We're waiting for tests now."

"She's hardheaded and stubborn," he injects, "she'll be okay. So will this one."

Ruben is a good man. Chase brought him on a couple of years ago to help out with the business end of things at the ranch. He handles operations and finances for us, and he's become very close to our family.

"Cantons are always okay," I agree, "as long as we have each other."

Just as the words leave my mouth, Aubrey starts wiggling in my arms and shouts, "Daddy!" I shift my gaze from Ruben to the entrance and see Chase striding in. His features are saturated in fear and anxiety as he approaches.

Aubrey reaches for Chase first, and I have to work to keep her in my arms until he's close enough to grab her. He reaches out for her, taking her weight off me with ease—only I see the small twitch in his eye when he bears her weight in his arms. That's something for me to bring up later, when we are out of here and we know our daughter is okay.

"Chase—" it's said on an exhale as relief floods my system. I don't need to be the only strong one now. We can tag team this, be here for both our girls and each other.

"Hey, Darlin'," he responds, shifting Aubrey to one arm and holding the other for me to fit beneath.

I move in close, slipping one arm behind his back and the other around his stomach and Aubrey's legs, laying my forehead against his chest and shoulder.

"I've got you now. All of you," he says, close and quiet enough that I know I'm the only one who heard. His breath is warm against my head and he kisses it before he addresses Ruben. "Thank you for being here for my girls, Ruben."

"I wouldn't have been anywhere else, Boss," Ruben answers. "You know whatever you need, I'm happy to help."

"I appreciate that more than you know. Really." He kisses my head again, it's natural, it's comforting and makes me melt into him even more. "I think we've got it from here, if you want to head back to the ranch."

"He brought my car," I pipe in, my voice muffled by Chase's chest.

"We'll take your car back, Aubrey's seat is in it. Ruben can drive my truck." Chase lets go of me and digs into his front pocket, pulling his keys out to hand to Ruben.

"Thanks, Mr. Cant—Chase," Ruben says, chuckling. I couldn't see it, but I know Chase gave him one of those looks that says, really? "If y'all need anything, let us know. I need to make sure Kip is okay, he was pretty shaken up when we left."

I pick my head up from Chase's warm, strong chest and look at Ruben. "Make sure he knows this wasn't his fault, Ruben. Because it wasn't. Not even a little. I saw it all happen. He did nothing wrong. You tell him that, okay?"

"Yes, ma'am. I'll tell him. I don't imagine it'll do much good until he sees Ava is okay for himself, but I will tell him."

Chase looks between us, the question of what we're talking about is written all over his confused face.

"Ava was riding under his supervision. She wanted to perfect her turn, so she could show you when she got home. Anyway, he signaled for her to stop, and I assume he told her to stop. And she did. But the second Kip's back was to her, she nudged Lightning on and took off."

I can see Chase's jaw clench and release. I know he's angry. So am I. But Kip didn't do anything wrong.

"You're sure he told her to stop?"

"I heard him myself, Boss," Ruben speaks up. "He told her to wait a minute while he talked to me. He wouldn't have let her ride without his watching. Not with the barrel out there."

Chase nods once. "We'll talk to her about it later. First, we make sure she's okay. Tell Kip none of us holds him responsible, and this wasn't his fault."

"Yes, sir." It's short, but Ruben knows Chase well enough to know less is more right now.

"We need to get to our daughter," Chase says matter-of-factly. "Thank you again, Ruben."

Ruben gives a final nod and turns for the door, leaving quickly and quietly.

"Where's Ava's room?" Chase asks, as he wraps his arm back around me.

"She's in twenty-two, that way." I point in the direction of her room. "A nurse is sitting with her now, I needed to check on Aubrey." I'm explaining to him why I'm not with Ava, and I'm not sure why. We have two daughters, I had to be here for both of them. But I still feel the need to justify myself.

"Babe," he says evenly, "I wasn't questioning because you aren't in there. I just wanted to know where to lead us. Right, Monkey?" He must've heard it in my tone. I tried not to be defensive saying it, but now that he's here, some of my adrenaline is tapering and I feel a lot less sure of myself, and what's happening, than I did before he got here.

"Right, Daddy!" she agrees, some of her fear ebbing away, replaced with happiness thanks to Chase's presence.

"I'm sorry," I sigh out, "it's all just starting to crash down on me now."

"It's okay," he says as we round the corner, and Ava's room comes into view. "I get it. I've got you." He gives me one of his patented, confident smiles. "Monkey, why don't you walk with Mommy now? That way I can make sure Ava is okay when we get into her room." He kisses her temple and winks at her, then sets her down.

Aubrey steps beside me and takes my hand, then Chase leads us into Ava's room.

"I hear my Pipsqueak had a pretty big fall today," it's the first thing he says the second the door opens, and Ava's eyes pop open instantly. She's still looking a little dazed, but her smile fills her whole face.

"Daddy, you're here!" It's the loudest, most outgoing she's sounded since we arrived, and it's the first sign I've seen from her that she really will be okay.

"Of course I'm here." He walks right up to her and bends over the bed, hugging her gently, but letting her wrap him up as tight as she can. He stays still over her, not pulling back even after her arms have gone loose.

I get it, baby. But she's okay.

Seeing our little girl, small and hurt, in a huge hospital bed with an IV in her arm and the lights dimmed, because if they were any brighter it would make her head hurt, is absolutely terrifying. I settle Aubrey in a chair with my phone and move to the other side of Ava's bed so I'm standing across from Chase.

He picks his head up and looks at me, not hiding a single feeling or thought at first, before he takes in a deep breath and puts a smile back on his face.

"Let's look at that head of yours," he says animatedly. He's put on a brave face for her and I'm so grateful. Ava turns her head to the side as best as she can with her neck brace on, so he can see the knot and bruise forming. "Whoa! That's one tough looking bump. Were you trying to prove how hard a head we Cantons have?"

"Nooo," Ava says, drawing out the word as long as she can.

"You weren't? Are you sure?"

"I'm sure, Daddy. I didn't mean to fall. I just wanted to practice."

"You know," he says more seriously, but still quietly, "practice is good, but only when someone is—" Before he can finish, Ava's nurse comes back in.

"We're ready to take her up for tests. Once those are finished, as long as they come back clear, you should be good to take her home."

Chase audibly lets out the breath I was holding, too. "Is there any reason to believe the tests won't be clear?"

The nurse shakes her head and responds, "No, Mr. Canton, we don't think so. Dr. Simms is pretty sure her neck is fine, and he just wants to be certain there are no skull fractures. Based on all the years he's been doing this, he said it's likely just the concussion."

I speak up first this time, "Thank you."

Anjelica Grace

A tech joins the group of us in the room and Chase and I kiss Ava, telling her we'll be right here when she gets back from her tests. I'm hopeful they'll be clear, especially after what we were just told, but if they aren't, at least my husband is here with us. We can figure anything out when we are together as a family.

Seven

Allie

F our words, that's all it took this evening to bring on a tidal wave of emotion and relief like I've never known before. Four words: "Her tests are clear." When the doctor told us, I turned into Chase, hid my face against his chest, and I cried. I cried grateful tears. Grateful our daughter is going to be okay. Grateful my rock was there, holding us all up. Grateful that after a few days or weeks, everything will return to normal.

When I watched Ava fall today, my world came to a crashing halt. Thoughts I wouldn't allow myself to think stayed at bay until it was clear she was okay, and then I drowned in them. The what-ifs were worse than what was really happening.

As I sit here with my family now, watching Ava sleep curled in Chase's lap, and Aubrey sleep with her head in mine, I can finally breathe. We are whole. We are healthy—minus Ava's head and sore neck, and Chase's arm—and we are home together.

I don't have to figure out what to do because my little girl is fighting for her life. I don't have to sit bedside, holding vigil until good news comes our way. I get to hold one of our babies while he holds the other in our home, while they sleep peacefully, and aside from a few headaches and some stiffness for the next few days, all is right in our world.

We got lucky.

Chase reaches over Aubrey's body, slipping his hand behind my neck, rubbing it gently, and whispers, "How're you doing?"

"Okay." It's all I can think of saying. I am okay. I'm exhausted, I'm relieved, I'm amped up, yet perfectly content exactly where I am. I'm okay.

"I'm sorry I wasn't here today. I left a little later than I'd planned to. Had I been here…"

I shake my head. Now isn't the time to play that game. "She still could've fallen. She's going to fall. She's going to make mistakes. There's nothing you could've done."

"But you said she was out there so she could show me when I got home. Had I already been here, then she wouldn't have been on the damn horse."

"You don't know that. In fact, I'd venture a guess that you're wrong, and she still would've been on the horse today. She still would've found the same determination to take the barrel with speed to prove herself, whether it was you, me, or Kip in the pen with her—she still would've gone down."

He closes his eyes and shakes his head, rejecting my words outwardly, even though I know they're settling in his mind and over his heart.

"She's you, Chase," I say with a small smile. "Nothing is keeping her from riding. Nothing."

He dips his chin down gently and kisses her head, careful not to bump her temple. I can tell he's thinking, and I'm not sure what he's going to say, but I don't think he is, either. So I give him time to work it out and run my fingers through Aubrey's hair.

"I don't know if her being me is a good thing," he whispers, and glances my way. "I couldn't take her being hurt worse. Not even a little. We know what the pain losing a baby we never even got to know feels like…" He breaks off and looks away, clearing his throat, gathering his composure. He doesn't break easily, but you put one of his girls in the hospital and it will bring him to his knees.

"Losing our baby, it killed me. But if something had happened to Ava today, if something ever happens to either of our girls, it would put me in hell. Death would be nothing compared to what I'd feel if I lost either of them. If I ever lost you…"

The tears welling up in his eyes render me speechless. This man, the strongest I've ever known in my life, the one who rides bulls for a living and puts his life on the line week in and week out, is crying over our daughter's calm, sleeping body because she could have gotten seriously hurt today.

I turn my head into his forearm, kissing it softly, and close my eyes, accepting my own tears as they slip out. "We didn't lose her. She's okay. She's a Canton, she's got a hard head, she's stubborn as hell, and she's full of piss and vinegar. A fall wasn't going to keep her down."

That brings a slight smile back to his lips, and he moves his hand from my neck to my cheek, brushing my tears away with his thumb. "She may be all me with her determination and stubbornness, but I watched the video you sent the other night, she looked just like a mini version of you up there. It took me back to when I first saw you ride."

I look at him and he's watching me carefully. We don't talk about my riding days. Not if I can avoid it. It's not that I'm ashamed to have ridden or been on the Junior Circuit. It's that I was forced to ride. My dad, a bareback bronc rider, started me at a young age—younger than Ava is now—and forced me to start training. Rodeo was going to be a family thing. Mom would support both of us and Dad and I would bring glory to the family name.

I hated it.

I wanted to cheer, or play softball, take up art, or singing. I wanted to try just about anything under the sun to see what would've been my passion, but I couldn't.

"She'll be better than I was," I whisper back to him. This isn't a conversation I want the girls waking up to. It's not one I want to have.

He looks over both girls and then whispers back, "Why do you hide it from them?"

There isn't a good answer. Not really. But I've never wanted the girls to know I did rodeo. I guess, in part, it's that I don't want to encourage Ava to focus solely on it—I want her to have a childhood and try everything. And, another part of it is, I don't want Aubrey to feel like she's the only one who doesn't like rodeo. Because she has zero interest in riding, and that's perfectly fine.

"It's not important," I say back, shrugging it off. "It has no bearing on either of them, and it's not who I am anymore."

He just shakes his head and drops it back on the couch, muttering something I don't quite catch beneath his breath.

"It helped shape you, though." He pulls his hand back slowly, then adds, "It's the reason we met. The reason we have them. That alone is worth shouting how great a rider you actually were from the rooftops…"

"Maybe one day, once the girls have decided what they want to do with their lives. I don't want my past influencing their futures."

"Okay." He turns his head toward the clock up on the wall and then looks back at me. "Are we going to sit here all night and watch them? Or should we get them into their beds?"

"Yes."

His gruff chuckle fills the room over my response. "Yes, we're going to watch them sleep in our laps all night? Yes, we're going to take them to bed?"

"I know they need to be in their own beds so they sleep better, I'm just—" I pause, searching for the right words. "I'm just enjoying this. For a split second earlier, I didn't know what life would bring us. Having you home, Ava is okay, I'm not ready to give this up yet."

"Then they can sleep in our bed."

That's a solution I wouldn't have even thought of. They sleep in our bed with me when he's gone a lot, but never when he's home. That's my and Chase's place. It's where we get our one-on-one time, in every form it comes in.

"Our bed," I repeat.

"It's why we got a king-sized mattress, isn't it? So we could all fit comfortably?"

He makes a good point. "Yes, it was, mostly. There's also the small matter of you being a bed hog."

His eyes go wide and he gives me an I'm gonna get you look. It hits me full force and awakens the butterflies in my stomach.

"I'm no more of a bed hog than you are a blanket hog."

"Am not!" I laugh loudly. His blue eyes are shining bright, smiling just as vividly as his lips are. Until Ava stirs in his lap.

"You're being too loud," she mumbles, still half asleep.

I cover my mouth with one hand, trying to muffle my laughs, when Chase mouths, "Bad Mommy."

"We're sorry, Ava," I manage to get out in a loud whisper.

65

"We'll move you to bed so we don't wake you again," Chase adds, still smirking in my direction.

Ava's response comes in the form of a soft snore and movement closer to Chase's body. "Let's get them to bed so we don't wake her, or Aubrey, again."

Chase

We lay the girls down in our bed carefully and cover them up. For the time being, they're in the center of the bed, but multiple occasions in the past tell me that as soon as we step away, their two small bodies will quickly take up every bit of space they can and leave little to no room for Allie and me.

Allie smiles at me over the bed, and the girls, then whispers, "Come shower with me? They'll be fine in here."

I walk around the bed and toward the bathroom, holding my hand out to her, waiting for our fingers to be linked before I guide her in and shut the door behind us.

"Was this your way of telling me I smell?" I ask her teasingly. I reach into the shower to turn the water on, letting it heat up, and turn to her.

"Yep," she quips, "I could smell you across the couch. I didn't want you in our bed until we hosed you down."

She pulls her T-shirt off and tosses it on the floor, then pops the button of her jeans open and shimmies them down her legs.

"My God, you're beautiful." I watch her wiggle and shake until her jeans are pooled at her bare feet, where she can step out of them. She's left in plain, cotton black panties and a matching black bra and the look makes my mouth water and heart race.

"Thank you." She smiles shyly, still, after all these years. "You're still completely dressed…"

I am. But watching her, unrushed and perfect, is far more important than removing my clothes at the moment. She's still looking at me expectantly, waiting for me to undress, but reaches behind her to loosen her bra before it slips down her arms and falls away.

"Chase, clothes…" She laughs and pushes her panties down. She starts walking toward me and my breath catches, watching her, anticipating what she's going to do. Much to my dismay, she continues right on by me, and steps into the shower, giggling beneath the spray of the water.

"That was cold," I half-groan, half-say, tugging my shirt over my head and dropping it where I stand. "So cold."

The sound of the water sloshing off her body to the shower floor nearly drowns her voice out, but I manage to catch her words anyway, "Then hurry up and get in here, it's nice and hot."

I do as she says and finish undressing as quick as I can, then join her in the shower.

"It's about time." She turns around beneath the water to face me, smiling. "Will you wash my hair? It's been so long, and your hands could literally put me to sleep with how comforting they are when you do it."

I reach for her shampoo, a white bottle labeled with the scents of vanilla and coconut. "It would be my pleasure. Turn around, please."

She turns away from me again and tilts her head. Her hair falls down her back, looking like a dark, smooth curtain with water dripping from the ends. I squirt the shampoo into my hands and lather it before I apply it to her head.

"Mmmm," she moans, "that feels so good." I'm working the shampoo into her scalp now, massaging gently, letting the soap build before moving my fingers down her long locks, combing shampoo from her head to the very ends of her hair.

"Please don't stop yet," she murmurs.

"I won't." I move my fingers back to her scalp and continue to work my magic, stepping closer so I can kiss her shoulder and whisper in her ear, "Rinse this out then I'll give you a massage. I felt the tension in your neck earlier. Let me take care of you."

She spins back around, facing me and lets the water cascade down her hair and body. "I've missed you. This."

"Me, too." I take the opportunity to bend and kiss her lips while the shampoo runs out of her hair. Her hands move to my chest and settle there as the kiss grows between us. A gentle meeting of our lips turns to a deeper pressure, then her mouth opens, or maybe it was mine first, and we each give and take. A leisurely pass of my tongue over hers is followed by a playful nip of her teeth over my lip. I wrap my arms around her and pull her tighter to me, loving the feel of her body, slick and hot from the water, against mine.

"Hit the other showerhead," I instruct against her lips. She reaches out to the side and turns the head behind me on so we are enclosed in a sheet of water. I revel in the feel of her lips and body melting into mine for a few minutes, then break away with a level of restraint I didn't know was possible.

"What, what are you doing? You don't want…" She's a little breathless, and her eyes are wide and dilated. It would be so easy, so damn hot, to take her right here and now. But we have days for that. Tonight, she deserves to be pampered.

"Oh, I do. But I'm going to do what I said I would," I respond, leaning in to give her a chaste kiss. "I'm going to rub the knots and tension out of your neck and shoulders. Then I'm going to wash your body, rinse you off, get you out of here and dry, and then I'm going to carry you to bed. I'm going to take care of you tonight." I take a deep breath and turn her away from me. "Tomorrow I will finish what was about to start just now."

She gives a little huff, but the second my hands press into her shoulders, it blends into a deep sigh. "I—why?" I know she's confused, I can hear it in the tone of her voice.

"Because I know what today did to you." I rub my thumbs into the knots in her shoulder and lower my head to kiss her heated skin. "I know what my being gone has been doing to you. I've seen it in every Skype. I've heard it in every call. I felt it when I finally showed up and you clung to me for dear life earlier."

"Chase…" It's all she says, but it's enough. My name on her lips in that tone is all I need to hear to know I'm doing the right thing. Her tone is laced with the weight of her feelings, frustrations, acceptance, and love. But most of all, it's laced with relief and exhaustion.

Allie lets her body relax beneath my touch, and the tension slowly releases from her shoulders the longer I work my fingers over them. I'd love to do this for her all night, but we've only got so much time before the hot water runs cold and all the progress I've made freezes back into her muscles.

"Pick your bodywash, Darlin'," I whisper to her. She reaches out and grabs the lavender one I love and passes it back to me.

"I'm so tired now," she says. "You've relaxed me so much I could fall asleep right here."

"I'm almost done. Then I'll dry you and get you to bed." I kiss the crown of her head and start washing her body. I work my way down her back first, bending to wash down her rounded, perfect ass, and along her firm legs to her heels. "Turn around so you can rinse while I get your front next."

She turns carefully and I look up from where I'm still kneeling at her feet. Every part of her that turns me on most is right here, open and exposed. All I would need to do is lean forward and kiss her, and she'd widen her stance and give me a part of her that only I've ever had.

She smiles down at me and threads her fingers through my wet hair silently.

Don't do it. Not tonight. This is about her, not you.

I mentally chastise myself for thinking with my dick rather than my brain and heart. Instead of leaning forward to kiss and taste what's taunting my body, I kiss her flat stomach, right where a child will grow one day, and soap her up again, massaging all of the tight muscles in her legs before I stand.

She's watching my every move with tired, happy eyes. I did that for her. I'm not going to fuck it up by being a horny man, now. But I'm not going to pass up the opportunity to move my hands over her chest, either. With the bodywash still on my hands, they both glide easily up her abdomen, and over her breasts. I brush my thumbs over her tightening nipples, drawing a small sigh out of her.

70

"Tomorrow. Tomorrow." I'm repeating it more for myself than her, but her answered agreement makes me happy, nonetheless.

I stand fully again and wink at her. "Turn and rinse, I'll get my hair and body real fast, too. Then I'm getting you to bed."

"Thank you," she says; then turns to rinse her body off. While her back is to me I grab my shampoo and work it into my hair quickly, giving my body an equally quick pass with the same shampoo on my hands, then rinse it all off beneath the other showerhead.

"I could've done that for you," she says, just before her hand touches my back.

"Next time. This time was about you, not me." I spin and reach for the handles, shutting the shower water off and then grab her big, fluffy towel and use it to dry her off.

"I need pajamas, please."

I guess we can't exactly walk out of here and climb into bed naked tonight. Not with our girls asleep in there. "I'll be right back, you stay put." I cinch my towel around my waist and head into our bedroom. The girls are both out, and taking up the whole bed, as I figured they would. I grab her clothes, and mine, then go back to her. She's wrapped in her towel and looking more gorgeous than should be possible.

"I hope these are okay," I say as I hold up what I brought for her.

"They're perfect. I love sleeping in your shirts." She steps out of the shower and takes the clothes from me, dropping her towel to dress in her pajamas, and then she winds her hair up into a bun.

"Funny, I love you sleeping in my shirts, too." I grin at her and dry myself off the rest of the way, then dress as quickly as I can and scoop her into my arms. She wraps her arms around my neck and lays her head on my bare chest while I carry her to bed. I lay her down beside Aubrey and bend to kiss her lips. "Good night, Allie. I love you."

"I love you too, Chase." Not long after the words leave her mouth, she closes her eyes, and sleep finds her nearly immediately. I plan on joining them in slumber soon. But first, I want to watch them. Take in my girls, and let the weight of the day and what might have happened melt away.

Eight

Allie

There are mornings when you wake up, and everything feels a little brighter, a little happier, and a little calmer. It's like a blanket of happiness has settled over everything dreary and sad, and all you can see are the stunning colors of the world. All you can see are the bright sun rising out of the east, peeking up behind our lands and the cattle. The green, open fields just beyond the grazed-over pastures. The rich, dark brown of the coffee swirling perfectly with the white of the creamer. It's all more vivid, more special than it's been in I can't remember how long.

Then again, I've had my Cowboy home for nearly forty-eight hours now, and he won't be leaving for another seventy-six at least. And that is enough to make everything perfect right now.

Chase walks into the kitchen behind me and slides his hands over my hips, pressing his body into the back of mine, and his lips into my hair, kissing me with a subtle groan.

"You showered without me this morning," he murmurs.

"I did, I'm sorry. You needed to sleep, though. And I wanted to get a jump on coffee and laundry." I turn in his arms so I'm facing him and we are pressed together, front to front. "You looked way too comfy with the girls snuggled into you to disturb you for something as mundane as a shower."

"Mundane? You call time spent with you wet and naked mundane?" He smirks at me. "You sure you weren't the one who hit your head a couple days ago?"

I nod and grin up at him. "Positive."

"Speaking of hitting heads, and Ava, how did the girls end up in bed with us?"

"They snuck in about an hour ago. I heard Aubrey stir first, she went into Ava's room, and then they both came and crawled in with us. You were out like a rock."

"I must've been. I didn't notice anything. Not them joining us or you leaving."

I slide my hands up his bare chest and link my fingers together behind his neck. "I stayed in there for about thirty minutes after they came in, I couldn't go back to sleep."

"So you showered, then got a jump on laundry and coffee?"

"Close," I respond. "I haven't gotten to laundry yet. You interrupted my morning flow."

He lets out a low, deep chuckle. "Morning flow?"

"Yep, my morning flow. I have to act before the girls are awake, otherwise what should take ten minutes takes an hour."

"Ah, I see." He leans in and kisses my lips, then smiles against them. "You know what, though?"

"Hmm?"

He kisses me again. "I'll keep the girls company this morning, so you can take a few minutes right here with me and not have to worry about your morning flow."

"You're a saint." I open my eyes when he pulls back a little.

He shakes his head and smirks. "Believe me, it has nothing to do with me being a saint. I just left the girls, and they were out cold. So, I'm thinking if I play my cards right, I can make out with my wife for a while before they wake for good and ruin *my* morning flow."

A laugh starts deep in my belly and bellows out into the open kitchen, and he slides his hand over my mouth, laughing at my laugh, much quieter than I was.

"Shhh. You'll wake them up before I get some time with you," he chides, lifting me by the hips up onto the counter. "And if they wake up, I can't do this..." He steps between my legs, sliding his hands up them and beneath my T-shirt, trailing a featherlight touch from my tummy, around to my back, before he pulls me closer to him and kisses me.

His lips claim mine with an intensity that steals my breath, and makes every part of my body tingle with need. "Chase..." It's a plea...and a warning.

"What?" He moves his mouth from my lips to my jaw, and kisses down my jawline and toward my ear.

"That feels..." He scrapes his teeth over the sensitive skin just beneath my ear and I moan quietly.

"How does it feel?" He does it again, and my breath catches.

"Too good, we can't... The girls could..."

He moves his mouth lower down my throat and starts working his way over to the other side. "We aren't. I'm just... giving you a little taste of what comes later. While I take a little taste of you now."

His teeth graze over my skin again and I shiver. "You're such a jerk."

His mouth moves expertly from my throat up to my jaw, kissing back around and up to my lips, until he's able to take them with his again. They flutter and dance over mine until I part them to breathe, and he takes the

75

opportunity to dip his tongue in for a taste. It brushes over mine then glances the roof of my mouth—teasing me just a little—before he pulls it back out and he kisses only my lips again.

I can't help the small sounds of appreciation, or lust, that escape in little bursts. He's assaulted my senses and kicked my body into overdrive in a way he hasn't been here or able to do in close to a month.

"Chase…" I say again, this time it comes out as a soft moan. "Please…"

He grins and asks, "Please what? Please stop? Please more?"

"More, so much more."

He nods and slips his hands back toward the front of my shirt and slowly walks his fingers up my ribs, but halts them in place when the sound of one of our girls coming down the hall alerts us to the fact that our alone time is up.

"More's going to have to wait," he whispers, sliding his hands back down my stomach and around to my back, just before Aubrey walks into the kitchen.

"I'm hungry," she says, rubbing her eyes with her hair wild and falling into her face.

"See," I whisper to Chase while we watch her, "this is why my morning flow gets ruined."

Aubrey pays us no attention while she finishes rubbing her eyes, and then she looks up and grins wide when she sees us here.

"Looks like someone finally noticed us," Chase says under his breath, resting his head against my chest while he watches her.

"Hi, Daddy." She waves, then walks around the island and climbs up onto a stool across the counter from us.

"Mornin', Aubrey," he replies and pulls his hands out from beneath my shirt where they had been resting on my back. "Do you two want some pancakes?"

I nod my head and reach for my cup of coffee again, then reposition myself so I'm angled toward Aubrey and Chase, and that's when I notice Ava walk into the kitchen, too.

"Did Daddy say he's making pancakes?" she asks.

"I did. What kind do you guys want?"

I look at both girls and ask, "What do you say, do you guys want them?"

Each of our girls nods their heads.

"On the count of three then," I say, smiling. Then I hold up my hand, using my fingers to help me count, one...two...three...

All three of us say in unison, "Cowboy Pancakes!"

Chase laughs and gives us a little salute. "Let me go put a shirt on, and then I'm going to need some help. Allie, why don't you get to your morning laundry going so when we're done, maybe we can drive up to Denver and go to their zoo."

"Don't you have to practice?" I ask, smiling wide.

"Not today. Today I'm taking the day off to spend with you three. So everybody better get a move on."

"But what are we supposed to move on to?" Aubrey asks, holding her hands up by her shoulders to show us just how confused she is.

I can't help but laugh. "You girls get the table set, and grab the stuff you want to put over your pancakes, while your daddy gets his shirt on, then the three of you can make the pancakes together. I'm going to go do laundry."

As the girls set out to grab plates and forks, and their toppings, Chase helps me off the counter and kisses my lips. "See, morning flow problem solved. Now get moving so we can have a fun family day together at the zoo later."

It's been one of the best days we have had together as a family in a very long time. Once breakfast and laundry were finished, Chase did take us to the zoo. And it was a blast. We don't make it to Denver's often, so to see the changes they've made, to watch the girls in awe by the animals and the shows, feeding the giraffes, it was everything.

Chase and Aubrey bonded over the monkeys, especially the ones out on the open ropes course in the new elephant exhibit. Aubrey was so hoping one would land on our shoulders, though it never happened. I suspect the zoo has ways of stopping them from doing that.

Ava loved the elephant show. She picked the seats right in front of the glass railing and got to throw some of their fruit chunks out for the elephant to snag and eat up. Even her headache didn't put a damper on the day.

What he did for me today, getting us in privately to see the sloths, and the new baby sloth—I'm certain I fell even harder for him than I already had.

Now that we're home, with two exhausted girls he's tucking into bed, all I can think about is spending some alone time with him.

I walk into our bathroom, washing my hands and face then get a washcloth out to wipe my sweat and sunscreen-covered body down. I strip out of my clothes and change into a navy lace bra and panty set, then I find his favorite body spray and spritz a thin coat over myself. A quick glance at the mirror and a pinch to each cheek and I feel sufficiently ready for the night I have planned with him.

I move back into our room, light a few candles throughout, and settle in our bed to wait for him. His approach is easy to see with each light that dims and cuts out from the living room, down the hall and the girls' rooms, until he's stepping through our door.

"Lock it, Chase," I whisper, watching him take in the candles around the room. He looks around as the flickers of each small flame cause shadows to dance across the walls, and then he reaches me with his gaze. I wish I could see his eyes clearly right now, whether they're wider or showing the possessive hunger I only know is real because he seems to always have it for me.

"Allie," he husks out. "The way you look in the candlelight, shit..." He steps farther into the room and closes the door with the quietest click possible, and then I hear the lock engage.

"It's been a while, we haven't..." Explaining myself to him makes me more nervous and my voice falters, "I don't know when we'll get to again... Is it too much?"

He steps beyond the door and into the first glow of light from the candle on our dresser, and the smile on his face stops my heart, then proceeds to cause it to not only speed up but pound against my chest like a drum.

"Why is everything always too much with you?" he asks teasingly, as he slowly steps toward the bed. It's a joke we've had for a while now. I'm always telling him he's too much. Honestly, I think it's something he takes pride in. Then he reminds me in his very special way, that with him, it's never too much.

"Because I like making you show me it's actually just enough."

He stops at the foot of our bed and lets his eyes lazily traverse my body, pausing briefly on my chest, and then stopping at my face, our eyes locking instantly. "When it comes to you, it'll never be just enough. I'll want and take more, as often as I can, until the day I die."

"Do you promise?" I'm not sure why I'm asking, except for the fact I know in the back of my mind, when these few days are over, he will be back on the road, away from me, and all of this will be a memory I cling to until he's home for a few days again

"I swear, Darlin'." He pulls his shirt over his head, using his one perfectly fine arm, and then he starts working his belt loose. His hands are large, moving over the buckle so quickly and precisely you wouldn't think it possible. I want them to move that way over me.

"Let me." I push forward to my knees and crawl to the foot of the bed where he's standing. I feel his eyes on me; know he's looking down my back and at my bare ass as it sways with each movement forward. It's highlighted by the black lace along my waist that disappears between each cheek.

"You're wearing a thong," he states, his voice gravellier now. "You're trying to kill me right where I stand, aren't you?" His hands are no longer moving over his buckle, he's frozen in place, watching me. As I kneel in front of him, I know as long as he's staring at me, he won't actually get his belt the rest of the way off. So I replace his hands over it with my own, and finish working the metal loose with a clank, then let it fall and hang off his belt loops.

"I'd never kill you. I need you too much."

He finally snaps out of his trance and forgets about undressing himself, choosing instead, to touch me. His hands move steadily down my shoulders and arms, and his lips find their purchase along my throat and collarbone as he murmurs, "You're so soft. Always so soft."

His hands, in complete contrast to my skin, are rough and calloused. They're the hands of a hard-working, bull riding cowboy who knows exactly how to use them. And use them he does. He moves them from my wrists to my body, barely touching my skin as he slides them from my ticklish sides, up to my covered breasts. "Always perfect."

His words make me move faster. I pop the button of his jeans open and lower his zipper so I can push his pants off his hips and down his strong, built legs; they fall in a heap at his feet. We're on equal ground now. He's in nothing but his tight-fitted boxer briefs, which are doing absolutely nothing to hide his growing erection. And I'm in nothing but my panties and bra. The same bra he's eyeing and licking his lips hungrily over.

I suck in a sharp breath when he pinches my nipples through the lace, then I look up into his eyes, breathing hard, needing to see what I couldn't before. Now that I can see what's in them, with the flickering of the candles behind me, I see every last thing running through his mind that his eyes give away. I see the heat of his stare, the desire, the love, and mixed within all of that is the obvious fight for the restraint and control he's holding onto—even though he really wants to let go.

Knowing I do this to him still, after all this time, is such a powerful feeling.

"Perfect for you," I moan, as he leans forward and closes his mouth over my bra, flicking his tongue over the lace before sucking gently. It's a sensation I can't even describe. The warmth of his mouth pulling gently, the coarseness of the bra rubbing over my sensitive flesh—it's the sweetest torture there is.

"God, baby, that feels—" My words are cut off and turn into a loud groan when his teeth sink into me and tug gently. It sends a bolt of need and pleasure through me, and I feel its effects between my legs where my body is already ready and desperate for him.

"Tell me, what does it feel like? Should I do it again?"

I nod my head and graze my nails over his skin, tracing over the dark lines of the tattoo draping off his shoulder and down his arm. "It feels rough and soft at once. And so, so good."

He obliges with a cocky grin and leans forward, paying the same glorious attention to my other breast, drawing out a cry of pleasure when his hands find their way down my body and between my legs.

His fingers move in perfect sync with his tongue, rubbing and flicking, causing every bit of lace between us to become wet, from his mouth or my excitement. I reach for the back of his arm, holding on, gently caressing the triceps I know is still pulled, and then guide it down to his wrist and hand placed perfectly between my legs. I slide my fingers over his hand and slip them between his, linking them together, guiding his movements over me.

Chase

Our fingers move together over the damp, abrasive lace covering her, and her head drops to my chest, lips parted as she pants against me. She's knows exactly what she wants, and she thinks she's going to show me. But I know better. I want to drive her to the brink, then pull her back, tease her and make tonight last.

"Let me work our fingers over you," I whisper commandingly to her, flipping our hands so mine is on top and in control of hers beneath it. "I know what you need. I'll guide us now."

She answers with a nod against my chest and her lips fluttering over my skin.

"Good girl," I praise her with a kiss to the head. Then I clasp her fingers tightly between mine, and move them from where they are—where she wants them most—over her pert little clit, up to her waist and into her panties. "These really need to go now," I mutter, as our hands move back down the front of her. We pass over the neat strip of hair leading back to her swollen nub, and just before we make contact, I lift our hands up just enough to pass right over it.

"You're teasing me," she whimpers, and grazes her teeth over my chest.

"I'm building you up in a way this will last and be fucking amazing," I promise. She lets out a little huff against me, but doesn't push back…yet. "Use your other hand to help me get rid of these," I add, hooking my free hand into the string of her thong and sliding it down her leg, waiting for her to do the same.

"So bossy," she says with a chuckle, then pushes the other side down.

"Now wiggle." She looks up at me, eyebrows raised. "Just, trust me."

Allie starts to wiggle her hips, and I move our hands back against her, causing her to wiggle right over our fingers, rubbing herself against our joined hands.

"Ohhh..." she sighs out.

If I thought the lace we just peeled off her was wet, it's nothing compared to the slickness now coating our fingers, allowing her to rub herself over the ridges from my big fingers to her small with ease. I press our hands tighter to her and she grinds down, fucking our hands without a second thought.

She's kneeling on the bed, legs spread, riding our hands while I guide them over her clit, her lips, setting a steady rhythm in time with her, and it's so hot my dick is throbbing in my underwear, begging for relief of any kind. But this isn't about me, yet.

"More," she groans out, "Please give me more."

"Don't you come," I say, moving our hands lower and slipping my middle finger over the top of hers. "Not yet." I guide our fingers to her opening together, her smaller curling beneath mine, as we press into her. We move our fingers in, and I swear on all things holy, her walls start sucking us in deeper, squeezing and pulsing around us like they've been starved of attention for years.

"Jesus," I groan out, "You're so damn tight. Do you feel that? Do you feel how bad your pussy wants us to fuck it with our fingers?

"Oh God, Chaaase."

"Not. Yet."

"Pleeease," she begs, and moves her other hand down my stomach, curling her fingers around my cotton-covered dick. "I need to, baby."

"We're going to fuck you together, now. Move your finger in and out with mine. Keep them together or it won't feel as good."

"O-o-kay," she manages to agree.

I slowly pull my finger back, waiting for her to follow suit, until we are both slipping out of her, and then I move mine back in, starting out slow, in-out-in-out, until she's gotten the pattern down. "Quicker now, until you can't keep up with me. When the time comes, pull out and let me finish while you work your clit. Got it?"

She's beyond words now, swallowing hard and nodding her head, breathing heavily as we start to pick up speed. Her other hand slips into the front of my boxer briefs and circles around my shaft, moving up and down it, driving me mad with need. I can feel the precum oozing from my tip, spurred on by her hot, delicate fingers moving over me. But her movements become inconsistent and shaky at best when we really get moving in her.

"God, Chase, I can't, I'm so close... I can't anymore..."

"Take your finger out, I've got you." She slips her finger from her body and I can feel her slip it beneath my wrist and the heel of my hand so she can circle herself, add the last little bit of friction she needs.

"You can let go now," I rasp in her ear, starting to move my finger in and out faster, curling it up in just the right place so I hit her sweet spot, the one that's sure to make her explode.

Like a stick of dynamite, she does. Her release is so forceful, it's rendered her soundless as her head and mouth fall slack against my chest. Her hand clenches around my cock, and her legs squeeze together, trapping my hand where it's at. Her walls contract around my finger like a vise, holding me in place while a surge of warmth and her juices coat my hand beneath her.

"That's what I wanted," I whisper as I slide an arm around her waist. "Let go of my hand, Darlin', let go so I can give you more."

Her legs part just enough for me to pull my hand free.

"Oh. My. God," she pants out. "That was…"

"I know." I chuckle. "While I'm holding you steady, pull my boxer briefs down. I need in you, now."

Her hands move shakily to my waistband and shove the constricting fabric down, allowing my cock to spring free. I use the hand she just came on and grip myself, stroking up and down, covering me with her release.

"Do that again," she says, eyeing my hand moving over me.

I nod my head for her. "Lie down…"

She drops backward, falling to the bed and pushing her panties still around her knees off, allowing her the room she needs to widen her legs. "Touch yourself again, just outside, let me watch for a couple of seconds."

Allie does as I say and moves her hand back down, touching herself, moving her fingers over the glistening flesh still wet from her release. I grip my length harder, sliding my hand up slowly, and groaning when her back arches into her touch, and her lips part on a sigh.

"Are you ready for me again?"

"God, yes. Hurry."

I crawl up the bed and over her body, raising one of her legs beneath her thigh and spreading her wide for me.

"Slow will have to wait," I warn her, lining myself up at her entrance. "I need to fuck you, hard, fast…"

"Stop talking and fuck me, then" she replies, catching me off guard and making me chuckle.

"Ask, and you shall…" I plunge forward, filling her in one, powerful thrust, then groan out, "receive…"

Braced on my good hand, and holding her leg with the other, I use my position as leverage for my movements, and draw back, then surge forward again. She fits around me like the snuggest leather glove, designed only for me. I thrust with reckless abandon, our bodies pound together with each movement. Our pants and moans fill the room. She's muttering and murmuring, but I can't make out a single thing she's saying. I'm too focused on the feel of her: accepting me, meeting me, moving with me, beginning to flutter and quake around me as a second release overpowers her. It doesn't take long before the tickle starts in my limbs, too, building like an uncontrollable pressure as it moves down my spine and through my body.

"Christ, Allie, I'm—" It's all I can manage to get out before the pressure is too much, and my release crashes out of me like a tidal wave, surging from me to her in long, forceful bursts.

"Holy shit, baby." Her voice breaks through the haze of my release, and I smile down at her, letting her leg go gently, so she can put it down. "That was…what came over you?"

I lower myself to her body, laying my full weight on her carefully, making sure she can handle it, then respond, "You in that God damned lace thong."

She lets out a laugh and moves her hand up into my hair, combing her fingers through. "I wanted to seduce you, instead I got…" her voice trails off.

"Thoroughly fucked?" I offer as a response.

"Yes. I got thoroughly fucked."

I can feel the rumble of her chuckle at my word choice, and the pounding of her heart in her chest beneath my head, and her fingers are slowly raking over my scalp. It's the most satisfying, content feeling on the planet. One that settles my mind just enough to start thinking. "Maybe we just—"

She grips my hair just enough to tilt my head so I'm looking at her, interrupting me before I can finish, "No…Don't… Tonight is about us, just us. Okay?"

I nod my agreement, even though the thought floods my mind. Maybe this time will be the time…

"Chase?"

"Yeah, Darlin'?"

"I'm not ready to call it a night yet. I got hard, hot, and fast. I still want slow and steady…"

"Mhmm," I agree, and turn my head in, kissing her chest like she always does mine. "Let me catch my breath first."

She lets out a soft laugh and agrees, then moves her hand from my hair down to my back and rubs gently.

I will give this woman anything she wants, from now to eternity.

Nine

Allie

Having Chase home has been everything the girls and I have needed for quite some time now. He's gotten work done here on the ranch, practiced a little, but let his arm heal a little, too. He's spent time with Ava and Aubrey, and he's put some time and focus into building our business here. Every night since the night after Ava's accident has been spent locked away in our room, talking, or reacquainting ourselves with each other's bodies and working for a baby, even though I won't let him utter the words. I can't take the letdown if I let him get excited about it again. I can't take the letdown if I start to get excited again.

More than all that, though, he's been present. Not once has he seemed ready to bolt out the door to chase the next ride and check.

For the past few days, his world ranking, and being the number one rider on the circuit hasn't mattered at all. He's been a husband and a father first.

It's helped me calm down. I've gotten caught up on my stuff, and I think our girls are angels again, rather than the predecessors to Satan.

I've gotten sleep, albeit not as much as I could—given our late nights together—but it's been better sleep than

I've had in a while. I've loved having my partner back here with me. The girls have been well-behaved, and I haven't had to be the "bad guy" when they have acted up. We've tackled all the problems together. It's made a world of difference.

Ava is still suffering from headaches, and having him here to soothe and comfort her has been what she has needed most. Not once has she brought up riding, or rodeo. For either of them. It makes me wonder if her fall didn't scare her a little more than we thought it did. She's been content to watch movies, read books, score Aubrey's gymnastics routines in the living room, and spend the evenings in Chase's lap or at his side, watching sunsets and talking about swimming and being able to run and play when she feels better again.

"Hey, Chase," I say, stepping out onto our porch where he's been on the phone with Cody. "Can we talk about something?"

He looks up from the rocker and nods, tapping his thighs. "Pull up a seat."

I move over and drop into his lap, feeling his muscles flex beneath me as we start to glide back and forth slowly.

"I'm worried about Ava." I look out over our property, watching the glare of the sun dance across the windshield of his truck.

"What's wrong with Ava?" His voice is tinged with concern.

"I think her fall scared her, more than she'll admit, and I think she'll be afraid to get back up on Lightning."

I feel his fingers settle on my bare leg and squeeze gently. "What makes you think that?" There's nothing there to make me think he's just humoring me, or he finds this a trivial matter, and it makes me feel justified in bringing it up.

"She hasn't mentioned riding or rodeo even once since we brought her home. When has she ever gone this long without mentioning either? She hasn't even gone out to watch you practice…"

He lets out a heavy sigh and stops the chair momentarily, answering in a strained voice, "I've noticed. I was just hoping it was something she started to do before I got home." Then we start rocking again.

I shake my head no. "Rodeo was a constant for her. She checked your standings daily. Multiple times a day. She'd ask for my phone just to pull up the site, then she'd give it back when she was finished."

He lets out a chuckle. "Our child is not normal. You know that, right?"

"Chase!" I giggle.

"Listen, I'm just saying, even I do more on the phone than check my standings. She's nine. Shouldn't she be playing games or something else, too?"

Before I can respond, a warm breeze picks up and blows some dust our way, and he guides my head to his chest and tucks it beneath his chin so I'm breathing in him, and not the dusty air. He smells of sweat and the mahogany teakwood cologne I bought him. It's addicting, and I don't want to pull away yet.

"Enjoying your sniff?" he teases.

"Mhmm," I respond against his neck, then nip at it playfully and pull back. "I love eau de Chase."

"And now we know where Ava gets her weirdness from…" he says, too seriously to actually be serious.

I smack his chest playfully then focus my attention on the girls' bikes in front of the porch. "Seriously, I'm worried about her."

"We won't let this fall hold her back. When the time's right, we'll get her back up in the saddle. And I'll be right there with her, every step of the way."

I look up at him and flip his baseball cap backward, so the brim can't hide his eyes, and say very seriously, "You can't make that promise. You're gone a lot. And she's not ready to get back up yet. Her head is still hurting her too much."

He closes his eyes and presses his forehead against mine. "I'm making you that promise, Allie. I will be here for her when she's ready to get back on Lightning. I won't leave her hanging, and I won't let her be afraid to the point that she gives up on her dream. Because I think riding really is her dream. Right?"

"What do you mean?"

"She's not just doing it for me, is she? Like you did…"

I ponder his words silently, really thinking them over. My dad forced me to ride. I went along with it because it was a way for us to stay connected, but is that why Ava is riding now? She feels the same need to stay close to Chase, even if it's by doing something she doesn't want to?

"Tell me she isn't just riding for me. To make me happy and to make sure I notice her."

"No, baby, I don't think she's riding just for you. I think Ava loves everything about riding. She loves the control, the danger, the challenge. The fact that you're one of the world's best bull riders, and love rodeo as much as she does, is just a benefit to her loving it."

"Are you sure?" he asks, whispering so quietly I almost miss it.

I take gentle hold of his face, making sure our eyes are locked, and nod my head slowly. "I'm positive. When we were at gymnastics with Aubrey the other day, she asked if I thought she could do what Aubrey was. It caught me off guard, honestly."

"So how are you so sure now, then?"

"Because I told her she could do anything she wanted to, if she set her mind to it. All you and I want is for her to do what she wants to do, no matter what it is."

"Good, that's good." He exhales, relieved, and leans forward to kiss me. "Did she say she wants to try anything else?"

I laugh. "Nope. She got that scrunchy faced look that's so adorable, shook her head no, and said she would never stop riding because she loves it. And she made me feel a little insane for suggesting anything else."

"Which is why you're so worried she hasn't said anything about riding since her fall…"

That's exactly why. That and I know she's going to need his help, and as much as he wants to, he can't guarantee he's going to be keeping that promise.

"That's why," I respond easily.

"If she really loves it," he says with a smile, "she'll get back up. I always have. It's in our blood. It's who we are."

He's so certain about it. His faith in our girls is unwavering, and it puts me at ease where Ava is concerned. If he's that confident, I need to be, too.

"Speaking of riding," he says, interrupting my thoughts, "Will you go for a ride with me tonight? We can pack up a little basket, head up to the lake, play some country music, maybe explore the bases a little…"

"Are you asking me on a date, Cowboy?" It's crazy, but I can feel little, giddy flutters in my stomach where the butterflies have taken flight. How does he manage to do this to me, even after all this time?

"I am."

"Then I accept. I'd love to go for a ride with you." I lean in and kiss his lips, then slip off his lap. I have a date I need to go get ready for.

Chase

I get Thor and Jane's blankets and saddles over their backs, securing our little basket in place on Thor and making sure our Dixie cups and wine are in there, along with our sandwiches, then dust my hands off on my jeans.

"It's been a long time since we've done this, huh, boy?" I ask Thor, gliding my hand down his neck. "I'm sorry I haven't been around to ride you as much lately, I know you need to get out and fly sometimes. I promise we'll do some of that this evening. Okay?"

Thor turns his head into my hand and makes me laugh. "That's what I thought."

"Who ya talkin' to?" Aubrey's little voice rings out in the otherwise silent barn.

I turn to look at her, smiling wide at her little pigtails, denim shorts and tank top, and her cowgirl boots. "I was having a talk with Thor."

"You were? What did he say?"

"He said he's looking forward to getting out for a ride with Jane and your mama. And he wants to run fast."

She steps up to me, putting both hands on her hips, and looks up at me very seriously, whispering, "But horses can't talk, Daddy. Duh."

I look at Thor and drop my jaw dramatically for Aubrey's sake before saying just as seriously, "Don't listen to her, boy. I know what you were saying. Just because she didn't hear it, doesn't mean it didn't happen. Your secret is extra safe with me."

Aubrey starts to laugh and steps closer. "He didn't talk! He can't! You're so silly!"

"Me? Silly? I'll show you silly!" I bend down and lift her, tossing her into the air above my head and catching her, then hold her over my shoulder, tickling the backs of her legs while we walk out of the barn. She wiggles and squirms from my tickles, laughing loudly.

"Stop! Stop! It tickles so much!" she shouts between bursts of laughter. Before we reach our patio, I let her slide down, holding her on my arm and side instead.

"Okay, I'll stop, but only because I need your help with something extra important. Can you help me?"

Aubrey bounces her head up and down enthusiastically.

"Okay, I need you to help me pick a flower from your mommy's rose bush. The perfect one. So I can give it to her. Can you do that?"

With the happiest smile and widest eyes, she agrees, giving me a thumbs up. "A red one or a pink one?"

I set her down on the ground and she looks at both of Allie's rose bushes, waiting for me to decide. "What about one of each?" I ask, looking at them.

"Yep, that's a good idea." She squats down in front of the roses and looks carefully. Her sparkly purple fingers reach forward carefully, touching one of the reds. "Not this one. It's not pretty enough." She keeps looking, and giving me her own commentary on each rose until she stops on one. "This one is perfect! Mommy will love it."

I kneel down next to her and pull out my pocket knife. "This one right here?" I point to a rose that's not completely open yet, and wait for her to answer before I cut.

"Yep. Mommy said these grow prettiest in the house."

Okay then. I should've known Allie would've told Aubrey, who joins her out here all the time. I cut the rose how Aubrey very carefully instructs me then hold it up for her, and my, inspection. "You picked good, Monkey. Now how about a pink one?"

She shuffles to her right and starts to search through the roses again. "Oh, I think I like this one," she says, reaching forward.

"Be care—" Before I can even finish she pulls her hand back and shrieks out in pain.

"I poked my finger. Owie. I poked my finger." She pulls her hand back and examines her finger, then her lips form a pout and tears spring to her eyes. "Daddy, it's bleeding, make it better."

"Let me see," I say, squatting down beside her again. She stands to her full height, leveling our heads out, and holds her finger up. There's a big bubble of blood pooling over where she poked herself, and her eyes shine brightly behind her tears.

"It hurts so bad," she whimpers.

"I'll make it better, Monkey. Give me your hand." She lays her tiny hand in mine and I swipe my thumb over the blood, wiping it away from her finger, then rubbing my hand over my jeans, getting the blood off. "I'm going to give it a big kiss now. It'll make the stings go away. Then we will go in and get you a Band-Aid to hide the blood."

She nods her head and watches her finger expectantly as I bring it up to my lips and kiss it. "There, does that feel better? Or do you need one more?"

"One more, please."

I press one more kiss to her finger and then gently boop her nose with one of my fingers. "All the pain will

96

go away now. But let's get you in and wash your hand so we can put a bandage on."

"Thank you," she whispers, and rubs the back of her arm over her nose, dropping it back to her side covered in tears and snot.

"We're going to wash your arm, too. That was gross," I tease.

It gets a little laugh out of her and I stand up, rose in one hand, holding my other out for her to hold while we go inside.

Once we cross the threshold, Allie appears from the office. "Head into our bathroom, Aubrey. I'll be right there."

She lets go of my hand and does as I said, and I step up to Allie. "Mrs. Canton," I say, smiling and holding the rose up. "For you. I'd planned to do this differently, pick you up with two roses at the door, but Aubrey poked herself something good, so I've got to go get her finger cleaned up, and change my jeans, then I'll be ready for our date."

"Thank you for my rose. It's beautiful. I'll wait right here for you, go do your daddy thing. I'm in no rush."

I brush a quick kiss over her lips and mutter, "You look beautiful. I'll be right back."

When I get to the bathroom Aubrey has her Band-Aids pulled out, *Moana* characters included on them, and has the soap on the edge of the counter.

"I washed my hands, and my icky arm," she states, proudly. "Can you cover my owie now?"

"Gladly." I open the box and pull out one bandage, carefully wrapping it around her finger. "One more kiss for quicker healing?"

"Oh yes," she responds, holding the finger up for me to kiss. "I don't want it to hurt at gymnastics next time."

97

With a kiss to her finger and a pat to her backside, I shoo her out of the room, happy and on her way to fully healed, so I can change my jeans and get back out to Allie.

"You know," I say as I walk down the hall. "I think these are my jeans from a few years ago. And my a—" I stop myself short when I see Ava, Aubrey, and Aubrey's teenaged gymnastics big sister, Michelle, sitting on the couch. "Hi, Michelle, I'm sorry, I didn't realize you were already here."

"Hi, Mr. Canton. I just showed up about five minutes ago. Mrs. Canton is in the office, ordering our pizza, so you can get going."

I nod and smile at her. "Thank you."

"Yes, thank you, Michelle," Allie says, walking up behind me and slipping her hand over my ass and around to my hip while she ducks under my arm. "And sorry for his commentary on his jeans."

Michelle blushes and shakes her head. "It's okay. I know you said you wouldn't be late tonight, but just in case. Bedtime for these two?"

I answer before Allie can, "Nine thirty, tonight. They can stay up later." I wink at the girls on the couch then smile down at Allie. "Special night. Staying up later won't hurt anyone."

"You heard him," Allie says, shaking her head. "You two, listen to Michelle. Your pizza should be here within the hour. It's all paid for, tip is covered, you're all set."

"Sounds good, thank you. You two have fun, too."

Michelle is a good kid. She's in high school; she's an honors student, an elite gymnast who volunteers with the young girls Aubrey's age, and very trustworthy. I'd leave the kids with her ten times out of ten.

"We'll be back in a few hours," I say to her, and the girls. "If Ava's head starts to hurt, her Tylenol is in our bathroom. I left it on the counter. I'll have my phone, too. The number's on the fridge."

I wrap my arm around Allie's shoulder, spotting her rose already in a vase and on display on the coffee table, and we head out on our stay-date.

Ten

Chase

There are some sights and sounds in this world that have the ability to stop me in my tracks, bring me to my knees, and make me thank God for the life I have been given. Lucky for me, tonight is one of those nights where I'm getting a little bit of every one of them.

Allie is perched atop Jane, smiling back at me while she moves at a slow trot along the property line. Her hair is in loose waves down her back, her jeans are stretched tight over her ass and legs, and the laugh spilling from her lips is the purest, most angelic sound I have ever heard in my life. She is the most stunning, incredible woman, and I have the backdrop of a perfect Colorado skyline to highlight every single feature on her.

"Hurry up, slowpoke," she calls back, teasing me. "Jane and I are itching to kick your ass racing to the lake, but we can't go until you've caught up to us."

"Listen, ma'am," I say with my most convincing drawl, "I'm quite enjoying the view back here, so you're just going to have to wait."

"In that case," she calls out, looking back with a smirk on her face now, "you can keep enjoying it!" With that, she takes off like a bullet, nudging Jane on and putting a quick twenty to thirty-yard gap between us in nothing flat.

I could take off, try to catch her and beat her, and knowing Thor like I do, he'd get us ahead in no time, but I'm not ready to yet. I haven't seen Allie ride like this, carefree and like the professional she is, in years. Her hair is blowing back in the wind, she's riding hard, and in such control of Jane I can see flashes of the teenage Allie I used to know—the rodeo winning, barrel racing, bad-ass cowgirl—I first fell in love with.

"Come on, Chase!" she shouts out, having slowed up and turned to find me. "Let Thor loose! You've neglected him lately." She doesn't really believe that. I know she takes him out for rides, too, just to be sure he gets what he needs. But she knows saying that will get me moving, which is all she wanted anyway.

I bend over his neck and give him a gentle pat and scratch. "What do you think? Should we go catch our girls?" He doesn't answer, but he looks in their direction, and that's answer enough for me. I sit back up, loosen my grip on his reins, and urge him forward. "Let's show 'em who rules this place."

Thor takes off after Allie and Jane, and once we're close enough, Allie surges them forward again, picking up speed, trying to outrun us.

"Keep going, Thor, faster, we've got them, faster," I urge my horse on and start to catch up. "Last to the lake is first to skinny-dip," I shout over the sound of our horses galloping at full speed.

"You're on!" Allie hollers back, raising out of her saddle just a little more and shifting forward, silently commanding Jane to push it.

I do the same and Thor turns his speed up a notch, jumping a neck length ahead with ease before we break away and put a small distance between us.

I can hear Allie laughing behind me, undoubtedly still pushing Jane as fast as she can, but I turn the corner of the property that leads to the lake and slow Thor down when I've clearly won. "Atta boy, Thor. We did it."

A few seconds after me, Allie brings Jane to a stop beside us, laughing and smiling wide. "I should've known better than to stop and taunt you."

"Yep, you should have. It's okay, though. We still would've won. Thor here is as strong and powerful as the god he's named after."

Allie rolls her eyes and shakes her head. "You're teaching him to be as arrogant as you are. It's not an attractive quality. Jane doesn't like it."

"Yeah, right. She likes it as much as you do, and we all know it."

"Keep dreamin', Cowboy." She dismounts Jane and stretches her arms above her head, the action tugs her tank top up just enough to let a thin strip of her stomach peek through.

She's perfect.

Flawless.

And she's going to be needing to strip out of those clothes and taking her dip into the water to make good on our bet.

"I won, you realize that, right?"

"Yes, cocky one, I do. What's your point?" she retorts, clearly not realizing where I'm going with this.

"I won, therefore you arrived last..."

Realization flashes across her features and she looks up at me, where I'm still perched atop Thor, with her hand providing shade over her eyes and her lips slightly parted. "You can't be serious. Right now?"

"Mhmm, right now." I nod my head and fold my hands over the horn of Thor's saddle. "I need to see you gloriously naked and getting into the water."

"You really are serious." She shakes her head and starts to pull her hair back. "You can tell me you're joking anytime."

"Allie, I'm serious as a heart attack. You agreed, last one here is the first to skinny-dip. And I want to watch every second of you doing exactly that."

"My God, you are so full of yourself. I suppose you're going to stay there on top of Thor, like you're the ruler of the lands?"

My only answer is to smile at her.

"Impossible. You're impossible." She pulls the band off her wrist and secures her hair into a messy pile above her head then she works her boots off with a huff. "How am I supposed to dry off?"

"I brought two blankets, we can share one so you can use the other to dry yourself."

"And what are you going to—you know what—never mind." She steps up in front of Thor and slides her hand over his face. "You're a traitor, Thor. You should've lost for me."

She makes me laugh loudly. "He knows whose horse he is. Now, quit stalling"

She steps back away from Thor and holds her arms out, "Fine. I hope you're happy with your race winning self." A small smile pulls at the corners of her lips, letting me know she is absolutely fine with doing this, as she reaches for the bottom of her tank top and pulls it agonizingly slowly up her body, then tosses it up to me.

"Don't let it get dirty," she commands.

"It'll be safe with me," I reply, bringing it up to my nose and inhaling the scent of lavender and vanilla coming off the warm top.

"Too much, always too much," she chuckles out after watching me sniff her shirt. She then proceeds to wiggle out of her jeans, leaving her in socks and matching black panties and a bra.

"Just enough, always just enough." I wink at her. "I can hold all of that, too, if you'd like. Just toss them on up."

"You don't expect me to take these off, too?" she asks, referring to the black still clinging to her body after she removes her socks.

"You can keep them on, but we both know you don't want to ride back commando. And neither of us wants you to experience any…chafing."

She removes her bra and tosses it up with her jeans, muttering incoherently as she bends to step out of her panties, then tosses them up to me, too.

"Will you strike a pose for me before you take your dip of shame?" I ask.

"You want a pose?"

I nod my head. "Do I ever."

"Fine, here's your pose…" She juts a hip out with one hand bent over it, then lifts her other hand, every finger but one curled in, and flips me the bird. "There's your pose." She gives me a sarcastic smile, turns her back to me, and marches toward the water.

Her hips sway with every step, and the sun casts a glow over her skin that has me licking my lips. She's my angel sent from heaven with a wild side. My God, I love that side of her. There isn't a challenge in the world she would back down from, and when she takes it on, she'll do it with a fearlessness and determination nobody else on this planet could match.

She pauses momentarily when her feet hit the water, and her back stiffens, then she continues forward, calling out, "This water is cold, Chase!"

I chuckle and watch her move forward. "You can back out."

"Not a chance in hell, Cowboy. But you better get your ass off Thor, strip down, and join me in here."

"What about your clothes?" I holler back, chuckling to myself.

"Screw the clothes. Get off your horse and get in here. Now!"

"Yes, ma'am," I mutter quietly to myself, dropping off of Thor's back and folding her clothes, dropping them over a tree stump nearby.

She walks out until she's deep enough that the water is up to her neck then she turns to face me. "I'm waiting…" she says impatiently, grinning wide.

"I'm coming, I'm coming. Just let me undress. I don't need any chafing, either." That gets a laugh from her. Then I start to undress, pulling my black T-shirt off, kicking my boots and socks to the side, then pushing my boxer briefs and jeans down.

She lets out a loud, appreciative whistle with her fingers to her lips, not taking her eyes off me for a second as I stride toward her, dick swinging in the wind.

"Holy fuck," I say, surprised. "This water is cold. You just wanted to see me shrink, humiliate me, didn't you?"

She giggles and shakes her head. "No, I didn't want to humiliate you. And trust me, the cold water won't make you any less of a man."

"Better not," I say back, walking in deeper, grinding my teeth together as my body adjusts to the cold. "It's the dead of summer, why the hell is it so cold in here?"

"Beats me," she responds easily, moving toward me until she's able to wrap her body around mine. "It feels good once you're used to it, though."

I wrap my arm around her back and wade us out a little deeper, holding her above the waterline so her hair doesn't get wet, and stop when the water is up to my shoulders. "Now that you've got me out here, what exactly do you plan on doing with me?"

She leans in, her breath hot over my lips as she answers, "See how much we can get you to grow in this cool water." Then she presses her lips to mine and kisses me hard, showing me even more of that wild side I love so much.

Allie

"This date couldn't be any more perfect," I whisper, reaching for Chase's hand. I'm settled between his jean-clad legs, leaning back against his bare chest, wearing nothing but my panties and his T-shirt while we watch the sun slowly start to set in the distance.

"No, it really couldn't," he replies, extending his fingers so I can trace the lines of his palm with mine.

"Ava asked me something today, while you were getting ready," he says into my hair.

"What's that?"

"She asked if I would stay home from the next rodeo."

I tilt my head back on his shoulder so I can get a look at him, and feel the stubble from his five o'clock shadow scrap against my temple as I do. "What did you say?"

"I told her I would…"

I nod my head, letting each thing he just said settle. The fact that Ava asked him to stay is concerning, all on its own. As we discussed earlier, our little girl is the most supportive, rodeo-obsessed kid on the planet, and there's no way she would ever ask him to risk his standings. Not unless she's scared and her fall has her fearing for him now, too.

"What you said earlier, then her asking me to stay…" he sighs, then flattens my hand against his so he can close his fingers around mine. "Before I go anywhere, I need to make sure she's okay. I need to make sure she knows she doesn't have to ride another day in her life, if she doesn't want to. But if she does, and she's just afraid now, I'm going to get her back up on a horse before I leave you three here alone again."

I'm still watching him, even though his eyes are glued to the lake. There's a hard set to his jawline right now, almost as if he's clenching his teeth. I reach up and slide my hand along his stubbled jaw and rub. Easing his eyes back down to me. "She'll be okay, we'll make sure of it together. So put it out of your mind for now. Let's enjoy what time we have left out here tonight, and then tomorrow, we tackle Ava. We will work it all out together."

"Together," he repeats, smiling down at me. "I like the sound of that." He brings our linked hands up to his mouth and kisses the back of mine. It's one of those simple things that makes my heart skip a beat and brings a smile to my face without fail.

"Are you really okay with missing the next rodeo?"

"She needs me here more than I need the check. It's smaller, anyway. It'll be fine. Plus, it'll give Cody a better chance of winning. Poor guy needs it more than I do this weekend." He smirks, then winks at me and reaches for our basket of food.

"Good Lord. Are you two still at that?" I laugh and shake my head.

"We've been competing for what, seven years now, if you want to go back that far. Of course we're still at it. And I'm in the lead, thanks to my progress this season."

"You two set such a fantastic example for the kids," I tease him. "Does Ava know all about this competition between you two?"

He reaches for the bottle of wine and the little cups he packed, ignoring my question and asking instead, "Are you thirsty? Or hungry? I made your favorite sandwich."

"She knows," I muse, shaking my head. "I'd love some wine and your home-cooked meal."

"Coming right up." He pours the wine into the cups, hands me mine, and then offers me a bite of my sandwich.

"Don't turn her against Cody, rooting for him to fail so you can beat him," I advise. I know our daughter, and current situation aside, she'd root for her dad to win at all costs, no matter what.

"Would I do that?"

"Yes," I say on a laugh. "You would, just to get under his skin. You know he loves the girls, and turning Ava against him, even for fun, would be amusing to you."

He adjusts and drags his hand up to his chest, gasping exaggeratedly, "You wound me."

"I do not. Drink your wine, Cowboy. And don't turn Ava against your best friend. Otherwise, he'll try to kick your ass. And... I think he could possibly take you."

His jaw drops, and I wink. There's no way Cody could take Chase, but to put his overinflated ego in check, I figured I'd add that just to drop him down a notch or two.

"Take it back, Darlin'. Take it back right now."

I shake my head and take a drink of my wine.

"You really think Cody could take me? I mean, yeah, he's put on some more muscle lately, but not that much. I'd still kick his ass."

"I don't know. He's feisty."

"Feisty? What the hell does that mean?"

"It means he'd find a way to win. He's resourceful."

"So you mean throw dirt in my face, wait until I'm blind, then take me out. Feisty?"

Wine launches out of my mouth and nose when I crack up hysterically, and I strangle a bit, which forces me to cough up a lung. But it's worth it. Absolutely worth it to get this reaction.

"He wouldn't cheat, Chase. My God, you're dramatic. I see where Aubrey gets it from now."

"You really think he'd beat me?" He looks like a wounded, sad puppy, pouting like someone just took his most favorite bone.

I can't help it or fight off my smile any longer. He needs to be put out of his misery. "No, Chase, I don't think he'd beat you. You could and would still kick his ass."

"Then why'd you...are you just yanking my leg right now so I quit pouting?"

"Good Lord!" I set my cup down and carefully move to my knees and turn to face him. "No, I'm not pulling your leg now. Yes, I was when I said he'd beat you. You needed your ego put in check, especially after our race out here. Cody wouldn't beat you. Just like he's never beat you before."

"Just so we're clear," he says, cocky tone and features back in place, "we are talking about in the standings *and* if we were to fight. Right?"

"I'm not sure how Thor will get you home with your head that big and heavy... I'm talking about fighting.

109

Cody is a damn good rider. He could very well beat you, if you don't drop the ego a little."

"No way," he says, reaching for my hips and pulling me into his chest. "He'll never beat me. At the end of the day, I'll always be the best. The biggest winner. You know why that is?"

"Do tell."

"Because at the end of every day I'll go home knowing that with you and the girls, I've already won life. Nothing and no one in this world will ever top that."

"Smooth. Very smooth." I wrap my arms around his neck. "I love you, Chase."

"I love you too, Allie. Always have, always will."

I lean in and kiss him, reinforcing my words with my actions, then pull back a little. "Let's finish up here so we can get back to our girls. I'd like to have a fire, s'mores, and fun night before they go to bed."

"That sounds like the perfect end to this date night." He reaches back for my jeans and my tank top. "You may want to put these on before we finish up, too."

I nod and stand in front of him, slipping my jeans on and his shirt off, then sit back down, pulling my tank into place. We still have to finish our main course before we can go back and have dessert with our girls.

Eleven

Chase

I don't remember the last time I missed a rodeo. Not for something other than injury and a doctor advising me it would be in my best interest to take the weekend off, so I didn't permanently damage whatever I had hurt. Yet here I am, sitting at home in our big recliner, with my daughter on my lap, watching my best friend on a shitty internet feed while he rides his last ride.

It's fucking torture.

Correction, missing the weekend is torture. Missing the adrenaline, the pull of the arena, the thrill of riding for eight, even the smells, dust, and roar of the crowd—it's all painful.

But the reason I missed is greater torture. Knowing my daughter is afraid enough to ask me to miss, and I can't make her fear go away with the snap of my fingers, is torture. However, being here with my little girl when she needs me is a pretty good balance to missing out on my other love, my living, and my job. I'm just glad I was in a position in the standings to be able to be home this weekend. Getting to watch with Ava, see her reactions, hear the hesitation in her voice when I asked her to come watch with me—before we go for an easy ride tonight—was important. Very important.

I'm genuinely happy for my best friend. He deserved the win this weekend. He rode his ass off. At least, it appears he did. This is the first time the video feed has worked, so I've had to rely on texts from other riders and some commentary on social media.

"You ready to head out for a ride, Pipsqueak?" I ask Ava, shutting the laptop.

"We don't have to." She looks down at her hands and starts picking at the pink nail polish on them.

"I think we do, though." I put my hand over the top of hers, stilling her fingers, and waiting for her to look up at me. "I have a very, very important question to ask you. And I want you to be honest. Because no matter what your answer is, I won't be mad, and I will love you more than the universe."

She looks up with worry in her eyes and her lips pressed together in a tight line, then nods her head.

"Do you want to ride in the rodeo still? Or do you want to try something else?" I give her hands a gentle squeeze and smile at her. "Be honest. Anything you say is okay. There isn't a wrong answer."

All she does is nod her head, not giving me anymore than that.

"I need you to talk to me. Because Mommy and I are worried about you."

"I still want to ride," she says quietly, her voice shaky and unsure.

"You don't have to ride ever again, if you don't really want to, Ava. I won't be upset."

"You won't?" she asks, surprised.

"No, I won't. I only want you to ride if it makes you happy. I never, ever want you to ride because you think that's what I expect."

She looks forward again, hiding her eyes from me.

"I thought you loved riding, otherwise, I would have put you into dance or piano lessons."

She scrunches her nose up and shakes her head. "Ewww. I don't want to dance. Or piano."

"No? You don't?" I tickle her a little bit, drawing out a laugh. And a smile. They're really great to see on her. "When did you stop liking riding?"

She stops laughing and smiling almost immediately when I ask, and then she clams up, shaking her head no.

"You can tell me anything. So will you tell me that? Please?"

She goes back to picking at her fingers and takes long enough to answer me that I'm about to give up, when she finally says, "When I fell."

And there it is. That's what I needed to know for sure.

"It scared you." It's not a question. The first fall—the first injury causing fall—is fucking terrifying. I still remember mine, too. I was a little older than her when I had my first trip to the hospital from a ride gone wrong. It took me a while to get back up once I was out of my cast.

"I don't want to get hurt again," she admits.

"I don't want you to get hurt again either. And I was scared, too. Did you know that?"

She looks at me with wide, surprised eyes.

"I didn't know what happened, and when your mom called me, it scared me to death. Can I tell you a secret?"

She nods her head.

"I'm afraid to let you get back on Lightning."

"You are?" she asks, repositioning herself on my lap.

"I am. But do you want to know something else?"

"Yes."

"I think we both need you to ride again. Lightning won't hurt you, and we both need to prove it again."

113

"What if I fall again?" She has never sounded more worried in her life, and I want so badly to take that fear for her. But I can't. Not until she agrees to ride again.

"You might. But it doesn't mean you'll get hurt like last time. How often do you see me fall off the bulls?"

"A lot." She says it so matter-of-factly that I can't help but laugh.

"Yeah, a lot." I press a kiss to her temple where the bruise has faded and the knot has all but disappeared from. "But I don't always get hurt. And you won't either. You won't fall as much as me, either. As long as you follow the rules, especially until you get better."

She looks down to her lap now, not answering. Which tells me the other thing I've needed to know since her fall happened.

"Kip told you to hold still until he came back, didn't he, Ava?"

"Yes," it comes out as barely a whisper. "I'm sorry I didn't listen, Daddy."

I let out a sigh and kiss her head again. "You're not in trouble, this time. You paid the price with your head, right? But I need you to apologize to Kip tomorrow. He felt really bad for letting you fall. Even though it wasn't his fault."

"I will," she agrees easily.

"That's my girl." I rub her back then help her slide off the chair. "Do you trust me?"

"Of course, I do, Daddy." She crosses her arms over her chest, watching me intently as I lean forward and brace my forearms on my legs. "We're going to go out and saddle Lightning, and get you up for a ride. And I promise you I will stay right there. I'll even lead him for a while, if you want. Okay?"

She doesn't look sold, at all. But she's my daughter, and Allie's, and she won't back down from a challenge

114

if she can help it. She's stubborn like that. And I'm going to push her a little. I stand up and stretch out, sitting for a while does leave me sore, not that I'm going to say it to her tonight.

"I'm going to go out and get started, Lightning will be really sad if you don't come out, too. But if you can't do it, I'll lead him around the pen for a while to get a workout in."

I walk out of the house and to the barn, getting started on saddling Lightning, waiting for Ava to join us. It takes her about ten minutes, but she comes out in a pair of jeans with her boots on, and her hat in hand.

"You all set?"

She nods and approaches Lightning slowly. She hasn't come out to see him since she fell, and I know right now she's got a lot of things going through her mind.

"Just give him a little loving and a few bites of apple. Show him you aren't afraid. He's still your same horse, he just needs to trust you're the same adorable little girl who always rides him."

Ava grabs some apple slices from the fridge in the office then comes back out to us, holding her hand out, waiting for Lightning to take them. He does, munching them out of her hand like it's the best treat he's ever been given, and then he nudges her hand with his nose and leans into her touch.

I step back quietly and lean against the stall door, watching them, giving her a little bit to feel comfortable around him again, and smile when she speaks up.

"Hi, Lightning. I'm sorry I haven't come out to ride you. Will you forgive me?"

I move around to grab the halter, so I can lead them around, and Ava sees me. She keeps rubbing Lightning's head and moves around to the side. "Can I use the bridle?"

"You want to ride him alone, no lead?" I'm not surprised, but I don't want her to feel pressured, either.

"No lead. But will you and Thor ride with us?"

That's my brave, brave girl. The amount of pride I have in her right now, watching her tackle this head on—get back up on her horse by herself—my heart feels ten sizes bigger in my chest right now.

"You bet. Let's finish getting Lightning ready, then I'll lead Thor out and we can ride together."

She walks over and grabs the bridle from me, taking it over to Lightning, and starts explaining to him what she's going to do. I help get it over him and secured in place, then tell her to lead him outside.

As they start to walk away, I make my way over to Thor and saddle him, getting done as quickly as I can so Ava doesn't have to wait, and then we set out for the pen.

Allie

I'm not sure what I expected to see pulling in after dropping Aubrey off at a birthday party, but I am sure it wasn't the scene I'm watching now. I put the car into park and sit, still buckled, frozen in place, staring out the windshield toward the pen. Chase and Ava are out there with Thor and Lightning, and it looks like they're about to mount and ride.

Chase squats down to Ava's level, grinning wide, and says something to her. She gives him a nod, and the second he puts his hand up to give her a high five, she claps hers against his. But they don't part right away like usual. Instead, she keeps her hands there and I can see him talking again, then her tiny fingers slip between his, and their hands clasp together.

Never in my life has our ritual brought tears to my eyes, but when I see the smile stretch over our daughter's face as they let go, right before Chase lifts her into her saddle, I start to cry. I knew he wanted to talk to her. I know she's afraid. After a fall like she had, it's normal.

But watching him teach her our ritual—the one we've always done so he stays safe during rides—so she would feel safe getting back up, melts my heart. Seeing him teach her something that is so special and private, a secret for our family to hold onto together for life, it hits me in a way I couldn't have ever imagined. Once she's perched on Lightning with the reins in her hands, Chase gets on Thor, and they start a slow walk around the pen.

She's doing it. And he's right by her side, just like he promised he would be.

Twelve

Chase

"I really wasn't sure you'd make it here after missing last week," Cody says, sitting beside me at the hotel bar in Cheyenne with a drink in his hand.

"You're joking, right?" I reply after swallowing hard.

He just looks at me and grins. The fucker.

"How's Ava really doing?" He signals the bartender for another round.

"She's okay. The headaches have stopped, we rode a few times this week, just light stuff. I don't want to push the jarring motion until she's been headache free for a while longer."

"That's good. No need to mess her brain up like yours is, she's far too smart to have your dumbs."

I laugh. "You're such an asshole. But you aren't wrong about her being smart. And we don't want to fuck her future. Not for riding."

He raises an eyebrow in my direction, looking at me like I really have lost my wits, and possibly my mind. "Say that again? Did you really say riding isn't worth it?"

"Don't look at me that way. I did say that. Do you really think I want this life for her when she grows up? Rodeo, riding, being on the road, it's good enough for us, yeah. She deserves better. I want better for her."

"Christ, Chase, who are you and what the hell have you done with my best friend? You love this life."

"Damn straight I do. But I want her to have even more, Cody. I want her to grow up, find a good man—if that's what she wants—have kids, have a career, live in one home steadily. She's so much better than a life on the road."

"What if she wants to live this life? Are you going to tell her she can't?"

"I'm not going to tell her shit if she's following her dreams and safe. But... I'm not going to sugarcoat shit, either."

"Where's all this coming from?"

"Allie's...she started...she's still not pregnant."

"Fuck, I'm sorry." He pushes my new beer toward me, then asks for a couple of shots of whiskey. "Why has that got you all sentimental about what Ava does for a living, though?"

"I was home this time when she started. To see the disappointment. To watch her go through the fucking calendar, marking down days, seeing if when I was home and we were together corresponded with when we could've made a fucking baby."

"And you weren't?"

"Shocker, right?"

"Because you've been on the road, making a living, doing what you love, you weren't there to get your wife pregnant at the right time..."

I shake my head and toss back my shot, letting the burn of the alcohol slide down my throat and into the pit of my stomach, fueling the fires burning deep inside of me. "I wasn't home when she needed me. I wasn't home when Ava needed me. But I was there for the aftermath this time. To see the shit she hides."

"That's tough. It really is. I'm not saying you're wrong for feeling the way you do. Hell, I can't speak to that, because I'd rather fuck my way through rodeos with willing women, who want nothing more than to say they were with me, than settle down and have to worry about being a good man, or a good father. But, Chase, dude, I've known you nearly all of my life, and you are a good man. The best fucking man I know. And you're a damn great father."

"Thanks." As much as I don't feel like either right now, it feels good hearing it from him. He knows everything there is to know about our lives. He knows Allie, he knows me, there is no other person in the world I would tell this stuff, other than him. We have a history that goes back even before I met Allie. They have their own history, too. He'll defend her as fast as he will me. He'll protect her, too, even if it means putting me in my place when I'm in the wrong.

"It's just the truth. As much shit as I love to give you, when it comes to this, I'd put you up against any other man and you'd win every time. Allie and the girls would agree, too. Even with the struggles y'all are having right now."

"Sometimes it doesn't feel like it." It's hard to admit, to see that throughout my time riding, my family has suffered, but it's true. I could be a better man, a better father. And I will be. I'll be there for them. I'll keep my top spot, finish this year, and we will be okay. It'll all be okay. Then we can afford any sort of treatment it takes to make our dream come true. IVF, adoption, whatever the hell it takes to add to our family—I just need to win it all this year. Bring in the big check after finals in Vegas, and we can have what we want. That's why I'm doing all of this.

"That's just further proof you're the good man I'm saying you are." He drinks his shot and looks over to my left, grinning.

"See your next la—" I look where he is and smile just as wide when I see Allie walking toward us.

"Nope, I see your forever lay. So stow the pity party shit, she doesn't need it," he mutters, then rises from his stool. "There's my favorite girl!" he hollers across the bar, waiting until she's close enough before he wraps his arms around her and lifts her up, spinning and hugging her.

Her laugh fills the room and she hugs him back just as tight, kissing his cheek before he puts her down. "There's my second favorite bull rider," she says easily, winking at him. "I've missed that easygoing smile and demeanor. You don't visit…ever."

"I know, I'm sorry. Texas isn't so close to Colorado, and going home after long weekends is needed."

"Colorado *was* home, in case you forgot. Then you up and left…and for what?"

"Don't do that, please," he replies, shaking his head. "You know why I left, and there was a damn good reason for it, Allie. Shit didn't work out, but she was worth leaving for."

Allie snorts. "Until she wasn't… You could come home now, ya know? There's land, ranches, and family, our family, for you back in Colorado…"

I should step in and stop this argument before it really gets started, but hell, she's like a sister to him, she has every right to share how she feels. He can defend himself.

"Whatcha drinking, babe?" I ask instead, trying to diffuse things a little, even if I have no intention of stopping it entirely. They both look at me, Cody with a look that begs for me to save him, and Allie with a look that says 'Really? You had to ask that now?'

"So your usual, got it," I add, smirking and turning toward the bar as they bicker over Cody's living arrangements, location, and reasoning behind me. I listen to them while I wait for her drink, smiling at the accusations and rebuttals they're both tossing out, and risk a glance behind me once they go silent.

They're both smiling at each other, amused looks on their faces, and Allie's hands are on her hips while she looks at him expectantly. "So you're going to spend Christmas with us this year, then?"

"Yes, I will spend Christmas with you this year. My God. Arguing with you is like arguing with a lawyer. And you know how I feel about lawyers."

Allie steps closer to me and slides her hand over my back, chuckling softly at his jab. "I do, but unlike your old man, you love me."

"Yeah, yeah. Lucky for you, I do." Cody shakes his head in exasperation then turns back to the bar to grab his beer. "I've missed you too, Allie. And those girls. So where are they?"

"They're up in our room, Mitch's daughter is watching them for us. She wants some spending money for the rodeo this week, and she agreed to watch the girls when she's not out having fun."

"I'll make sure to have cash for her," I say, handing Allie her drink.

"I guess I'll wait until tomorrow to see the girls then." Cody holds up his bottle, waiting for Allie and I to follow suit. "To lifelong friendship, and the family you choose. Even if they're a pain in your ass." He gives Allie a pointed look then winks.

Allie and I both laugh at that and tap our glasses to his. "To the family you choose," we add, in unison.

Thirteen

Allie

I haven't been to a rodeo in a long time. I haven't been to this rodeo in even longer. It's even bigger and more spectacular than I remember, yet it feels like coming back to the home I grew up in. Since we arrived in Cheyenne yesterday, I have run into so many people I used to know well. Past barrel racers I competed with, other cowboys I remember from all of Chase's events, and even from my dad's. It's such a jolt to the system.

They all remember me for some reason or another associated with rodeo. For some, it's as the young up-and-coming star daughter of Rhett Bowman, Junior Barrel Racing champion two years in a row. Others remember me as girlfriend of Chase Canton, the tag-along to his and Cody's duo, and established rider in my own right, too. And they all remember my dad and his career, God rest his soul.

None of them know my dad forced me to ride, keeping me from ever doing anything else, going to school with my friends, or experiencing life like any normal teen. None of them know I despise rodeo, as far as my riding and everything it took from me, so much that I hide the fact I ever rode from anyone I meet now. I hide it from my own daughters, because I don't want it to put pressure on either of them to feel like they have to follow in our footsteps in order to be loved.

Aubrey has zero interest in rodeo, and if she knew she was the only one in our little family not to ride, it may make her feel like she has to do it one day, and that's the last thing I want. I don't want Ava to hear I rode and think she can't ever quit because it's in her blood. I know what that pressure feels like. It's suffocating.

I won't do it to them. For most of my young life, except for during the second half of December after National Finals and over Christmas—the only holiday we celebrated—I felt like the only way for my dad to be proud of me, or love me, was if I was riding, too. He put the thrill and notoriety of our family name over me. And I hated him for the longest time for it.

Only Chase, and Cody, know that. Everyone else just thinks I quit to raise our family. That's fine with me, because once I got pregnant with Ava, I would have quit anything to be her mom, Chase's wife, and his number one fan.

The truth is, I will support my husband until the day he decides to retire, but there is a lot about rodeo I resent, both from my childhood, and even now. It was my dad's pride and joy, and he forced me into it so I could fit his mold. It is the mistress who keeps my husband away from home far too often.

Rodeo has stolen a lot from me. Being back here reminds me of everything I ran away from years ago. I didn't expect that. Yet, Chase and our girls are so happy this week being here together, that in spite of everything, I'm loving being back with them.

I'm a mess. That's all there is to my conflicting feelings.

"Earth to Mommy," Ava says, poking my arm. "Can I have more money to get some cotton candy before we go watch Daddy?"

"I want some, too!" Aubrey enthusiastically adds.

"Haven't you two had enough sugar today?" I respond, grinning at them both while I get more money out. "You'll be bouncing off the walls with any more in your systems."

Ava shrugs, then throws Chase's words from earlier back at me. "It's a special occasion, remember?"

"Your father is going to pay for saying that." I chuckle and hand her some money. "Get one for you both to share, and hold Aubrey's hand while you walk over there. I'll wait here and watch."

Ava rolls her eyes but takes Aubrey's hand anyway, guiding her over to the cotton candy vendor across the walkway. They get in line behind the others there, and start talking to each other. She may hate having to hold her sister's hand, but they're still close as can be—sometimes—when they aren't at each other's throats. And it warms my heart.

"Allie Bowman, is that you?" a woman's voice rings out amongst the crowd. I look around for it and spot the prissy, rhinestone and jean wearing blonde I could never forget, even if I wanted to.

Missy Wynkoop. She rode at the same time I did, though she was a couple years older than me, and she was absolutely obsessed with Chase. I'm pretty sure she drooled and panted like a dog over him anytime he was in her proximity.

"Missy, it's nice to see you again," I say with a polite, albeit forced, smile. "It's actually Allie Canton, I was sure you knew that, though."

"Oh my God," she drawls out, "Yes, you're absolutely right. I had heard you snagged Chase up for good. I must have forgotten."

I'm sure she did...not.

"I did. We've been married for years now."

125

"That's so incredible for you," she says, smile plastered on her face. "Why are you here? I haven't seen you at a rodeo in forever."

"We thought we'd make this rodeo a family outing. We brought our girls out to watch Chase and have some fun."

"Your girls?" she says, looking around. "I don't see them."

"They're in line for some cotton candy before we head to our seats."

"Isn't that nice. I'm sure they love being here to watch. And to hear the stories about how great their mom was back in her prime. It is a shame you couldn't keep up with his career, having a family, and your own. I would've loved to take your title from you once you went big."

"We try to focus on Chase's career. I stepped away from rodeo because I wanted to be home for my family, and that's what I've done. I didn't need the notoriety that came with wins, nor did I want it. I'm more than happy to support my husband."

"That's so sweet of you." Her response is sugar sweet, and fake.

"He means more to me than rodeo ever did, as do our kids. I saw you had a couple really successful years a while back though, good for you. I didn't notice your name on the leader boards, are you riding this week?" I know she is. I also know she's not scoring well, and her times have significantly dropped off since she was in her prime.

"I am, but you know how it is. Sometimes rides don't go your way, especially while you're changing up tactics and horses."

"Mhmm," I nod, catching the girls paying and coming back toward us with their treat. "It was so nice seeing you again, Missy, but I need to go. We need to get to our seats."

She looks up and forces an even bigger smile. "Oh. My. God. Are these Chase's girls?"

Ava and Aubrey stop in front of us and look between Missy and me. "They are. Missy, this is Ava, our oldest, and Aubrey."

The girls each hold out a hand to shake hers, remembering their manners like they were raised to. "Nice to meet you Miss Missy," Aubrey says first.

"I know who you are," Ava adds after. "I saw you ride once."

"You did?" Missy beams down proudly. "Did you think I was good?"

Ava nods, but doesn't answer verbally. She'd never say no to a question like that, she knows better. "Your horse is really pretty," she says instead.

"Oh, well, thank you," Missy replies with far less enthusiasm. "I guess I'll let you all get to your seats. Tell your daddy I said hi."

Ava looks to me with wide eyes at Missy's words, and I respond, "We'll be sure to do that, Missy. Good luck with the rest of your rides. It was nice seeing you again."

Missy clears her throat. "Yes, you too. Thank you." Then she turns her back and promptly walks away.

"Who was that, Mommy?" Aubrey asks, reaching for a chunk of cotton candy.

"Daddy and I used to know her a long time ago. That's all. Let's get to our seats."

Ava stands in place and watches until Missy is out of sight, then looks up at me curiously before she turns toward the arena entrance. "I'll lead us."

Ava guides us through the crowd of people and to our seats. Front row, right by the bucking chutes.

"I can't wait to watch Daddy," she says, bouncing in her seat, looking all around. "Uncle Cody is coming to sit with us, right?"

"I think he will for a while, but he'll probably be down with your dad for his ride. They help each other get ready."

"Ohhh," she draws out, looking back to me. "Does he know Missy, too?"

"He does."

"Does he like her?"

"Why do you ask that?" I look over to her, curious.

"Because you didn't, and she was weird."

I have no idea what to say to any of that, so all I can manage honestly is, "I don't know if Uncle Cody likes her. You can ask him, though."

That's answer enough for Ava for the time being. Hopefully, she'll forget about Missy before Cody starts answering questions I don't want her having the answers to.

Cody has been sitting with us for the last hour and a half or so, watching the events, playing silly games with the girls, and talking to all the women that pass by gawking at him when he's got my daughter giggling in his lap. Aubrey has my phone and has the app open where you can do funny things with your face. Cody has his arms wrapped tight around her body, and he dips his hatless head down to hers so they can take a puppy picture together. With him here, I'm actually starting to think Aubrey is beginning to love this rodeo gig. I'm hoping he's starting to see how much the girls miss him. This could be a double win.

Then Ava remembers Missy. Naturally she would, barrel racing is happening now, and Missy does race. "Uncle Cody," she chirps out, leaning in to take a picture with him and Aubrey. "Do you know that lady, Mmm, um, Missy…"

I sigh out then help her finish. "Missy Wynkoop is her name, baby girl."

Cody looks over at me with his eyes raised and I nod my head slightly, saying he can tell her, but giving him that look, too, the one indicating he better not say too much.

"Yea, I know her. Why?" He shakes his head at me then looks down at Ava.

"Well, she was talking to Mommy, and I don't think Mommy likes her, but Missy said to tell Daddy she said hi."

"Did she now?" Cody smirks, and I angle my head, not finding the amusement he seems to have found in it.

"Mhmm, she did. Mommy said you all used to know her. How?"

I clear my throat loudly, warning Cody once more I don't want Ava knowing how, then turn my attention to the action in front of us.

"Well, when your daddy and I rode Junior Rodeo, right after we met your mom, we all ran into Missy. She rode, too." He glances over at me. "So we all knew her. And, no, I don't like her very much. She wasn't very nice to your mom. I know it's not polite to keep secrets, but I don't think you need to tell your dad she said hi, either."

"Okay." Ava nods in agreement. "If you guys don't like her, I don't either."

Aubrey pipes up then, too. "Me needer!"

"Neither," I correct her, smiling.

Cody chuckles and kisses Aubrey's head, and then Ava's. "All right, my favorite girls, I need to get down there, bulls are up soon and I need to be there to help Chase."

"'Kay, Uncle Cody," Aubrey says as she slides off his lap.

"Will you do something for me?" Ava asks as he stands.

"Sure thing," he replies easily and squats down to her level.

"Will you give him a high five? Tell him it's a special one from me, he'll know what it is."

A huge grin overtakes Cody's face and he nods his head, glancing up to me and winking. "I'll give him one, and I'll tell him it's from you."

"Thank you," she says.

As Cody starts to walk toward the steps I call out, "Tell my Cowboy it's from all of us, yeah?"

Cody puts his hat back on his head and tips the brim down with a subtle nod, and then he disappears.

"Mommy," Ava says, "I'm nervous."

I am too, Ava. This will never get any easier.

"He'll be okay, he's the best, right?"

Ava nods her agreement and both girls settle on the bleachers, filling in the gap left from Cody's departure.

Chase

The bulls have been rank today. All of them. I don't know if it's in the food, the water, the heat, or if they're

130

just really fucking tired of having riders on their backs, but very few of us are staying up for the full eight. I will be the one that changes the pattern. No bull will best me when my girls are all here to watch.

But I need my damn friend to get his ass down here. Superstition isn't something I take lightly, and I start every damn ride the same way. He helps me. I help him.

As though he could feel my thoughts shouting at him to unbury himself from whatever pussy he was balls deep in and get over here, he comes strolling up, shit-eating grin firmly in place.

"I hope she was good, jackass. I didn't think you'd make it down here in time."

He throws his head back and laughs. He fucking laughs like I just told the best joke in the world.

"Relax, asshat, I wasn't going to miss being here. And, for your information, all three of them were great to hang out with."

"You sick fuck, three of them? Really?"

"Christ, having your family here makes you uptight about rides. Your ego can't handle anything going wrong while they're watching, huh?" He shakes his head, still smirking. "Tell me, genius, how many girls did you come here with today…"

Realization smacks me square in the face when he says that. "You were with Allie and the girls?"

"No shit, Sherlock." He steps up beside me. "So pull your head out of your ass, ask what I know you want to ask, and let's get focused on your ride."

I exhale and let out a little chuckle. "How are they?"

"Missy run-in aside, they're all great…"

I look at him, clenching my back teeth together. "What did she say?"

"From what I can tell, nothing too terrible. Ava wanted to know if I liked Missy, and she told the girls to

131

tell you hi. Allie wasn't thrilled, but she's fine, too. And Aubrey, is having a blast. Between rides and events we were taking silly pictures together."

"Good, that's good. Thanks."

He pats me on the back and clasps my shoulder. "Now get your head on straight. It's about time."

We move up to my assigned chute and I get ready. Trying to steady my breathing and tamper the adrenaline starting to course through me as the bulls are brought into the chutes.

"Oh, before I forget, your girls sent you something."

I look at him, and he holds his hand up like a fool.

"What the hell are you doing?" I ask, completely lost.

He nods his head up toward the stands, in the direction of their seats then says, "Ava asked me to give you a high five and tell you it's supposed to be the special kind. Allie said to include her and Aubrey in on that, too."

I smile up, finding the girls in the front row and nod my head once for them, then give Cody a high five.

"If you ask me to clasp your hand like they do, I'll push you into the chute with Freight Train and let him stomp your ass before you even get out."

That draws a deep, loud laugh from me, one that turns everyone's heads around us. "You try it, and you'll be the one getting stomped…"

"There he is," Cody teases, "I was starting to think you left your balls in Allie's purse."

"Fuck you," I retort. "They're right here and still bigger than yours, just so we're clear."

Cody doesn't say anything. Instead, he turns his attention to the ride going on right now. "Has anyone hit eight today?"

"I don't think so," I glance at the board to see the standings, and there are no riders up there. "Take home this round may be huge."

"It will be."

Cody steps over and shakes hands with another rider we've seen around, he's new and young, but he's good, and they talk for a few until I'm ready to get set on my bull. When Cody comes over to help me get set, we run through our normal routine, he pats me hard, "Eight seconds" leaving his mouth, just like every ride. Before I nod my head to indicate I'm ready to ride, he adds in one last thing, the push he knows will make me fight even harder. "This one's for your girls."

I nod my head, for him, and for the gate to be opened. I will fight harder for every single second tonight, for my girls, than I have all season. They're who I'm riding for always, but with them here, I want them to know I'm the best.

I want them to know I will always be the best, for them.

It's that silent vow that lets me hang on long enough. I fight for every point, squeeze my fingers, roll and turn every time Freight Train does, and get my time.

With my family here, I'm damn near invincible.

Fourteen

Allie

"Mom, mommy, look, looooook," Ava says dramatically, pointing her finger in the direction of the Ferris wheel. "Who is with Uncle Cody?"

I look up where she's pointing and see Cody talking to a young woman. He's standing with his chest puffed out, arms crossed over it, flexing like a damn fool. You'd think the man would avoid sexual contact for a night, considering his first ride of the rodeo is tomorrow, rodeo day four. The final day of the first round.

"I don't know, but you can go see if you want to." I grin down at her.

"Okay, I'll be right back!" She takes off in Cody's direction.

A deep, gruff chuckle vibrates in my ear right as two strong arms wrap around me from behind. And then Aubrey appears momentarily before she's chasing Ava.

"That's cold, Darlin'," Chase says, still laughing.

"He'll survive. She may even find the girls cute and endearing." I rest my head back on his shoulder, feeling the heat from his arms through my tank top, causing a warmth that is equally comforting and also unpleasant in this heat, to spread through my body.

"She won't. You just sent the girls to chase his piece for the night off."

"Now really, would I do that?" I ask, feigning innocence and smirking up at him.

"To him? Hell yes, you would."

"He can go one rodeo without getting his dick wet," I say, shrugging, and Chase laughs. It's a loud, full laugh that warms my heart. It's a laugh I know has his eyes squinting with the spread of his lips, giving him a smile that takes up his whole face.

"Allie Anne," he tries to chastise me, but fails when he laughs some more. "I can't believe you just said that."

"We both know it's true," I reply, still watching Cody, Ava, Aubrey, and the woman who's quickly losing interest in him.

"It is," he says, turning me in his arms to face him. "But you haven't talked like that since, shit, I don't know? Maybe when you were still riding every weekend, or joining me on the road. Your old habits are coming back on you."

I scrunch my nose up and shake my head. "No, they aren't."

"Yeah, they are. And I love it. Not everything about the life you lived growing up was bad. Our two daughters, accompanied by a pissed looking Cody, coming our way are proof of it."

I sigh and kiss his chin quickly. "You and the girls are the only good that ever came from my riding. Now protect me from your angry best friend."

He wraps his arms tight around me, resting his chin on my head, a light laugh still bubbling out of him the closer Cody and the girls get. "You're going to need it," he says in a whisper. "I think he was looking forward to a night with her."

His safe embrace is starting to get too warm, too suffocating in the summer heat, but Cody can't get pissed at me while I'm here. Once I see the tiny boots of our daughters' feet beside us, I chance a quick look at Cody. He's glaring, but he's also smirking, well, trying not to smirk. He wants to be pissed at me. But I don't think he can.

"Old habits die hard, huh, Allie?" Cody says. "That's fine, I'll pay you back. Just like the old days. And this one," he juts his chin out toward Chase, "won't be able to protect you."

"What does Daddy need to protect you from?" Aubrey asks innocently, completely unaware of the childish game I just unwittingly entered into with Cody.

"Your Uncle Cody," Chase answers for me, chuckling and letting me go.

"Traitor," I accuse, laughing. "You're my husband, protector, for better or worse…"

Cody laughs, and the girls look back and forth between the three of us, utterly confused.

"Don't use our vows against me. I at no point said I'd protect you from the games you always start with our best friend… I stuck myself in the middle once. Exactly once. And we all know how that ended…"

I huff, Cody laughs, and the girls step closer. "We'll protect you, Mommy," Ava says, smiling wide.

"Thank you, Sweet Girl." I squat down and pull the girls to stand in front of me, letting my head pop up between their shoulders. "You wouldn't dare go through these two," I say, grinning at Cody.

"Wanna bet?" He crosses his arms over his chest, staying silent momentarily, then winks at me.

What does he have up his sleeve?

"What do you girls say I tell you all about your mama when she was a teen?"

The girls look at each other, and then at Cody, and they nod.

"You should come with me then, we'll ride some rides, eat all the junk food and sugar we can, and I'll tell you all about her before I take you back to the hotel tonight."

"Cody," I say sternly, giving him warning.

"Can we go with Uncle Cody, Mommy?" Aubrey asks, completely missing the tone of my voice.

"Please, Daddy," Ava adds, knowing he'd never say no to her spending time with Cody.

I look up at Chase and he's smirking down at me. He's going to let them. Of course.

"Yes, you can both go with Cody," he says easily. Then he looks at Cody, and Cody looks at him, and I swear to God they just had a conversation with that one look. Cody nods slightly and Chase laughs and bends down beside me, looking the girls in the eyes. "You two listen to him. Have fun. Don't eat too much junk, I don't want either of you sick tonight."

"Okay!" they both shout. It's scary how in sync they can be sometimes. But I love it.

"And don't force your sister to go on rides she's afraid of, Ava," I add. She smiles and nods her head, indicating she understands, but I'm sure Aubrey will be pushed to go on something she doesn't want to anyway.

"They'll be good," Cody pipes in. "You two should try to get to the concert tonight. I'll keep them until you're ready for 'em. It's not like I have any plans tonight or anything…" He raises his eyebrows and pins me with a look that very directly conveys that's my fault.

I hug each of the girls and then stand back up. "Thank you, Cody. And I'm…" I should say sorry. I really should, but it's just not our style. "Glad you have the night free. The girls will love spending some extra time with you."

"Just couldn't do it, could ya?" he asks, shaking his head.

"Nope, never." I smile at him.

"Good. Life would be way too boring if you started apologizing for your behavior now, after all these years. Besides, I'll have fun telling the girls everything tonight, too. Just remember you started this."

"You wouldn't dare…"

"Wouldn't I?" he teases. "You're the one who's being obnoxious and acting like you're sixteen again, being a giant pain in my ass."

"You love it," I toss back as a weak argument, hoping he keeps his mouth shut about the things he should keep to himself.

"Yeah, actually, I think I do," he says. "Have fun tonight, you two."

"Thanks, man," Chase says, then hugs the girls. "You two, have fun, be good, and I love you."

They each throw their arms around his neck and they each say back, "Love you, too."

Once Cody and the girls are gone, I turn to Chase and put my hands on my hips. "You don't think he'll really tell them everything, do you?"

"No, Allie, he won't betray you. But Christ, what would it matter if he did? You're hiding shit that doesn't need to be hidden. Be proud of the girl you were, the accomplishments you achieved, and how they shaped you into the woman you are now."

"It's not that—" My mouth zips shut when he cuts me off.

"It is that easy. You rode rodeo. You were really fucking good. You won junior championships and you probably would've been a title holder in the pro ranks, too." He steps into me, sliding his index finger beneath my chin and tilting it up so I'm looking directly into his eyes. "Just because you resent your father for making you do it, doesn't mean it was all bad. What you accomplished was all on you. He didn't make you the great rider you were, that was you. He didn't pay for your championships. You earned them."

I open my mouth to speak, but I don't know what to say. He's never seemed angry about me keeping that part of my past from the girls, but right now, he does.

"This life is as much a part of you as it is me, Allie. It's how we met, it's what brought us closer, and we have a ton of amazing memories at events like this together. It wasn't a bad life for you. So quit acting like it was."

"Chase, that's not... I'm not trying to say it was a bad life."

"But you are. You act like you don't know people here because you rode with them. You act like you're above the lifestyle they chose to live. That I fucking live still."

"I don't... I've never.... I've always supported you riding. You know that."

"You do, and you don't."

He drops his hand from beneath my chin and crosses his arms over his chest defensively.

"What is that supposed to mean, Chase?"

He looks around us, and I do, too. Some people are minding their own businesses while others are staring openly. Catching every word we jab at each other with.

"Not here, we aren't having this conversation here." He reaches for my hand and laces his fingers through mine. It's not the gentle, soft touch he used earlier. I can feel the tension in him, it's rolling off his body in waves, and the firm grip of his fingers, even as he rubs his thumb over mine, gives away how upset he really is.

He's not hurting me. He'd die before he would ever purposefully hurt me. But he's firm as he leads us through the crowds and out to the parking lots. We trudge through the stifling heat and dust and make our way to his truck.

He yanks the door open and helps me up into the cab, then circles his way around the front of his truck and climbs in beside me.

"What's this about, Chase? What brought all of this on? And how dare you say I don't support you? That's all I do. Day in and day out."

He backs out of our spot and pulls out of the lot, turning onto the road and driving.

"Where are we going?"

"I don't know, okay. We're just getting away."

"Okay…" I look out the window, biting the inside of my cheek. Where the hell did all of this come from? I really don't understand a single bit of it.

"You support me," he finally breaks the silence after fifteen minutes of just driving. "But you also resent me."

I what?

"Where the hell are you coming up with that?"

"It's obvious." He turns off a main road and down some back road that's more dirt than road.

"I need you to elaborate on how it's so obvious that I resent you. Because I don't know what you're talking about." I look over to him, watch his fingers flex over the steering wheel and the veins of his arm pop out due to the force of his grip.

"Talk to me, Chase. Because I'm really fucking confused right now."

"We're almost there," he mutters, but says nothing else after.

140

Chase

She says she's confused, and hell, so am I. I don't know what it was about her being so bent about Cody maybe telling the girls she rode, but it set me off. I am so damn tired of her acting like she didn't ride. I'm tired of her acting like it wasn't a huge part of who we were. I'm tired of her acting like rodeo is beneath her. And, fuck, I don't know. I'm tired of her shunning it because it was so awful for her when it's all I've ever done. If she hates it so much she can't talk about it, what does she think about me riding?

What's going to happen when I tell her about an offer I got this morning to ride a few exhibitions, unsanctioned events that would bring in some good money, but will keep me gone for a while again?

I haven't even told her about it, but I already know she's going to be pissed off. After the last couple of weeks together, I don't want that fight. I especially don't want it when she realizes it falls on the day of Aubrey's first big gymnastics meet. The one she begged me to go to.

Then again, look where we are now. Fighting anyway.

I pull into a deserted field, one Cody and I used to come shoot at a long time ago, and throw the truck into park.

"Are you going to tell me what the hell is going on now?" she clips out, clearly annoyed and on edge.

"You resent me. You resent my being gone, my goal, my dreams to win," I say, pushing my door open and dropping out of my truck, pacing back and forth.

She follows me out of the truck and stomps around toward me.

"Say that again, because it sounded a lot like you said I resent you and your dreams."

"You do, don't you?" I shout at her.

"No!" she shouts back. "I've never resented you, or your dreams. Do you really think I would've stuck around this long if I did!" It's not a question, not how she shouted it.

"I can see it every time I am gone and we Skype, Allie. I see it when I walk out the door before every rodeo. I saw it when you started another God damn period again."

"Oh no you don't." She steps up to me, standing as tall as she can, pointing her finger right in my face. "You don't get to use the baby we can't seem to have against me. I swear to God, Chase, if you even try to bring up the child we lost, I will walk away from you right now and I may never turn back again."

Those words cut me short and render me absolutely speechless.

"What, you don't have anything to say to me now? Caught you before you could get the words out so now you have nothing else to say?" Her voice is shaking with her anger, and the hurt I've managed to cause her.

But for her to think I could or would ever do that to her pisses me off, and hurts me, too. "How could I say anything?" My voice is low, and piercing. "You think I would ever hold losing our child over you? What kind of man do you think I am? I lost our baby, too. I was hurt, too. I would never, not in a million fucking years, take that pain and turn it on you. But apparently you would turn it on me. Showcasing the fact that you do, indeed, resent me. Or maybe you blame me? Is that it?"

She drops her finger and takes a step back, shaking her head. Tears pool in her eyes and spill down her cheeks. "I would never blame you for us losing our child. Ever."

"It sure doesn't feel like it," I say, clasping my fingers behind my neck and squeezing, feeling the tension in my own muscles build with every passing second.

"I wouldn't. Not that. I may hold a lot back, but blaming you for our baby…" She wipes at her eyes and turns her back to me. "You weren't there. How could that have been your fault?"

There it is. The one thing she does hold against me, and as it turns out, it's the one thing I hold against myself, too.

"I'm never there, that's what you're not saying."

"You're gone a lot, that's for sure. When were you planning on telling me you are going to miss the one thing Aubrey asked you for?"

"You know?"

She laughs a cold, sadistic laugh. "That's what this is about, isn't it? You wanted me good and mad so when you told me you were failing our daughter, I didn't beg you to stay. You wanted me mad enough I wouldn't want you home."

Is that what all of this was for? Does she know me so well that she knows, even if I don't consciously, I'm trying to hurt her now so me being gone later hurts her less?

"I can't turn down that money," I say quietly. "It's too much."

"We don't need the money, Chase. We live a good life. We need you."

"We do need the money, Allie. There are things I want for us that won't work if I can't afford them. That's the fact of the matter, plain and simple." The only way we can put out thousands of dollars to try to have another baby is to have thousands of dollars in our account that won't be used for other bills, and life.

"So you're going to let Aubrey down, then you're going to accuse me of resenting you and your dreams, and you're going to turn this on me…for money?" She turns back to me and if looks could kill, I'd be dead where I stand.

"No, not for money. It's more than money. It's for us."

"No, it's not for us. If you were acting for us, you'd be home, you'd realize I don't give a shit whether you have the title of best in the world or not beside your name. If this were for us, you'd realize your daughters love you, in spite of the fact you're a rodeo going cowboy who leaves them constantly."

"It is for us!" My head is reeling and everything she's saying is swirling around inside it, creating a storm of uncertainty and confusion. She doesn't know. She doesn't get it.

"It's not! We don't want the money. We want you! We want our family whole!"

"Don't you understand? That's what I'm riding for!" I can't hold it in anymore. I can't. I didn't want to put that on her but I can't keep it all on me now, either.

"The money? I know, Chase. You're riding for the money. I got that."

"No, Allie, I'm not." I step up to her so we are toe-to-toe and look down in her face, lowering my voice so I'm not screaming at her anymore. "I'm riding to make enough that we can comfortably follow through with IVF. I'm riding so maybe the one thing I've managed to fuck up and fail can be righted. I want to fix it."

144

She opens her mouth, primed to argue again, I know. Then she closes it, and lets what I just said to her sink in. "You want to go through with IVF?"

"If you still do," I respond, swallowing hard. "It's expensive. With the cost of everything else we have on our plates, we need me to have the best year of my life so every extra cent I make can go to our future baby."

"Why didn't you tell me? Why did you just disappear every weekend, stay gone, and leave me hanging?" Her tears are falling more freely now, and all I want to do is hold her.

"Because I didn't want you to feel like the same failure I feel like every month. I wanted to save up quietly, come home one day, and say let's do this. I wanted to protect you from disappointment if I failed this season."

"Oh, Chase," she sobs out and reaches for me. I pull her into my chest and hold her tight. "I'm sorry I can't give you that on my own. I do feel like a failure every month. Don't you know that? The one thing you want, and I can't give it to you."

She buries her face in my shirt and cries. Her tears soak through and I can feel their cool, wet effect against my skin.

"You aren't failing, Darlin'. You aren't. You've already given me the world." I kiss the top of her head and squeeze her tighter, holding on for dear life.

"Had you just told me," she cries into my chest, "I wouldn't have started to resent you. I wouldn't have been so mad."

"I knew you resented me," I say, shaking my head back and forth, letting my mouth and nose pass over her hair.

"I don't resent you, Chase. I resent the rodeo for taking you from me."

"Nothing could ever take me from you. Not rodeo. Not all the money in the world. I'm yours. I will always be yours."

She lifts her head from my chest and looks up, leaving our mouths inches from each other. "If you'd told me, I wouldn't have been as mad."

"If I'd told you, you would've said we'd find another way. And, baby, I don't think there is one. I wasn't ready to give up on our dream yet. Fulfilling my dream is just a means to give us ours."

"Don't lie to me, Chase," she says quietly, the warmth of her breath against me causes a shiver down my spine.

"What do you mean?"

"Winning and the money you bring in may be a means to trying for another baby, but rodeo is still your passion. If it weren't for our future baby, you'd still ride. You'd have another excuse for why you need to do it. Another reason you have to be out, putting your life on the line every weekend. You can't walk away from it any more than I can walk away from you."

"Does that mean you want to walk away from me?" I ask, closing my eyes, afraid of what she may say.

"No, Cowboy, I don't want to walk away from you. I love you too damn much. I just wish you'd walk to me and the girls, and away from rodeo, a little more."

"I love you, too. You know that, right?" I should address rodeo and my need for it. But right now, I don't have it in me to come to terms with how she sees me. To terms with the fact she believes I can't walk away from the one thing she wishes I could walk away from, just like her dad.

"I know."

I tentatively slide my hands up and along her jawline, then close the small gap between us and kiss her. "You need to tell the girls about your past." Now probably isn't

146

a great time to say that, given everything. But it is what started all of this in the first place.

"I'll tell them about my past riding the day you walk away from rodeo as your full-time job." She takes a step back and reaches for my hands. "We should get going before we miss the concert," she says.

I nod my head. There isn't much else to say here. She knows why I'm riding this year and I want her to stop lying to the girls. I know she wants me to be home more. However, we're at an impasse as to whether either of those things will ever happen.

Fifteen

Allie

We went back to the hotel to get ready for the concert after our little trip to the middle of nowhere so we could fight. Though we both said a lot, I don't think we actually resolved anything. We just opened up wounds that are going to need time to heal.

While he gets our drinks between the opening act and Josh Turner going on tonight, I can't help but think about everything that's happened today. I can't help but think he's going to disappoint our daughter so he can go and ride. And make more money. That upsets me, but there isn't much I can do about it.

I guess it helps knowing, even beyond riding because it's in his blood, he has a plan for us in mind that will be a direct benefit of his riding. One he never shared with me, but I wish he would have. I can't help but think of the fact that I don't need that, either, though. I don't want him to make me, our family, an excuse for him to leave us. Even if I know he really does want to have another baby still. I know he loves us. I know he wants our family to grow and thrive, and he absolutely means it when he says he wants his earnings this year to go toward infertility treatments and trying to have a baby.

I know, too, that even if we'd already had our baby, he wouldn't quit riding. He wouldn't quit trying to be the best. He wouldn't quit chasing the dream. Garth Brooks has it right in his song. I want Chase as much as he wants rodeo. He will never give it up. He will give anything to continue to ride. He needs it like he needs air to breathe. I know that. I knew when I married him. He would give anything to have the challenge and rush each go round. He lives for the thrill of every ride, hearing the buzzer, riding in the short every Sunday because he's that good.

It's being as good as he is that allows him to continue riding every weekend. He does make money. It is his full-time job. On top of our business at home, he doesn't have to scrape together any entrance fees, hope and pray that he'll make enough to feed, clothe, and provide for our family every weekend. He's given us a life we can sustain until we are old and gray. He's given us a life where we want for almost nothing.

I just fear he won't be living it with us, because the abuse his body takes, the knocks and danger could rip him away from our family now, or earlier in life than he should be taken after he retires. It terrifies me.

I saw what could happen when rodeo sucks a man in and doesn't give him back. My parents fought constantly, Dad dragged us from rodeo to rodeo, made me ride, and put it above all else. It tore our family apart from the inside out. To everyone else, we were the perfect family following dreams. But behind closed doors, we were broken. Irreparably so. I resented Dad. I resented my mom. I resented a sport that I may have loved, had it not been forced upon me relentlessly. I resented the culture and everything rodeo put families through.

Yeah, maybe Chase is right. Maybe I do resent him a little. He knows how I feel about it. He knows I blame rodeo for the broken home I grew up in. He knows I blame rodeo for taking my parents away from me too early in life. And he still rides.

For all that I do resent about rodeo, I don't resent him, not as the man he is.

He isn't my father. He is so much better than my dad was as a father to our girls. He doesn't force rodeo on us. He and my dad are night and day, polar opposites.

Chase is a good man. A good father. He's a good husband. He loves me with a fierceness I never knew possible growing up. I certainly didn't see it in my parents' marriage. He makes me feel it daily, whether he's home or on the circuit.

I love him more now, even with everything, than I did as the awestruck fifteen-year-old girl that was taken by the older, blue-eyed cowboy, twelve years ago. I can still picture the first time I noticed him, while he was watching me from beside the stripping chute where he was helping strip the broncs. He kept staring, and I couldn't help but stare back.

Even right now, as I see him coming down the aisle with our drinks in hand, and the tenseness in his body I know our argument caused, I can't help but stare again. And like he was that day, he's staring back. His black hat is hooding his gorgeous blues, but I can feel them on me, nonetheless.

"Darlin'," he says when he gets to me, handing me my drink. "Sorry that took so long. Everyone had the same idea I did and the lines were long."

"It's okay," I say, taking a sip from my straw and closing my eyes as the vodka and lemonade burn their way down my throat. "That's strong."

Chase smiles at me and tips his bottle of beer back for a drink before he answers. "I got you a double. I thought, after earlier, maybe you could use it."

I take another drink, enjoying it a little more now that I'm expecting the kick of the alcohol, and nod my head. "Thank you."

"You're welcome," he says and takes another drink. He lifts his hat off his head and runs the back of his arm along his forehead, wiping the sweat there away.

"I'm sorry," I say to him, watching him cover his head once more. "For earlier. This weekend wasn't the time or place for that conversation."

"Allie," he steps closer. "I'm the one that should be apologizing, not you. You're right. Now isn't the time. But I think we have a lot to talk about once I'm home for a stretch again."

"I think so, too. But tonight I just want to enjoy the show and being here with you."

"I'd like that. He is your favorite, after all."

"Yeah, there's just something about those blue-eyed country boys that know exactly how to steal my heart," I say, grinning at him.

"All blue-eyed country boys?"

"No, not all. Just one, actually."

"He's a lucky man."

"Ya know, he may not know this, especially today, but I think I'm the lucky one to have caught his eye a long time ago."

"You sure you still feel lucky?"

I slide my hand down the buttons lining the front of his light blue shirt and nod my head. "I'm positive. We'll talk through everything else when we're home."

Just as the crowd starts to scream in delight at Josh Turner taking the stage, Chase dips his head and whispers in my ear, "I'm the lucky one. And I know it."

Chase

Raw. That's the only way I can explain how I feel after this afternoon. The things that were said in anger between both of us were…unacceptable. But I think that was the most honest she's been about how she feels in a long time, too.

There is resentment there. Resentment I could feel, that I brought on myself. I know my being gone has created it. I know she also thinks I'll never pick her and the girls over rodeo. I can't even fault her for thinking that now.

But to think I would ever hold the child we lost over her…had she stabbed me with a real knife through my heart, it wouldn't have hurt as bad as the words did cutting through me. I've replayed them in my head repeatedly since we left the field.

I can hear her telling me that if I use our lost child, she'll walk away and never come back. I hear her say I couldn't have caused her miscarriage, because I wasn't there. I can hear her shouting I'm never there, even though she didn't even say those words. I hear, over and over, how I'm failing the girls. And I know that in failing them, I'm failing her.

Every dream I have, every goal I've tried to reach, every cent I've made riding has come at their expense. I'm no better than her father was. I may not force the girls to go with me, to live the rodeo life on the road, but I've made them live this life. The life where I'm gone, and they're home.

It's a tough pill to swallow. Because she was also right when she said, even if we had already had the baby, I would still be riding. That fact makes me the biggest asshole to walk this earth. I would be chasing this title, all-in, and not looking back even if we had a baby here.

That doesn't mean I can't still be there for my family. I need to be better for them. Even if it means exhaustion because I'm traveling around the clock. I can fly home more. I can be better.

They deserve that. I want to be the man all three of my girls need. Rodeo won't last forever; I know that. But my family, they will. They're mine until the day I die. I owe it to them to be there, like they're always there for me.

I watch Allie sing and sway to "Firecracker." The lights from the show pass over her, illuminating her in yellows, reds, and flashes of blue and white. She's lost in the music, putting everything behind us, and she looks every bit the beautiful, strong woman I've been in love with since I was seventeen years old.

It's time I start showing her how in love I am again.

I slip in behind her, sliding my hands to her waist, moving my body with hers, and nipping at her neck playfully so she'll throw her head back and laugh. And she does. She drops her head back on my shoulder, smiling wide, her cheeks noticeably flushed from the drinks she's had and from dancing and moving in the hot night air.

Her eyes land on mine and I tip my head down, kissing her lips. And then the song comes to an end. Our bodies quit moving, stilling while he speaks up on stage, talking about the next song he's going to sing, how it's dedicated to all of the couples in the audience tonight. Then the music starts again.

It's slower than "Firecracker" and the second I hear the first words of "Soulmate" being sung, I slip my hands from her hips around to her stomach and settle them there, holding her protectively, caressing the spot our children have all started at. The spot we lost our last child from.

I start to sing along to the song, quietly in her ear, swaying slightly. Every single word he and I are singing is absolutely true. Halfway through the song I stop singing and start talking.

"You are my soul mate, Allie. The woman who lifts me up. The woman I will grow old with. And I hope to God that I do go first when the day comes, because I could never and would never love anyone like I love you." I kiss her temple and rub my hand over her stomach. "I'm so sorry I wasn't there for you, baby. I am so sorry you have gone through some of your hardest days alone. I will be better for you. I'll be better for the girls."

She spins in my arms and wraps her own around my neck, then looks up at me with tears in her eyes. She opens her mouth to speak and I silence her with a quick kiss.

"I'm not done yet." I kiss her again and let her pull my hat from my head before I wrap her tighter and lower my head so my mouth is pressed to her ear again, and then I continue, "You were right about a lot you said. I'm not going to quit. I wouldn't have if we had had another ten children. But I swear to you, I'll be there for you. I wouldn't be the man I am, the rider I am, or anything if it weren't for your love."

Allie lifts her head and kisses my lips, letting the taste of her tears and the drinks she's had tonight mix with the taste of the beers I've been drinking, then nods her answer. We start swaying to the song again, and I pick back up with the end of the song, singing quietly about how I will never find another soulmate in my life because she's it. She will be it through the very end of time.

Allie

I slide my fingers through Chase's hair and hold his hat against his back, listening to every word he's singing in my ear. I don't hear the band. I don't hear my favorite country singer. As far as I'm concerned, the only two people here tonight are Chase and me, and he's serenading me with a song all about how we are each other's soul mates. Between verses of the song, he told me he heard everything I said earlier, and he wants to be better.

As the song rolls to an end, I move my hand to his cheek and guide it so his lips are pressed to mine again. While I kiss him, I mumble against his lips, "I love you."

He mumbles it back and keeps kissing me, even though there is no music, and it's possible the people around us are watching. He poured his heart out to me, and I haven't even apologized for the terrible things I said to him.

"Chase," I pull back just enough, and exhale when he rests his forehead against mine.

"Yeah?" he whispers, slowly moving his hands up and down my back.

"I'm so sorry I said what I did, about the baby, about you…"

"I forgive you." He wraps me up tighter and buries his face in my neck. I can feel his lips moving over my skin, and then feel his tongue slide over the place my pulse is beating harder for him.

The next song starts, and he chuckles into my neck, then starts moving our bodies quicker to the beat of the song.

This time he doesn't sing to me. No, he lets his mouth dance over my skin, holds us together so our hips roll and swirl with each other, and lets me feel him between us, reaffirming with each second of song that passes how much it really does turn him on to be mine.

A raspy moan travels up my throat and it's my turn to whisper now, "Take me back to the hotel? Cody and the girls won't be expecting us yet."

His stubble passes over my neck as he nods, and then he turns me back around, letting me walk in front of him, keeping his midsection hidden behind me until we are free of the crowd and in the parking lot. Then his hands are all over me again until we get to his truck.

Sixteen

Chase

Never in my life have I been happier to have a bench seat in my truck than I am right now. Allie wasted no time scooting as close to me as she could when we got out here, and as we pass through the dark, empty streets leading to our hotel, I can hold her close and touch her all I want with nothing between us.

"Don't lose focus on the road," she murmurs, while sliding her hand up my leg. It's really hard to follow her command when her fingers graze over my crotch. My cock twitches beneath her touch, and the painful strain against my jeans becomes unbearable torture as she continues to move her hands agonizingly slowly over me.

"Maybe—" I swallow hard, then try again, "Maybe you shouldn't do that, then. I don't want to crash."

She lets out a little giggle, and pulls her hand back, laying it back on my thigh again. Allie isn't usually so reckless with us driving, but I imagine she's feeling a little looser than normal with the drinks in her system. When she asked for another drink, I knew she needed a night of freedom and letting loose, so I stopped.

"Drive quicker, then?" There's a quiet, sultry rasp to her voice that tells me that for as hard and in desperate need of her as I am, she's equally needy of me.

"I'm going as fast as I can," I reply, then slide my hand back from around her and move it to her lap, dipping my fingers between the denim valley created by her jeans and rubbing over her inner thigh. "We'll be there in ten."

I pull off the highway and we get caught at the red light at the bottom of the exit, so I lean over to her and kiss her lips. She kisses me back slow and steady, teasing my lips with her tongue and playful nips over my lips, and she moves her hand back up my leg again, making me groan against her when her fingers pass over me, tracing the obvious swell in my jeans. She smiles triumphantly, then says, "The light's green. Get us home."

Home. That's not where we're going. Not even close. But the sentiment lodges in my chest and settles there. It's a hotel. Her ease of calling it home, simply because we are going back there together, to stay, means that even with the way the night started, everything said, everything thrown out into the universe, I'm still home to her. Just as she is to me.

We pass through the streets of Cheyenne in a hurry. Her perfume fills the cab of my truck, and her breath is coming in deep, heavy bursts. White lines over black pavement blur together, and neon signs over businesses turn into a passing rainbow of lights. The way she can't take her hands off of me—my leg, my achingly hard cock, my neck, her lips on my arms, her fingers playing with the buttons of my shirt—they all mix to stimulate each of my senses in a way that builds the deep-seated need in the pit of my stomach into a tight knot ready to unravel as soon as we're in our room.

I feel like a horny, desperate teen again—and it's so fitting—being here with her, in the same place we shared our first kiss together, where we first met. I squeeze her thigh gently, yet possessively, and whisper, "I love you, Allie."

"I love you, too."

I get us to the hotel and pull into the first parking spot I can find, vaguely hoping it's not reserved or valet, as I lean back into my wife and plant another kiss on her lips. "Let's get upstairs."

I open my door and drop down, helping her scoot over my spot and taking her by the hips, lowering her down in front of me. I let her slide down the front of my body then move my hands to her neck, holding either side and framing her face with my thumbs, then lay a featherlight kiss over her lips, her nose, her forehead.

She releases a small sigh and blinks up at me, smiling softly. "Upstairs…"

I scoop her into my arms, drawing out a shocked gasp and then a laugh.

"Chase!"

"Hush," I say, kissing her again, raising my boot up behind me to nudge the door closed before carrying her inside.

She pulls my hat off my head and runs her fingers though my hair, letting my hat hang down from her side, discreetly covering my obvious hard-on as we walk through the lobby to the elevator.

"Your fingers are magical," I murmur into her ear before I trace its shell with my lips.

"So are your lips." She keeps stroking her fingers through my hair and then along my jaw, back up to my hair, repeating the same path. "Kiss me, please?"

We step into the elevator and once the doors close, I oblige. Our mouths form together, lips parting, tongues dancing and tasting, until we reach our floor.

The doors open after the ding and release us into the hall, not far from our room.

"Back pocket, my key's there," Allie says, then grazes her lips over my neck, scraping her teeth right

159

over the spot where my blood is thumping hardest against my skin.

Her lips, tongue, and teeth are a tantalizing combination of heaven and hell over my skin. The way she nips and sucks causes the hair on the back of my neck to stand on end and makes my dick swell further in my pants, straining so hard against the zipper I'm surprised it hasn't forced it open yet. I moan and slide a hand beneath her ass, rubbing over the denim before I dip my fingers into the pocket and withdraw the little plastic card that will give us entry to our room.

"Give me," she commands, placing my hat back on my head and taking the key from me, expertly sliding it through the reader and opening our door with a click so we can pass through.

As soon as it's shut behind us, I set her down, roaming my hands over her back and ass, reaching for the hem of her tank top and tugging it up and off. Her fingers move in a practiced, precise pattern starting at the top of my shirt and working their way down, popping each button free, exposing more and more of my bare chest to her.

"My jeans, free me," I grind out, working the clasp of her bra open and then moving down to her jeans, loosening the button and zipper at the same time as she does mine.

"Chase," she says reverently, as she works my jeans and underwear down my hips and sets my member free. I look down between us, watching as the last of her clothes fall down her legs, seeing the effects each of us have had on each other up until now. My cock is harder than stone and in desperate need of her touch.

"You did that to me, you always do." I kick my boots off and step free of the clothes surrounding our feet, holding her hips to balance her when she does the same.

Instead of letting me walk her back to the bed, she guides us in a slow turn, then with her hand to my chest, she directs me back to the bed, giving me a gentle shove once the mattress is behind my legs so I fall onto it, landing with a thud on the mattress.

"I want—" she starts to say, before I cut her off by tugging her hips and bringing her down on top of me.

"I do, too," I nod, tracing my fingers over her back, dipping them into the little dimples just above her ass.

She moves her hands to the mattress and uses it to pull herself up over my lap, sliding her slickened flesh over my thighs and coming to stop just before my dick. Then she puts her hands on my chest and pushes herself up so she's seated over me. She smiles down on me, like a queen perched on her throne, and takes my length in one of her hands, stroking and holding it upright like a scepter before her.

"Christ," I hiss out in approval, watching her hand grip and squeeze from root to tip until another bead of arousal oozes from the head. "Fuck me... Ride me until you can't move anymore. Take what you need and give me you in return."

Allie

I lift up onto my knees and move forward, angling him so I can lower myself over him. I move slowly, relishing in the feeling taking him in gives me. He's so hard. Even with moving slowly and deliberately, there's a subtle sting of pain that comes with accepting him deeper and deeper, one that slowly gives way to full, powerful, pleasure.

He isn't rushing me, or taking control of this; he's giving himself—his power—to me. He's showing me how much I mean to him, how much he loves me, how much he respects me, even though if he could, he'd fuck me senseless right now. It makes me love him even more.

Once I'm fully seated on him, I bend forward, sliding my hands over his chest, and wrap my fingers loosely around his neck, pressing my lips to his in the softest of kisses I can manage.

"You feel so good," he growls against my lips.

I can feel his hands roaming over my back—with his fingers tracing down my spine slowly—and chills erupt in their wake. His body is firm and strong beneath mine. The perfect balance to my soft spots and curves. And all I want is to melt into him, to lose track of where I end and he begins. I kiss him again and push myself back up, keeping my hands on his chest, so I can start to move over him. I rock back and forth slowly, finding the perfect rhythm that makes him rub me in the places I need most.

"God, Chase…" I hum out, then slowly raise up and glide back down on him. Repeating the same rocking, lifting, lowering motions over and over. "I need more. I want you, all of you."

He smiles up at me, and his eyes—bright and stunning, even in the dimly lit room—are the window to his soul right now. There isn't a single thing behind them that he's hiding from me. The look on his face makes my breath catch, and causes a stutter in my movements over him, throwing my rhythm off.

"You do have all of me, you always have." He sits up slowly, wrapping an arm around my waist to keep me from falling off his lap, then nuzzles his nose against mine. "I love you Allie."

"I love you too," I murmur into his neck. "Help me. Take control."

He nods silently and his legs shift a little beneath me, finding their footing on the ground, then his hands move to my hips and guide me. He lifts me, then pulls me back down while he thrusts up, setting a new, quicker pace.

I use my knees, planted on either side of his legs, and start to move up and down at his pace on my own. I lift. I drop. He thrusts. I roll my hips toward him. With every new start to the pattern I get closer and closer. His lips flutter over my collarbones, his tongue dips into the hollow of my neck. His hands fall between us and his fingers rub in steady circles over my swollen, sensitive bundle of nerves.

"I'm. So. Close." I stutter out. With my eyes closed I can feel every tiny sensation firing in my body. Every brush of his five o'clock shadow over my skin. Every circle of the rough pad of his thumb over my clit. The sweet nothings he's whispering, telling me how beautiful I am. How perfect. How I was made for him. It's all a complete system overload. Instead of shutting me down, it sends my body into overdrive. All it takes is his mouth sealing over mine, taking my breath and giving me his own, to set me off.

Then I fall.

My body trembles around him, and little bursts of light flash behind my eyes, mimicking the jolts of pleasure zapping through me. He swallows my moans until they start to blend with his own as he comes with a shudder, filling me completely with his release.

He kisses my lips, my cheeks, my chin, and then buries his face in my neck, so I feel each hot, panted breath he takes.

"Do we have to call Cody right away?" he asks after a few minutes of silently catching our breaths. "Or can we take a while to just be? I'll grab a shower before they come back."

I glance at the clock on the nightstand and shake my head. "We have a little. I don't think I can move just yet, anyway."

"Then don't, not yet." He carefully lifts me so he can scoot us back onto the bed, and then he cradles me to his chest, rubbing my back, and kissing the crown of my head.

His heart is beating steadily beneath my ear. It's hypnotizing. It's comforting. It lulls me into such a calmness that my mind starts to wander just a little to earlier. To our girls. Our lives together.

"Chase?" I whisper, almost hesitantly, after a couple of minutes pass us by.

"Yeah?"

"I understand your need to be out there." I pause, listening to his heart again, using it to gauge his reaction to what I'm saying. "I know what you're doing, what you're trying to accomplish this year, but, baby?"

"Yeah?" he replies, his voice is quieter and gravellier this time, almost like he's afraid of what I'm going to ask and say to him.

"You don't have anything to prove. Not to me, or the girls. Not to anyone. We will find a way to bring another beautiful baby into this world. But—" I break off, not finishing my thought as his heart starts pounding beneath me.

"But what?"

"But you've been gone so much that maybe, when all is said and done, you will have to prove you do love your girls, more than you love rodeo."

"Allie…"

"I know, Chase. I do," I say, turning my head in to kiss over his heart. "But they need time with you. Aubrey isn't all about rodeo or riding, she loves her gymnastics and dance. And Ava, well, she's all you, but she still needs you to be there and present for her. During the school year it isn't as bad. They're at school and long days and early nights full of school and activities make your absence from home easier."

I pause, drawing my fingers over the tattoo on his shoulder, continuing, "During the summer, they notice you aren't around. Aubrey especially. She won't watch you ride; it scares her. So she doesn't see you at all. You're just...gone. Maybe that'll change now that we brought her out here for the week, but it still may not."

I don't know how much time has passed since I finished talking. It's long enough that I think I'm not going to get an answer from him at all. The only indication I have that he even heard me is the pitter-patter of his heart, speeding up and slowing down, based on what I'm saying.

"I'll be there more," he finally says. "I'll find ways to get home more. Even if I have to fly in for a day and fly back out. I don't want the girls to question my love. I don't want them to ever feel they aren't the most important parts of my life."

I lift my head up and look at him. His eyes are darker now, an Aegean blue instead of ocean blue, and the lines on his face are pulled down with the frown on his lips. "Aubrey's gymnastics?"

He combs his fingers through my hair and nods his head. "I will find a way to be there. I'll fly in right after I finish my ride, and I'll take a red-eye back to ride the day after."

"You will?"

"Yeah, I will. I don't want the girls to grow up feeling about me the way you did your dad. I don't want them to hate rodeo and me because I was absent. I told you I'd be better. And I will."

"Oh, Chase…" I scoot up his body and kiss him hard, then hold onto him for dear life. "I promise we will try to be there for you more, too. I'll ask the girls' friends if they can spend a couple nights over now and then. I'll go to rodeos when I can, support you and make the same efforts."

I don't know why that thought didn't hit me before now, but I can be there for him. I love him more than I hate rodeo and what it stripped from me growing up. I've been punishing him for the sins of my own father, and that's not fair.

"We'll make it work, Darlin'. I promise. But don't feel pressured to come out with me. The girls need you more."

"I'll travel when I can. They need me, yes. But you do, too. More than that, I need you. I need us."

He doesn't say anything to that. He simply kisses me again and hugs me as though letting go means losing me. Though he won't, I love the feel of his arms around me, cherishing me like I could disappear at any minute.

Seventeen

Chase

Nine days, over eighty riders to compete against to start, and here we are, only seventeen of us left. Today is the short go and my final ride of this rodeo. Sixteen other cowboys and I had good enough scores between the first round and second combined to be here right now. Only eight of us will take home a split of the average pot at the end of this.

I won the first round, and raked in over five grand for my ride. But I finished lower in the standings second round, barely making my eight, and not winning any money for it. That's all okay. I just need to ride well today, get a good score, and hope Cody and one of the other guys jockeying for the top spot in the average with us don't beat me. We're the top three right now. As long as we make our eight, first through third should be ours.

I'm going to be in the top three. My girls didn't come out here for nothing. The fight, the words exchanged, the promises made—none of that was for nothing. With them here, cheering me on, I may as well be super human today. I have something to prove to them. And to myself.

First I have to watch my best friend take his ride.

I pat Cody hard on the back and watch him nod, starting his ride on top of a fierce bull that has a reputation for bucking riders off. He's not impossible, but he's damn hard to stay on. He bucked me off last time

I drew him. Cody maneuvers on the bull, moving every way he should to make his time.

The crowd is loving it. They're loud and cheering him on. The announcer and lead clown have gotten them going tonight, and all of us riders soak it up.

Dust flies beneath the force of his bull's feet with every leap and kick. Snot flies out of the bull's nose.

He's pissed.

Cody is determined.

Fans are anxious to see if he'll make it. The eight seconds fly by for all of us. But I know what Cody is feeling.

Adrenaline is coursing through his blood. He feels stronger than at any other normal time. He's hearing nothing but the sound of his heart pounding in his chest and the bull's body and grunts beneath him. It's like a tunnel vision he can't snap out of until he hears the buzzer. He will claw and squeeze his way through until the very end.

Same as me.

Same as every rider out here.

When the buzzer sounds, he works to set himself free. Loosening his grip, and trying to dismount as safely as possible, all so he can avoid being speared, stomped on, kicked, or charged by the fearless animal he's mounted on.

He lands hard, but jumps to his feet in a hurry, and he's able to dart away from the pissed-off bull and climb up on the rails of the gate to avoid any further contact.

Watching him has only taken twenty or thirty seconds since he left the gate. Riding, for him, has felt like an eternity.

As he hops off the gate and looks up at the Jumbotron, seeing a damn good score flash over the screen, every decades-long-second he spent on that bull is worth it. The roar of the crowd. The pride in his chest. Knowing he wasn't bested by the bull—or himself—is what makes us come back and ride day in and out. It makes us get back up on the bull, even if we've been bucked off. Even if we've gotten hurt.

It's why, as I mount my bull right now to take my final ride here in Cheyenne, I know no matter what happens here, I'll be back at it next weekend and as often as I can be, until I can't anymore.

As I look up toward the grandstands, searching out my wife and daughters, finding them and holding my hand up—a distant gesture of our ritual that they return to me—I know, too, that unlike Cody and the others, I will also seek the thrill of fatherhood more often from here on out.

I will make every ride the most important I've ever had, all so I can get big points and big money as often as possible, but still be home for my family. That new plan, my renewed determination to be better everywhere, starts right now. Tonight. On this bull.

Allie

Ava is going insane beside me, cheering and hollering for Cody, being his biggest fan like she promised him she would be. Aubrey is playing with her favorite Barbies at my feet, not paying attention to anything going on with the bulls or the cowboys riding them.

In the nine days we have been here, so much has happened. The girls have grown obsessed with their uncle again. Ava is back on the rodeo wagon, steering it herself, and more determined than ever to compete here one day, too. Chase and I have experienced some of the highest highs and lowest lows we've ever had. Especially our fight six days ago. But we've come out on top and we have a plan. And it all starts with him winning here.

Once I see Cody is fine, I turn my attention to Chase getting prepared in the chute and I watch him close.

"Aubrey," I say, reaching down to tap her shoulder, "Daddy is about to ride, do you want to see him before he starts? I think he's going to wave at us."

Aubrey stands up and turns toward the chutes, following my and Ava's lead. If he's going to do it, it's going to be just before he gets his rope in place. So I lift Aubrey into my arms and stand up, helping Ava stand on top of our bleacher seats.

"Daddy's waving!" Aubrey shouts, throwing her arm in the air excitedly.

"Yes, he is."

Ava and I each raise an arm up, palms facing him, fingers spread as though he could slip his between their gaps, and wait for him to drop his hand again.

"He did it," Ava says in awe. "He saw us and he did it again. He's going to ride so good. I know it."

"He's going to do his best," I agree, and take my seat again.

There is very little comfort in knowing Chase is one of the best bull riders in the world, when I also know, sometimes it doesn't matter how good the rider is. It does nothing to abate the absolute fear that this ride could go wrong. Any ride could.

I watch Chase adjust his hat on his head then reach his arm out to steady himself, holding on lightly to the gate before he nods once, indicating he's ready to start.

The gate pulls open and the dark, chocolate brown bull with big, shaved down horns rips out of the chute. He's rank. He's a good bull. Which means he's a bad-ass that could get Chase a good score, if he stays on, and if he keeps his form.

With every turn, my stomach drops.

With every leap and kick, my heart skips a beat.

Chase's free hand stays high above him, and he's staying over the top of his grip well. But one weird turn or hard buck and he could topple over the bull's head, or get caught up in the rope and not break free.

Ava is counting the seconds ticking by in the quietest whisper, changing to, "Hold on, Daddy. Hold on," around the six second mark.

By seven she's up to her feet again, and in the second that follows she's shouting her head off, so excited that he did it.

Three rides.

Three scores.

He will make a good chunk of money and build on his lead in the world rankings.

Aubrey jumps up with Ava, sensing what happened and cheering him on too, and I stay seated to watch them and let my heart slow down.

Eight seconds.

An entire life on the line.

It doesn't matter how many times I see him ride and dismount safely, the fear I've always had that he will get hurt is the exact same as the first time I watched him.

He loves the danger.

He loves the challenge.

He loves the rush.

For me, I love the man who chases his dreams with near reckless abandon. Who will go from being one of the shit-talking, bull riding, bad-ass cowboys with the guys right now, to the silly, soft, playful daddy the girls adore when we get back to the hotel later.

I hope he keeps his word. I hope he puts the girls first. I hope he wins it all this year. If he's willing to work harder to be what we need, I will damn sure work harder on making it to more of his rodeos and supporting him, fear and all, to see him accomplish everything.

This week was awful and amazing, and it was the wake-up call we both needed to realize we've each made mistakes and we each need to try harder.

Eighteen

Chase

Cheyenne was a fantastic rodeo for me this year, for many reasons. I barely beat Cody, one point was all that separated us, but my last ride put me over the edge. To receive the check, the one for winning round one, and the average, to see the proud smiles on my girls' faces when they saw my new buckle, I feel like the richest cowboy in the world.

My buckle hasn't left Ava's hands since we got home four days ago. She holds onto it as often as she can, tracing the engraving over the buckle, telling me and Allie all about how she's going to win one day. She's so in awe. Her new future plans include standing in the Champions Circle with me.

I have no doubt she will be there one day, but I don't know if we will ever stand in it together, not in nine more years. My body will probably have long since given out, and I'll be retired. But I'll be there, watching her, and so will Allie.

Speaking of Allie, I can't fight the smile that hits me when I feel her arms wrap around me from behind. She scratches her nails lightly over my stomach and presses her lips to my back, and I feel lighter than I ever thought I could.

"Hey, Cowboy," she says quietly.

"Hey yourself," I say back, dropping my jeans in my bag and rubbing my hands over her arms. "Whatcha doin?"

"I just finished making the girls dinner. I had to put your buckle up on the mantle, she wouldn't let it go."

I laugh and shake my head. "She loves that thing even more than I do."

"She's so proud of you. She got to be there with you when you did it, and it makes it even more special."

"It's more special to me for the same reason."

"I've been thinking," she says, stilling her hands on my lower stomach and slipping her arms around as tight as she can until we're pressed together, my back to her front, with no room between us.

"About?"

"What we discussed in Cheyenne."

"Which part of what we discussed?"

"All of it, truthfully." I feel her cheek press into my back, her hair tickles it a little as it brushes over my bare skin. "I feel like I've neglected Ava because I've been so hard on rodeo and going to watch you."

"You've done nothing of the sort…"

"No, I have. Have you seen her with that buckle? She won't let it go. She clings to it because she got to be there and be a part of you winning it. She got to hold her hand up before your rides, guarantee you were safe. She felt special. She was so excited and happy."

As much as I'd love to keep her behind me, I want to see her while we talk, so I gently peel her arms loose and turn around to face her, guiding her hands behind my back and tight around me again. "She's always been special," I say. "And you all being there gave me extra motivation to be the best. But, Allie, you've done nothing wrong by giving the girls a stable life here. School, friends, activities, they need those things."

174

"They do. But they need to see that love, support, and loyalty are important too." She rests her chin on my chest and looks up at me. "I already told you, I'm going to go to more rodeos with you when I can. But when the girls don't have weekend activities, I think I'll give them the choice to come too."

"I would love that," I tell her, leaning down to kiss her lips. "You aren't obligated to come. I don't want resentment to build because you feel like you have to be there. Okay?"

Allie shakes her head and closes her eyes, breathing deep before she responds, "There won't be resentment. I'll be going because I want to. And the girls will, too. If Aubrey wants to stay home sometimes, we will work something out."

"Only if you're sure," I say to reiterate this is entirely her call. "I'll never say no to having you three with me when I ride. Ever."

I kiss her lips again, letting it linger and grow, until Aubrey walks into the room. "Ewww," she says dramatically. "Don't kiss Mommy, that's icky."

I laugh and let Allie go, then squat down and crook my finger at Aubrey. "Come here, Monkey."

Aubrey walks over to me and I grin wide. "I have to kiss your Mommy, ya know why?"

She shakes her head no and asks, "Why?"

"Well, because I can't tickle her like I do you," I say, as if it were the most logical thing on the planet, right as I draw my hands up and start tickling my little girl relentlessly.

"Daddy!" she squeals and shrieks, trying to wiggle out of my grip and get away from me. Her laughs fill our bedroom and she doubles over, trying to protect herself from the tickle attack she can't escape.

"Say the magic words and I'll stop," I say with a chuckle, continuing to tickle her until I hear them.

"I love you, Daddy," she manages to get out between laughs.

I stop tickling her and pull her to me, wrapping her in a hug. "I love you too, Aubrey."

"Do you love me bigger than the stars?"

"I love you bigger than the whole wide universe."

She pulls back with wide eyes and an even wider grin. "That's a lot."

"It is. And I'll always love you that much."

"Always, always?"

"Always, always," I confirm and kiss her head. "Did you finish your dinner?"

"Mhmm, 'cept for the yucky green things."

Allie stifles a laugh behind her, and I glance up to see if she wants Aubrey to go back out and finish what I assume are her vegetables.

"Aubrey, did you eat any of your green beans?" Allie asks.

"They're not beans, Mommy. They're long and gross."

"You need to eat them so you can grow big and strong and be the best gymnast in the world," I tell her. "Go back in there and eat half of what your mommy gave you, or no s'mores by the fire for you."

Aubrey scrunches her nose in disgust, and I know she's about to argue. It's there, on the tip of her tongue, before I cut her off with a pointed look. "Go now, Aubrey Jane. I won't tell you again."

"Okay. But...Daddy?"

"Yes?"

"Will you come to my gymnastics this weekend?" she asks innocently.

"I'll be there," I confirm.

"And Daddy?" she asks again.

"What Aubrey?" I say, a little irritated, knowing what she's trying to do.

"Can I have two s'mores if I eat half my icky green things?"

"We'll see. Now go finish dinner."

"One more. Daddy?"

Allie is standing, amused and smirking, behind Aubrey, watching this whole exchange.

"No more questions. Go eat your dinner. We'll be in there after I finish packing my bag to make sure you ate what you were supposed to."

Aubrey pouts her bottom lip out and turns around, walking past Allie as slowly as she can, literally dragging her feet to put off finishing her vegetable as long as she can.

"How often does she refuse to finish her dinner?" I look up at Allie and ask.

"Depends on the night," she says, shrugging her shoulder. "Some, she eats everything like I've starved her for an eternity. Other nights, she refuses to eat anything on her plate. And the rest of the nights are like tonight, where she'll finish most and then refuse the stuff she really needs to eat."

"And the arguments like they've been having today?"

"They're pretty typical. The only difference is they listen to you more when you put an end to it than they do me."

"I'm sorry," I say, knowing there isn't much else I can say. "I'll be here more often, even if it's only a night, I'll be a better parent and not just the fun dad who saves the day."

"Thank you." She walks over to me where I'm still squatted and slides her fingers through my messy, damp

177

hair. "I need to go heat those yucky green things or she really won't eat any at all."

She kisses my head and turns to walk away, adding "You smell good, Cowboy," as she walks out of the room.

Allie

Chase and the girls are all passed out on the sectional couch together with half-finished glasses of milk and water, the plates their s'mores were on, and the cards they used for Go Fish on the table in front of them. I can see the sticky remnants of Aubrey's s'mores on her face and hands from where I'm seated in the chair.

Ava has her arm flung over her face, with her hand dangling just over Chase's head. He has Aubrey in front of him, with his arms wrapped around her tiny frame, holding her close so she doesn't roll off the couch.

He's going to leave tomorrow, and he's made all these promises to me. We both have made them. But it's easy to say one thing when we've settled into our normal home rhythm. When we are all together and things are great. It's easy to say you're going to fix what's broken while you're doing everything you can to stop the break from getting worse.

Actions, on both our parts, will speak louder than our words. It'll start with him coming home Saturday night to see Aubrey's gymnastics. It will continue when I make it to his rodeo in Wyoming next weekend.

Hold on Tight

We've made so much progress I didn't even realize we needed to make until we had our disagreement in Cheyenne last week. That's why, even though I should wake them all up and get them into their own beds, I think I'm going to leave them here for the night.

Nineteen

Chase

"You seem lighter than you have in a long time," Cody says, as he sits down on the stool beside me. We just got back to the hotel from tonight's "extravaganza." Thirty of the world's top bull riders roped into coming out and competing for an independent pot of money, which has nothing to do with pro rodeo. It's all about having fun and growing the sport for everyone, according to the event holders.

"I feel lighter," I answer honestly, signaling the bartender to get Cody a beer, too.

"Megatron thought you were, too, if how high he sent your ass flying tonight was any indication."

I let out a laugh and shake my head. "Fuck you," I say around the bottle I'm tipping to my lips. I take a long pull and set it down, then glance at him. "My grip was shit, I had no chance of making my eight tonight. I could feel it the second we were out of the gate."

"And you're okay with that?" he asks, seriously.

"Yeah, I am. This isn't counting toward our world rankings since it's not PRCA sanctioned, so..." I shrug my shoulders to prove I really am okay with it.

"Right, but it's still worth a ton of fucking money. Isn't that this year's primary objective?"

"It is, but..."

"But?"

"I didn't tell you, but the night you took the girls for us in Cheyenne, Allie and I had a pretty good argument."

"No shit? What over?"

"Rodeo…"

"Fuck, dude. Does she want you to quit?"

"No, she doesn't. And we worked it all out. It started with her refusal to acknowledge the part she once had in rodeo. Then it spiraled from there. The amount of time I've been gone, the baby we lost, the fact we haven't conceived, her resentment, we hit it all."

He raises his brows and asks for two shots of whiskey. "So what happened?"

"Well, for starters, I'm going to go home more often. Tomorrow, after I finish my ride, my ass will be speeding to the airport so I can fly into Denver and make it in time to watch Aubrey's first gymnastics thing."

"You're not staying here tomorrow? You do realize your ass will be tanked by the time you ride Sunday, right? And your arm is finally healing, not taking care will increase the odds of you fucking it up again."

"Being there for the girls will be worth it."

"Wow."

He doesn't mean that in a bad way, I know. It is pretty amazing. And he's not wrong. Traveling like that, two flights in less than twelve hours, no time to ice down, give my body a break, it's going to make Sunday more difficult.

"If that's for starters, what else came of your argument?"

"Allie knows why I've been so hell-bent on winning everything."

"You told her about your plans to aid the baby-making process?"

"I did. I had to."

181

"What did she say?"

"She appreciated it. Hell, that's a bad word to use. It's not enough to convey how she really felt, but she also called me on it and told me to quit using her and a baby as an excuse, because we both know I'd be out here anyway, even if she'd already had another."

"Was she right about that?"

"Maybe, yeah. I love riding, you know that."

"I do. It's in your blood, same as it is mine." He glances around the bar, taking in the group walking into the room.

"It is. But…"

He looks back at me again. "But what?"

"I'm having thoughts, brother. There's shit I need to sort out, but once I do… this year may be my last full time."

"If you win?"

"If I win. Maybe even if I don't. Only time will tell what I ultimately end up doing, but I'm working out a few scenarios, and I'm meeting with someone who may be able to help me clear some things up in the morning before we ride, too."

"Do I want to know who you're meeting?"

"Yeah, probably. You should come with. Because if I end up following through with all of this, I'll want to bring you in to partner with me."

"Well, shit, I guess we better get another beer, because it sounds like I need to be filled in on whatever the hell it is that has your head spinning."

Cody orders us another round, and sends one to the table of women across the room. His mind is going to be blown when I tell him everything I'm thinking. It could possibly change both our lives forever.

Twenty

Allie

"**A**va! Aubrey! Get in here, we need to leave soon." Oversleeping was not on the to-do list this morning, yet it happened, and I'm so behind because of it. Aubrey has her gymnastics meet this evening, and we are going to meet her coach and the other little girls and their parents on her team in Denver to spend an afternoon having lunch and exploring before we go to the competition.

Aubrey runs into the kitchen first, still in her pajamas, brushing her teeth. "What, Mommy?" she says, spraying toothpaste all over.

"Why aren't you dressed yet?" I ask, walking her back to her room, and passing Ava's on the way. "Ava, are you dressed?"

"Yep, I'm putting my ponytail in now," she answers from their bathroom.

At least one of them is almost done.

"Aubrey, we need to go. Why aren't you wearing your leo yet?"

She gets ready to answer, but I stop her. "Go finish brushing your teeth, you're spitting all over us when you talk."

She giggles and goes into the bathroom. I hear the water run, then Ava mumbles about getting splashed, before Aubrey walks back in.

"Try again, why aren't you in your leo?"

"My purple one isn't here," she says, frowning. "Daddy got it for me, and he's coming. I want to wear that one."

"Baby, it's dirty, you need to wear another one. He won't be upset. I promise."

"But I want to wear that one!" she shouts in frustration.

"Aubrey Jane, enough. You'll wear your black one, just like the rest of your team. Now get dressed. Put your jean shorts and shirt over the top, please."

I help her get her pajamas off and then her leotard on. "Now your hair. We'll just brush it out here, Coach Tatum said one of the other mom's on the team offered to braid everyone's hair when we get to Denver, so you all match."

"Really?" she says, bringing me her brush.

"Really." I run the brush through her hair, making sure all the tangles are out and she looks presentable, then hand her brush back. "Take this back into your bathroom. Ava," I call out in the same breath. "It's time to leave."

She pops into Aubrey's room, dressed in her jean shorts, her favorite Converse shoes, and a navy blue tank top.

"Daddy's coming to watch Aubrey, still, right?" she asks.

"When I talked to him last night, that's what he said. He has a flight out of New Mexico a couple hours before Aubrey starts. So he should make it just in time."

"Yay!" Aubrey shouts as she finishes putting her T-shirt on.

"So we can save a seat for him?" Ava looks at me expectantly.

"We have to save one. We'll make him sit right between us, front and center so he can see everything Aubrey does. How does that sound to both of you?"

Ava nods and Aubrey beams up at me.

"Good, then we need to make sure we have everything we want to take so we can go. It's going to take a while to get into Denver, and we're supposed to meet for lunch at one."

The girls each set out to grab the last-minute things they'll want for the long car ride and then meet me at the front door.

"Ready, ladies?"

"Ready," they say together.

Aubrey's meet starts in thirty minutes, and Chase should be here by now. Every call I've made to him has gone unanswered, every text left unread. According to the online flight tracker, his flight was a little delayed, but got in with enough time. It shows they landed in Denver thirty minutes ago. There are two thoughts on my mind. Chase either missed his flight, getting caught up in everything after today's ride at their exhibition, or there was a car accident with his Uber or Lyft coming from the airport.

One has me so pissed off I could throttle my husband, and the other has me so worried my heart is splitting in half in my chest.

Even Cody has gone silent. I tried him, too, and there was nothing. Not that it surprises me, necessarily. He usually picks up his dates after rides, so he's in all likelihood got some girl bent over his hotel room bed, gaining her little rodeo cred for being with him.

I dial Chase's number again and lift my phone to my ear. It goes straight to voicemail, as it has been all evening.

He turns it off when it's in his bag during rides so the battery doesn't die. He would've turned it on airplane mode for the flight. So even it's status doesn't give me any hint as to where he can be. So I dial again. Hoping maybe, just maybe, this time it'll ring.

C'mon, Chase. Just answer me.

After it sends me to voicemail, again, I give up and am ready to walk back into the little gym set up for the girls.

I don't make it two steps before my phone is vibrating in my hand, and I glance at the screen. The caller information displayed reads *New Mexico* and I answer in a hurry.

"Where are you, Chase? The girls are counting on you to be here."

The voice on the other end stops me in my tracks. It's not Chase's. The strain and fear in Cody's voice paralyzes me. "Allie, you need to get out here. Hurry. Chase is hurt. He's hurt bad. Oh God. I'm so sorry. You need to get here."

"What do you mean he's hurt, Cody?"

"It's his back and his head."

"That doesn't tell me anything!" I shout, panic filling every inch of my system. "How bad is it?"

"He's unconscious, and they fear he may be paralyzed. You need to get here now."

"Oh my God. Oh my God. I'm—I have the girls at Aubrey's meet. I can't leave them, Cody." I'm frantic now. I don't know what to do. I can't possibly take the girls out there. "What do I do?"

"Allie, you need to calm down. Breathe. Who can you leave the girls with?"

"Nobody, I don't know. Maybe one of the moms here. I don't know."

My voice must be carrying into the gym, because Tatum, Aubrey's coach, walks out to check on me.

"Mrs. Canton, is everything okay? The girls are worried, we all heard you in there."

I shake my head no, letting tears fall down my cheek. "My husband, he's hurt. In New Mexico. It's bad. I have to get there." Every word comes out choppy, full of agony and fear.

"Okay, okay," she says calmly, nodding her head. "Is that him on the phone?"

I only shake my head no.

"May I?" she asks, holding her hand out.

I pass her my phone then wrap my arms tight around myself, watching her.

"Hello?" she says, then listens quietly. "No, I'm Aubrey's coach. Mrs. Canton is scared and I want to help her."

She pauses again, nodding her head at what Cody is saying on the other side.

"Okay, can you repeat that so I can spell it out for her in a text?"

She pulls her own phone out and starts typing furiously with my phone pressed between her shoulder and ear.

"Albuquerque Regional, got it. Do you know what airline he was supposed to fly out on?" Another pause. "Okay, good. I'll call them and get an earlier flight in her name."

She goes quiet again, then smiles a little. "Thank you. Yes, I'll take care of the girls. I'll drive Allie's car home, and we will get her a safe ride to the airport as fast as we can."

Some of the other moms have filtered into the hallway and gathered around us. When Tatum hangs up the call, she hands my phone back and says, "I got all of the information you need. They are going to take Chase in for tests, it's imperative they know what they're dealing with. I'll keep the girls, but we need to get you a flight to New Mexico as fast as possible."

When the other moms hear what's going on, everyone springs into action. One hurries off to keep the girls occupied, others start looking up flight information, and Tatum explains to the other coach what's going on and asks if they can postpone the start a little. Then she busies herself calling the airline and steps away from us.

Everything happens so fast, but all I can feel are the miles spanning between me and Chase, the uncertainty of what's going on and what will happen.

"Allie," Tatum says, pulling me from my own thoughts of what-if and how bad. "You're booked on a flight leaving in forty minutes. You should be to New Mexico within the next two hours. Okay. You need to tell the girls what's going on before you go."

I nod. Then her words really hit me. Oh my God. My girls.

"Mrs. Finch is bringing them to you now. We will keep them here. Aubrey can compete if she wants or not. Do you have any family we can call to be with them?"

"I um," I stop and shake my head. "Chase's parents are in Florida, I'll need to let them know what's going on. But my family is gone. My parents died seven and a half years ago. It's just us."

"Okay, then I'll stay with the girls at your place, if that's okay."

"Yes, yes, please. Thank you."

The girls walk out into the hallway and Ava sees it instantly. She goes from smiling and moving purposefully to frowning, with her steps slowing, faltering beneath her.

"What's wrong, Mommy?" she asks.

"Is Daddy here yet?" Aubrey adds.

I bend down so I'm level with my girls and reach for their hands.

"No, baby girl, your daddy isn't going to make it after all. He got bucked pretty hard off his bull and he had to go to the hospital to be seen, to make sure he's okay."

"Is he hurt really bad?" Ava asks.

"Is it like when Ava fell off Lightning?"

I muster up as much strength and determination to lie and smile as I can and nod my head. "Yeah, it's a little like when Ava fell. So I'm going to fly out there to be with him, and see how bad he's hurt. I don't know much yet. But Miss Tatum is going to get you both home tonight, and she's going to stay at our house with you until someone else can take you."

Ava looks at me warily and asks, "Can we go, too?"

"No, not this time. I have to leave right now so I can catch my flight. But I will call you both as soon as I can. I promise." I pull them both into my arms and hug them, holding them as tight as I can. "I love you both, and so does your daddy. Don't forget, okay?"

I let them go and pull back so I can stand, and I see tears rolling down Ava's face. "Tell him we love him," she whispers, wiping her eyes.

She can't buy any of this, she's too smart, and she knows what can happen on a bull. But she won't say anything in front of Aubrey.

"Of course I will. You two, listen to Miss Tatum, I'll call when I can."

With that I step away and follow one of the other moms outside where a ride is already waiting for me.

Anjelica Grace

Hold on, Cowboy. You better stay strong and not give up on us now.

Twenty-One

Allie

The car pulls up to the hospital and I jump out before it's even reached a complete stop. My only focus is on getting to my husband as fast as I possibly can. Then I realize I never even paid the driver. I spin back around, fiddling with my purse, and lean my head in.

"How much do I owe you, sir?"

He shakes his head and waves me off. "It's already been handled, you get to your husband. I hope everything turns out okay with him. My thoughts and prayers will be with you and your family."

He has the kindest, grayest eyes I've ever seen. I didn't even pay attention to him during the drive from the airport to here, but I know I'll never forget the way his eyes held all the sympathy, or maybe empathy, in the world for me. Or how his hand was soft and reassuring when he squeezed mine.

"Thank you. For the ride and the kind words. We are going to need them."

"You're welcome. And ma'am?" he adds, stopping me again.

"Yes?"

"A wise person once said, 'When you feel like giving up, remember why you held on so long in the first place.' Don't let go when things get tough. Everything happens for a reason."

He says nothing else after, he only tips his head with a kind smile, and then he pulls away. I watch him leave for a moment, and then I take off for the doors, stopping long enough at the information desk just inside them to ask where I need to go, before going straight to the elevators.

As soon as the doors open, I follow the signs leading to the ICU. A left, a right, and then I jump out of my skin when a lullaby starts playing over the speaker system, announcing the birth of a child.

With every life lost comes a new life gained, my brain says to me. I have to shake that thought out. Chase isn't dead. He's not.

"Allie!" Cody calls from a seat just to the side of the closed, handle-less doors.

"Where is he? I have to see him."

"You can't right now. They took him for scans and tests. They said they'd come get us when he's back in there."

"Then let me go to his room and wait."

Cody shakes his head no. "You can't go back there right now, Allie. This is a secured unit. They won't let you in. Come sit with me. We'll wait. He'll be back soon."

"I need to see my husband, please, just let me see him." What little strength and hope I'd mustered up during my short flight and drive is dissipating by the second with the news I can't see Chase. That I can't check on him myself.

Cody walks up and wraps his arms around me. He holds me tight and mumbles into my hair, "I know you do. I know."

I slip my arms around his neck and hold on for dear life, letting go of the dam that was holding back all my tears. I sob into his chest. My legs go weak. I feel like all the strength in me has been let out. Cody's grip around me tightens and he holds me up, letting me cry against him.

Once I've stopped sobbing, and my body has stopped shaking, I ask him what I really need to know. "Wha-what's wrong with him? What happened?"

"Come sit. I'll explain all I can."

He guides me over to two chairs with his and Chase's bags in front of them. I look at Chase's on the floor, and he says quietly, "They just dropped those off for us. I came here with him, left all my shit there. I'm sorry I missed your texts and calls. I wasn't even thinking about my phone."

I shake my head, hoping he understands I'm not mad about that. I pull Chase's bag in front of me and run my fingers along the zipper.

"What happened, Cody?"

He lets out a deep breath and starts to explain, "He made his eight and went to let go, but his hand got caught, and then the bull bucked him. He was focused on his hand. He went ass to head to horns on the bull before he hit the ground, and then—" He stops speaking and closes his eyes, shaking his head. "The fighters tried to turn the bull, Allie, but he was hell-bent on getting to Chase. He reared up and came down right on Chase's back."

My hand flies to my mouth and fresh tears stream down my face. The only thought I have at this point is it sounds like there is a good chance I will be losing my husband.

"Is he going to live?" I risk glancing to Cody, even though I'm terrified the look on his face will say more than he will actually speak. There's pain and fear there as he nods his head lightly.

"They think he will, yes. But Al, they aren't sure he'll be able to walk again. They don't know for sure, he was unconscious when we got here. He hit his head somewhere in it all, too. There was a nasty gash there. They don't even know if he'll have swelling or bleeding in his head yet. They don't have many answers at all."

"What do they have, then?" I snap.

"They have the fact he's alive. That's what we have, too. We have to hold onto that."

I nod once and rise from my seat, starting to pace back and forth across the small, quiet waiting room. Thoughts I can't stop continue to fill my brain.

What if he's paralyzed?

What if he has brain damage?

What if he never gets to tell the girls he loves them again?

What if I never get to hear him tell me?

Those and so many other thoughts like them keep rolling through my mind on a loop. The longer we wait, the worse they get, until I have to stop walking because it feels like I have a two-ton bull sitting on top of my chest, keeping me from drawing air into my lungs.

I brace my hands on my knees and hang my head, trying to catch my breath. The thoughts keep plaguing me though. And my ability to breathe gets harder and harder.

"Allie, stand up," Cody commands, walking over to me.

"I-I can't." It's all I can manage to get out as panic starts to set in. This can't happen. My girls can't lose both of us.

"Allie, stand up," he says again, taking my hands off my knees and forcing me to stand up right. "Look at me."

Each breath is a struggle. My hands are shaking. My heart is racing. But I try to do as he says, looking at him and trying to stay there.

"You're having a panic attack. You need to try to breathe with me."

I shake my head no. I can't breathe. Doesn't he understand that?

"Yes. Watch me. Breathe in when I do, and out when I do."

Cody starts to breathe in and I watch him, wishing I could do that. But I can't. I know I can't.

"Allie, you need to breathe with me. Now."

He takes in another breath and waits for me to do the same.

It hurts. It's hard. But I can feel my chest start to expand outward as I watch his do the same.

"Good girl," he murmurs. "Now let it out, slowly. Then we'll do it again."

I exhale slowly and then breathe in with him again. His chest expanding just as slowly as the breath I take in. And then we exhale.

It's getting easier. Maybe I'm not dying.

We continue to breathe, in and out, with my hands locked in Cody's, until a short, brown-haired nurse with a pixie cut steps into the waiting room.

"Are you Mr. Canton's family?" she asks.

Cody lets go of one of my hands, but keeps the other firmly in his grasp as we each turn to her.

"I'm his wife, this is…um, this is his brother."

She gives a slight pity-filled smile. "Perfect, I need you to follow me. Mr. Canton is back in his room and his doctor would like to speak to you. His brother can wait here, if you'd like."

I look from her to Cody and then back, shaking my head. "I want him with us. I need another set of ears."

"Very well," she says, "you two can follow me now."

Cody puts his arm around my shoulder and gives me a reassuring squeeze. "He's going to be okay. You know Chase."

We follow the nurse to the locked, handle-less double doors and watch as she swipes her badge over the reader, releasing the doors with a gentle click. "While your husband is here, anytime you want to get back here, press the doorbell on the wall just back there and give his name and room number. We will buzz you in from the desk."

"Okay, thank you." I look up at Cody and he gives me a nod, and we follow her through the doors.

Immediately to our left is a door indicating it's a bathroom and shower, and to our right is the first patient room. It's got a long, clear sliding door with curtains hanging just inside it, offering a little privacy to the otherwise very small room.

"If you're staying here, and you need a shower, you can talk to Micha. She's the key keeper."

Her words hit me with the force of a bomb. Will we be here long enough that I'll need to shower here?

"Mr. Canton is in room eighteen," she says, as we continue to follow her.

The farther down the hall we get, the quieter things get. It's eerie. Each side of the narrow unit is lined with identical looking rooms. All of them have sliding doors, some of them are closed except for a small sliver, and others are wide open.

It's the wide-open doors that have my heart racing and palms going sweaty. In those rooms are people, young and old, hooked up to machines with tubes sticking out every which way, and family surrounding them.

Oh my God. Is that how Chase is going to look?

Cody looks into the same room I am and he holds on a little tighter, guiding me away and keeping up with our nameless tour guide.

"Ah, here it is. Room eighteen. Mr. Canton is in here. Dr. Montgomery will be right back with you. But it looks like his nurse, Breeze, is in with him now."

"You aren't his nurse?" I ask her.

"Oh, no ma'am, I'm a CNA on the floor. Maddie. I'll be in and out if you need anything."

"Oh. Okay." I look up to Cody, brows drawn together in confusion, and he just shrugs.

Maddie smiles at us and pokes her head in. "Hey, Breeze, Mr. Canton's wife and brother are here."

"Fantastic," I hear a voice say from inside the room. "Give me one second to check his catheter and then I'll be right out."

Maddie turns to us and smiles again. "She'll only be a minute or two, you can wait right here for her."

"Thank you, Maddie," Cody says, giving her a tight, polite smile back.

She looks down and blushes a little then scurries off, and I look up at him, expecting to see him watching her move down the hall.

But he isn't. He's staring straight ahead, through the little crack in the door, fixated on the heavy curtain obstructing our view of Chase.

"No matter what we see, how he looks…" Cody whispers so quietly I have to angle my head so I can hear him better. "We have to be strong for him. I'll do what I can for you, but he's going to need us strong and fighting for him."

I swallow past the lump his words just put in my throat and give him a little nod.

"Mrs. Canton, Mr. Canton?" the nurse says, as she steps past the curtain still hiding Chase from us.

"Cody, you can call me Cody."

"And Allie, please," I add.

"Cody and Allie, I'm Breeze. It's nice to meet you both. Before I let you in to see Chase, I'm going to explain a few things to you."

"Is he okay?" Cody asks right off the bat.

"Well, that's a hard question to answer. He is stable right now, and that's a good first step. But he's by no means out of the woods. He is still unconscious. We've got IVs in place, we are monitoring his vitals, and we are keeping a close watch on the pressure in his brain."

"What does that mean?" I ask, trying to make sense of everything.

"It just means that since he isn't awake yet, and we can't predict why or how long he will be unconscious, we want to make sure if any swelling or increase in pressure occur, we can get it taken care of as soon as possible."

"So you're not saying it will happen? It just could?" Cody clarifies.

"That's correct. We are keeping an eye on it, but he could just as soon wake up as have it go the other way."

That's good news. It has to be. A small win. But I'm sure the other shoe is about to drop, because it's in this moment I remember Cody saying they feared Chase may be paralyzed.

"But his back?" I ask, looking to her.

She lets out a small breath and nods. "His back is trickier, and his doctor will be speaking to you as soon as he's able to get away from the patient he was called to in an emergency."

"Can you give us any idea how bad it is?" Cody asks her, rubbing my arm gently as he speaks.

"Well, I can tell you he did suffer some bone fragmenting and there is swelling in his spinal cord. But beyond that, I really can't comment on prognosis or what to expect going forward. Dr. Montgomery will absolutely be able to answer those questions better, though."

"Okay," I say, feeling dejected and fearful. There is so much wrong. He's unconscious. His spinal cord is swelling. What else could be wrong?

"You can go in and see him. Maybe your voice will help rouse him a little. I must warn you with all of the tubes and machines, the tape, he will look different. It may even be scary. Just know those things don't necessarily mean worst case, they're all in place so we can monitor and help him get better.

"Is he—" I stop and take a deep breath of my own before continuing, "Is he breathing on his own?"

Breeze nods her head. "He is. That's a positive sign, but we will continue to monitor that closely as well."

I let out a little sigh of relief, and then take another breath in and open it when Breeze says, "You both can go in to see him now."

We follow her beyond the sliding doors and past the curtain and I freeze in place, my hand flying to my mouth. "Oh my God," I mumble into my hand. A fresh wave of tears hits me as I take my husband in.

He's still. Too still. There's a neck brace holding his head steady. And there's a little wire coming out of his head, with evidence of a shaved patch around it. He's got tubes coming out of his arms, and another coming out from beneath the blankets covering his legs, hanging over the side of the bed connecting to a bag filling with yellow fluid.

His hands are still at his sides.

His eyes are closed.

The strongest, most vibrant and virile man I know looks weak and broken. He has the face of my husband, but he's not the Chase I've known for almost half my life now.

"Allie," Cody whispers, making me look at him. The look on his face matches how I feel. He's never seen Chase like this, either. "Come talk to him, it's okay. Breeze said we should. And the doctor will be right in."

I look back over my shoulder and Breeze is gone. I didn't even notice her walk out. I didn't hear her tell us to talk to him.

"Cody, he's..."

"I know. He needs us right now. He needs *you*."

I step up to his bedside, trying to push everything I see now aside to focus on the Chase I know. I take his hand in mine and it's cold. Too cold. The weight of it is heavy between my fingers as I raise it up and kiss over his knuckles. The smell hits me hard. It smells like sweat and his leather glove still. They must not have washed it when they took his riding glove off.

"Hi, Cowboy," I whisper. "I'm right here, and I won't leave your side until you're awake and tired of me hovering. Okay?" I stop to try to wipe my eye on the shoulder of my shirt and sniffle back more tears. "But you have to wake up. I need to hear you tell me you're okay."

"She's right," Cody adds. His voice is thick, chock-full of emotion. I don't need to look up to know he's crying, too. "We need you awake, brother. Who else is going to give me shit for not making my eight today?"

I laugh a little around my tears and then look up at Cody. "I'll give you shit for other things. Who did you hook up with last night?"

Cody laughs, too, and he shakes his head. "No hooking up, I spent the night with him, talking."

"Your bromance is so sweet," I tease, then look back down at Chase. Even picking on Cody right now just doesn't feel right without Chase's input.

"Mrs. Canton, Mr…?" a deep voice interrupts us, and my thoughts. I look toward the door and see a man standing there. He's wearing a white coat over the top of blue scrubs, and he still has his hair covered, but I can tell he's older. Streaks of silver hair peek out from beneath his hat as he steps into the room.

"Yes?" I respond, angling my body toward him but keeping Chase's hand between each of mine.

"Hi, I'm Dr. Montgomery. I'm the head of neurology here."

"I'm Allie, please. And this is Cody."

He gives each of us a tight nod and steps farther into the small room, stopping at the foot of Chase's bed.

"How bad is it?" I ask him off the bat. I want to rip the Band-Aid off at once, because I know it'll hurt less if we get it all out now, than if we go through small chunks of pain.

"Well," he says, looking down at Chase. "We'll work from the head down. Based on our preliminary tests, and based on the scans we've done, we are pretty sure Mr. Canton has a moderate TBI. We are monitoring his intracranial pressure because his CT scan showed a brain contusion, likely from contact he had with the bull during his fall, based on what we've seen and heard."

"TBI?" Cody asks, and I'm grateful for it.

"Traumatic Brain Injury."

Those are words you never, ever want to hear. TBI sounds so much better. Less scary. Not as serious.

"Does that mean he's, he's…" I close my mouth while I search for the right words, not knowing how best to ask what I need to know.

Doctor Montgomery shakes his head, seemingly understanding what I'm unable to say. "I have every hope he will wake up sooner than later. Right now, the pressure in his brain is where we want it to be, which means it isn't swelling. He will likely have some memory loss, as is very common with these sorts of injury."

"But you said it's traumatic," Cody interjects.

"I did," Dr. Montgomery agrees. "An ordinary concussion is technically classified as a TBI, as well. But concussion is a far less scary word. It's a much milder form of injury, and there are typically no worries it'll get worse. With Mr. Canton, it could get worse. Given the circumstances surrounding his injury, over the next twenty-four hours, his pressure could increase, and we may need to take further steps to prevent brain damage."

"But you don't think that will happen?" I ask. My hands are clammy and damp over Chase's now.

"I'm hopeful it won't. But each person is different, and I can't speak in guarantees. With any of your husband's injuries."

I nod my head, in understanding, and trying to clear the web of thoughts forming. "What else is wrong?"

"He's got a vertebral injury, and we also fear he's got a spinal cord injury."

"What does that mean?" I ask, holding my breath.

"We will have a better idea when he wakes up what his status really is, but based on his scans, we are worried he may be paralyzed, and as a smaller hospital, once we're certain he is stable, we'd like to move him to a facility more equipped to handle any surgeries he needs to have moving forward."

"Surgeries?" He must think I'm insane, asking the things I have in the ways I have. But I'm just trying to hold it all together and understand everything he's saying all at once.

"He's got a fracture in his back, it's pretty severe. He will need to have his spine stabilized and bones fused together. But we don't want to move him until we are certain he can withstand a transfer."

I blink at him. Not nodding. Not shaking my head. Just blinking. I'm at a complete and total loss right now and I don't know how to overcome it.

Cody reaches over the bed and sets his hand over mine, squeezing gently, even though I'm still cradling Chase's larger hand, too.

"Where would you have him transferred? We have one of the best hospitals for his types of injuries at home, and if we could have him sent there…" Cody says, taking over for me because I'm incapable right now.

"Where are you from?" Dr. Montgomery asks.

"Colorado. Would Denver be a viable transfer option? I know it's a very short flight commercially…"

"You're talking about Craig Hospital?"

I watch both men during their exchange. Cody is taking Chase and me both on his back right now, and supporting us both by taking control of the things I'm not thinking clearly enough to ask myself.

"Would it be possible?" Cody asks, tilting his head slightly.

"I don't know if they handle the surgeries, but the rehabilitative process they offer would certainly give Mr. Canton the absolute best chances at making the best recovery he's able to."

"How long would it take to set that up?"

"I'll start making calls." He directs his attention from Cody, to me. "Ma'am, is that what you would like for your husband? All of these decisions are up to you, ultimately."

"Y-yes, please. I want to do everything we can to give my husband the best chance possible."

"I'll start making calls, see what they and we are able to do, and whether he will be able to be transferred anytime soon."

"Thank you," Cody says, and I nod this time.

"Yes, thank you."

With that, Dr. Montgomery walks out of the room and Breeze walks back in. It's as though they are a tag team and they just switched off.

"Can I get either of you anything?" she asks.

"We're okay, thank you," I reply. I take a step back when she walks over to check the numbers on all the machines surrounding Chase's bed, and then immediately move back to his side once she finishes.

"I'll bring another chair in so you can both sit with him," she answers with a smile. "Let me know if either of you need anything else."

Breeze brings another chair in for Cody to sit and we both settle on either side of Chase's bed, silently holding vigil for my unconscious husband. Everything the doctor told us is playing on a loop in my mind.

Brain injury.

Paralysis.

Transfer.

Surgery.

But he is alive. That's what I have to hold on to. It's the only hope I have right now.

Twenty-Two

Allie

Cody is sound asleep in the recliner in the corner of Chase's small room, and I'm still seated beside his bed, holding his hand, talking to him quietly, and willing him to open his eyes. He's been unconscious for close to seven hours now. But it feels like it's been an eternity.

I called Tatum to check on the girls and give her a heads-up about what's going on a while ago. She promised me she, and the rest of the team moms, are on top of everything and working out a schedule to keep the girls until we are able to bring them here, or until we get home.

She is going to spend the night at the ranch with the girls, and she's going to keep them distracted and entertained tonight, and then they'll start their tour of team homes tomorrow.

Ava knew immediately that it is bad here with Chase. She asked if she could look up what happened and I made her swear she wouldn't. I haven't even seen it. Cody refused to pull up video that was sent to him. He said there will be time later, but I don't need those images in my mind now, too.

Tatum swore she would keep the girls off the computer, and she would make sure every mom on Aubrey's team knows they aren't to have access to the internet while at everyone's houses.

I don't want the girls seeing what I know will be traumatizing and horrible.

Theresa, Chase's night nurse, walks in quietly and interrupts my thoughts, whispering, "I need to check his vitals again. Why don't you walk down to the vending machines, grab a snack, and stretch your legs? I only need a few minutes with him."

"Are you sure, what if he wakes up?"

"Then it'll be a happy surprise for you when you return," she quips, giving me a wink. "Just out the door and by the waiting room. It'll do you some good to move. These chairs aren't comfortable."

"Just the end of the hall. I'll use the restroom and grab a snack," I say, standing and rubbing my back.

I bend forward to kiss Chase's forehead gently and say as quietly as I can manage, "I'll be right back, then it's time for you to come back to me, Cowboy."

Theresa gives me a sympathetic smile and waits until I'm almost out of the room before she moves my chair out of her way and begins looking over Chase.

I turn right out of his room, giving the nurses at the desk across from his door a tight smile, then follow the hallway down to the double doors securing the unit. I press the little button on the wall, waiting for the doors to swing outward, and jump when alarms start to go off in the room to my left.

What I see when I look over is not something I'm prepared for. A mass of people, doctors, nurses, and family, are surrounding a young man, maybe even a teenage boy, and the two people who look to be his parents are crying. The woman is sobbing into the broad chest of her husband, and the medical staff appear to be shutting the machines off and down.

He died.

That's what this floor is for. It's the patients who have the slimmest chances of survival. The one's who are so hurt or sick they need special care and attention to maybe save their lives. But dying is such a real possibility here, too.

Chase dying is still a possibility.

That thought hits me hard, and my stomach churns. Bile rises up the back of my throat and another wave of tears rolls down my face, as I bolt away from the family experiencing the most painful loss imaginable, right to the bathroom.

I barely make it to a stall before what's left of my lunch from earlier, and all the bile sitting on top of it, comes up with a vengeance.

When nothing else comes up, I rest my head on my arms and let go of the tears and fear I've been holding in as much as possible, and I sob. We've always joked about it not being when, but how bad. But never, not even in my wildest dreams, did I think bad could be this bad.

When I hear the bathroom door swing open, I close my mouth over my arm and bite down, trying to hide my sobs, when a familiar voice says out loud, "Mrs. Canton, Allie, he's awake…"

I stand quickly, flushing the toilet and grabbing some toilet paper to wipe my face and mouth with, then push the stall open.

I don't care how I look right now. I need to be certain I heard Theresa right. "He's awake?"

She nods and smiles. "Splash some water on your face and collect yourself, he's asking for you."

She stands just inside the door and watches me until I've carried out her instructions, and then she pulls a stick of gum from her pocket. "It'll help get the taste out."

"Thank you," I mutter as I bite down and a burst of mint fills my mouth. "I'm sorry, I just…"

"I understand. You've had a lot happen today, it can be overwhelming." Her hand lands on my upper back and shoulder gently and she guides me out of the bathroom and back toward the ICU. "He's confused, agitated, and scared. We need you to help us keep him calm so we don't have to sedate him."

I nod my head and follow her through the locked doors and down the hall to his room.

The closer we get, the louder his voice is. He sounds angry, and he's arguing with Cody. I can hear the annoyance in Chase's voice while Cody pleads with him to stay still.

"What the hell is going on, dammit? Why can't I leave? Where is my wife?" Chase demands. Theresa picks up her speed and I follow close on her heels, rounding the corner and turning into his room in a hurry.

"Mr. Canton," Theresa says in the calmest voice ever. "Please, you need to relax. I don't want to have to sedate you."

"Sedate me?" he shouts. "Who the hell do you think you are?"

"She's your nurse, Cowboy," I answer him, stepping around Theresa and to the foot of his bed. I plaster a smile on my face and move around the side of the bed Cody's been sitting on.

"Darlin'?" Chase asks, anger still tinging his voice, but confusion makes its way in there now, too.

"Hi," I say, reaching for his hand as soon as I'm close enough. "You need to calm down. I don't want Theresa to have to sedate you, either."

"She can't—" he starts to shout again, and I lean forward over his bed and kiss his lips gently. They are so dry and chapped. I don't even know how it's possible, we've only been apart a couple days.

"She can, Chase. And she will. You need to calm down, okay? I'm here for you. So is Cody. And I won't be going anywhere, but you have to calm down. Please."

I feel his fingers squeeze around mine and he tries to nod, but he's stopped by his neck brace.

"Why can't I move my head? What's wrong with me? What's going on?" he asks, starting to get aggravated again.

I look up at Theresa, silently asking for her help, because I don't know how to settle him down.

"Mr. Canton," she says. "Do you remember what you were doing today?"

His eyes dart from me, to Cody, then to Theresa before he answers. "Did I ride today? What state are we in?"

I hear Cody mutter *shit* beneath his breath and then he steps up beside me.

"Yeah, brother, you rode today."

I nod and smile at him. I never realized smiling could be so hard to do, but now that I have to for him, even though it's the last thing I feel, I realize it's something I've taken for granted my whole life.

"Then what am I doing here?" he asks.

"You're hurt," I tell him honestly.

Then Cody fills in, "After you made your eight, you got caught up. You took a beating, we had to bring you to the hospital."

"Do you remember any of that, Mr. Canton?" Theresa asks him.

"No, not at all. What's today's date? What rodeo were we at?"

"It was an exhibition, in New Mexico," I answer, stroking my thumb over his knuckles.

"Exhibition?" he repeats.

209

"Mhmm. You came out to win more money for us. To save up so we can have a baby. Remember?"

Chase squints his eyes, no doubt trying to draw any memories forward he can, then lets out a frustrated growl.

"I don't remember anything. What's going on?"

Theresa runs the machines to check his vitals again and then smiles down at him. "You hit your head very hard, and then you got trampled on, and you sustained some pretty serious injuries. I really do need you to try to calm down, though. Your wife and brother can try to explain as best as possible, but it's important you stay calm."

"He can do that," I say, bringing his hand up to my mouth and kissing his palm. "Right?"

"He absolutely can," Cody says. "We'll be sure of it."

"Someone just please tell me what's going on," Chase responds to all three of us.

"I'll go and put a call in for his doctor," Theresa says. "You may struggle to remember what they tell you, Mr. Canton, but it should start to come back soon. You've got a concussion."

Theresa winks at me when Chase's lips form into an understanding "O," then she walks out of the room to give us some privacy.

"That's all that's wrong with me," he says, more amused than upset now.

Cody and I exchange glances, and his lips pull into a smile.

"Dude, you've always had more wrong with you than that, should I start listing everything?"

"Fuck you," Chase laughs, then winces and lifts his hand to his head.

"You need to rest, baby. We'll have plenty of time to go over everything."

Chase peeks at me through his fingers. "Everything?"

I let out a sigh and nod my head. I don't want to upset him, but I can't lie to him, either.

"There is more. A lot more." Cody reaches up and clasps his fingers over the back of his neck.

"Tell me?"

"You can't get upset, Chase. I mean it. We will tell you, but you have to stay calm."

"Just tell me," he says more insistently.

Cody exhales and then begins. "You hit your eight and you were ready to get off, but your hand got stuck, and then…" he pauses and shakes his head. "Jesus, this is hard."

"What happened after?" Chase says, sounding agitated again.

"Chase…" I warn, in the most soothing voice I can.

"After your hand got caught, Frosty bucked hard. You weren't expecting it; you were so focused on freeing yourself you never saw it coming. You went ass over end through the air, and he caught your head as you were coming down."

"You've got a bad concussion, Chase," I add. "It's a really bad one. But that's not all that happened."

"No, it's not," Cody picks up after me. "After you hit the ground, you were out. Unmoving, unconscious, out. And Frosty, he was moving too fast. The fighters tried to get between you two, but shit, it all just happened so damn fast."

"What happened?" Chase asks, going to reach for his head with the other hand, and I stop him so he can't disturb the sensor they inserted earlier.

"Don't touch your head on that side. I'll explain why after Cody finishes."

Chase just nods and sets his hand back down in his lap. The machine over his shoulder starts to beep, and a number starts to blink as it climbs higher and higher. It's the one with a heart by it, so I know that's his heart rate.

"Chase, baby, you need to calm down. Breathe. Slow down," I say gently, reaching up to his head and stroking my fingers over his brows. He closes his eyes and breathes slowly, and after a few minutes the number drops back down again.

"Cody, what happened?" he asks again.

"Once you were on the ground, Frosty dropped down right on top of you. You had your face in the dirt and he landed full weight on your back. Then he did a little spin when the fighters got his attention and his hind legs connected with you again."

I close my eyes and swallow hard. I didn't ask Cody for the details. So this is the first I'm hearing them, too. My stomach goes shaky, and nausea finds its way back in again. But I can't let Chase see that.

"Now tell me how bad I'm hurt," Chase says, managing to keep his aggravation at bay, though I can feel the frustration radiating off of him.

Before Cody can get the words out, a new doctor comes in and introduces himself as Dr. Pryor. His timing couldn't be any better, because once he gives Chase a complete neurological exam now that he's awake, he's able to explain everything going on.

Twenty-Three

Chase

I've never felt a throbbing in my head like I feel now. I raise my hand up to rub it, and Allie stops me, again. *That's right.*

I've got a hole in my head, and a wire attached to my fucking brain to make sure I don't keel over and die anytime soon. Though, if the pain gets any worse, it'll be enough to have me knocking on Heaven's doors all on its very own.

While Allie, Cody, and Dr. Whats-his-name all watch me silently, I run down everything I was just told.

Brain is okay for now, minus the literal hole they drilled in my head.

If everything still looks good tomorrow afternoon, they'll take the shit out of my brain and cover the hole back up.

My back is broken, and I'll need surgery.

There is pressure and swelling from the fracture and trauma compressing my spinal cord.

I will never ride again.

I may never walk again.

The doctor poked me. Prodded me. Looked at the scans they took while I was unconscious, and then he told me the news that has ended my life as I knew it. Everything I've worked so hard for—my goals, the life I wanted us to live—is all gone.

I'm paralyzed from the waist down.

Twenty-Four

Allie

I glance up at the clock and squint, trying to make out the time through the glare of the light coming from the hallway.

It's after two in the morning. Today has been the longest ever. Chase has been conscious and we have known for roughly four hours now what is wrong with him.

My husband hasn't spoken since then.

Chase shut down after Dr. Pryor came in to speak with him a few hours ago. He didn't say a word to me. Not to Cody. He barely managed to get a thank-you out to the doctor before he closed his eyes and tuned all of us out.

I can't imagine what's going through his head right now.

Only, that's a lie, because I have so much going through mine that pertains to all of us, I have to have some idea about what's going through his, too.

He's paralyzed.

Dr. Montgomery told us when we arrived that was a fear. I was so hopeful when Chase woke up, he would show them all how stubborn he is. How strong he is, and he would prove them wrong.

But this time, his body proved me wrong.

Dr. Pryor went on to explain that they will do further testing in the morning, and once they pull the sensor out of his head, they can start working on his transfer.

I followed him out of Chase's room before he left and asked him if there was any hope for Chase at this point. I didn't want my husband to hear, but I needed to know what to expect. I need to know what Chase is in for, but also what I'm in for. I need to brace myself now, find every ounce of strength I can possibly muster, and I need to be the pillar my family can hold on to as we go forward.

He gave me hope. That's what I get to cling tight to.

Dr. Pryor admitted spinal cord injuries aren't his strong suit, but from what he can tell—based on the early scans—Chase didn't suffer a complete injury.

Those words didn't mean much to me. But Dr. Pryor said with an incomplete injury, there is a very good chance for improvement, and living a fulfilling life going forward.

Adjusting to Chase's paralysis will be hard. For all of us. But I know he isn't going to die. Everything else I can take as it comes.

"You need to sleep," he mumbles, still not looking at me. "I'm sure the hotel we were at could give you a room."

"I'm not leaving your side," I respond, lowering the legs of the recliner I moved beside his bed, so I can sit forward and take his hand.

"You aren't sleeping here," he says with a tone so cool and harsh, it takes me by surprise.

"I just have a lot on my mind right now, I'll sleep when I can."

"No, Allie, I mean I don't want you here."

"You don't... Why? Why would you want me to leave?"

"Because we have two daughters who need you a helluva lot more than I do, at home. Because you can be useful to them. You can't do a damn thing for me. So you need to go."

Silence fills the space between us, interrupted only by the steady beat of the machines telling us he is very much alive. I stare at him, stunned silent. He's looking at me now, but his eyes are cold, they're dark. There isn't one ounce of remorse for his words in them at all.

"Get. Out."

"No, Chase, I'm not leaving you."

"I don't want you here, leave me alone."

Every time he says it, more of my heart breaks. His words are like a knife, jagged and fatal, slicing through the little bit of hope I had.

"Nurse! Nurse! I need you!" he shouts, making Theresa rush in as fast as she can.

"What's wrong, Mr. Canton? Are you in pain? What can I do for you?"

"I want you to get my wife out of here," he says forcefully. "I do not want her in this room. I want her gone. Now."

Theresa looks at him, then at me, and back to him.

"Mr. Canton, surely you don't mean that?"

"Did I stutter?"

"Well, no, sir, you didn't."

"Good. Then kindly escort her out."

Theresa looks at me with eyes full of pity, and she opens her mouth to speak when I cut her off.

"I'll leave, Theresa," I say, wiping away the lone tear in the corner of my eye.

She nods at me and moves to the head of Chase's bed, running his machines again so they'll capture a fresh set of vitals while she's in here.

I reach down for my drink and my purse, then stand and make my way to the door. I turn to look at him, and he's watching me, not saying a word.

"I'm not leaving the hospital, Theresa. I'll be in the waiting room with Cody if you need anything."

Theresa looks back at me and nods her head, while Chase closes his eyes and ignores me completely again.

"I love you, Chase. I can't imagine what you're feeling right now, just know I'll be here for you when you want me again."

Chase

The hurt in her eyes and her words do more damage than any bull ever could have to me. But I need to protect her from what comes next. I have to. When I want her again? She said it as though I don't want to cling to her with every last bit of strength and energy I have right now to get through this shitstorm.

But I won't. I can't. It's not fair to her.

"You know," Theresa says once Allie is long gone, "you may think you're doing the right thing right now, but you aren't."

I grunt out an acknowledgement at her words, and say nothing else to her.

"Be mad, Mr. Canton. Take the night if you need to, but when the sun comes up in the morning, and you've accepted all that's happened tonight, let her in. You won't come out of this with any chance of a good life without your wife by your side. I can promise you that."

With that, Theresa turns her back and walks out of the room, leaving me alone in the dimmed shoebox I get to call home from now on. What I wouldn't give to be able to get up and run the hell away from here without ever looking back.

Twenty-Five

Allie

What Chase didn't know last night when he kicked me out, but Theresa figured out pretty quickly once she left his room, was I didn't go far. In fact, I didn't leave him at all. I turned out of his room, stepped past the small window that allows the nurses to see him from their little desk and computer between his and the neighboring room, and then I slid down the wall and parked it there all night.

I was close enough I could hear every word Theresa said to him last night. And his lack of response to her.

I was close enough when his machines started to beep loudly a while after that, and she rushed into his room, I could hear his heart rate had increased because he'd worked himself up into a fit of anxiety and hyperventilation.

I could hear her tell him she was going to give him something to sleep. A mild sedative that wouldn't do anything more than relax him so he could rest and let his body heal.

I heard everything.

I wanted to go to him. I wanted to hold him and promise him we'd get through this together. I wanted to help him settle down and relax.

But I did none of that.

I sat here on the cold, hard floor and did something I haven't done earnestly in years—I prayed.

I prayed Chase would come to terms with what we've been told, and he would choose to fight as hard as imaginable so he can have the life he wants going forward. I prayed I will have the patience to endure the long, hard days to come. I prayed my husband would stop pushing me away, because whether he is in a wheelchair or up on two feet, I will love him with every bit of my heart and soul until the day I die. What he's able to do will never change who he is to me. I prayed for the strength to hold on through the ups and downs we will undoubtedly face before this crazy ride comes to an end.

While I'm on the floor, watching the hustle and bustle of morning rounds and the nurses' shift change, a cup of coffee is held out to me.

I look up to find Cody standing there, coffee in hand, tight smile in place.

"Thanks," I say, shifting to get the pressure off my tailbone again.

"Theresa said you'd need it," he whispers, then squats down in front of me. "Why didn't you come get me when he was being a prick last night?"

I take a sip of the coffee and swallow hard, the pain of the liquid burning my mouth is almost soothing at this point.

"He's not a prick," I say, shrugging. "He's terrified. He's angry. And he's going to take it out on me because I'm safe to take it out on."

"That's bullshit, Allie," Cody says, tapping my knee with his finger. "If he wants to take shit out on someone, he can take it out on me. I can take it. I will take it. But it should never be you. Do you hear me?"

"Don't worry about it," I say to him, covering his hand with my own over my knee. "His doctor should be in soon. Breeze is back with us today, she said we have a lot to discuss. If he doesn't want me in there, will you stay with him?"

"Christ," he says and closes his eyes. "I'll be there."

"Thank you."

He leans forward and kisses my forehead. "You may as well be my baby sister, you know that? There's nothing you could ask me for that I wouldn't give you right now."

His words mean the world to me. Having him here for me, for us, is everything. For all of the crap I give him about his womanizing ways, Cody is the second best man I know, and when push comes to shove, he will have our backs no matter what. I set my coffee down and lean forward to wrap my arms around his neck.

"I love you, Cody. He's going to need you now more than ever. So am I."

Cody wraps his arm around me and answers simply, "I'm not going anywhere."

Chase

My room has been a revolving door of nurses and staff for a solid hour now. But not once has Allie come back, and I don't know what to think about it. She's my resilient girl. She always has been. But maybe this really is asking more of her than she can handle. I wouldn't blame her. She never signed up for this. She will have to care for me, and the girls. She'll have to learn things no woman should ever be asked to learn and do for her husband.

221

But I'm still shocked she didn't come back.

"Good morning, asshole," Cody says, walking into my room with a coffee in his hand.

"I take it she told you what happened last night."

"Nope, she didn't say a fucking word to me. Your nurse told me when she was leaving a few minutes ago. I haven't seen Allie since I said goodnight to you both last night."

"What do you mean you haven't seen her?" I ask, feeling a pinch in my chest again, same as I felt last night. "Where is she?"

"What the hell do you care? You kicked her out, remember?"

"Cody, I'm not fucking joking. Where is my wife?"

"So now you want her here?" he asks me, raising an eyebrow. "You are a real piece of work, you know that, right?"

He is pissing me off to no end. But I'm also terrified by what he's saying. The first thought that comes to mind is: what if she got hurt leaving here? Then it dawns on me, she's out there in a city she doesn't know, because of me. Why did I ever ask her to leave? Why didn't she go to Cody?

Why is all of this happening to me?

"What did you gain from kicking your wife out last night, Chase?" Cody prods again.

"You think I gained something from that?" I all but shout at him. "You think I don't want her? When have I ever not wanted Allie?"

"Then what the fuck were you thinking?"

"I was thinking she can do a lot better than being stuck wiping my ass and caring for me like a child for the rest of her life. I was thinking that if I set her free she could still live a good life. She doesn't need this, Cody. She never once signed up for any of this."

"You're such a dumbass," he says, and sits down with a smirk on his face.

"What the hell is your problem? Are you not worried about her?"

"Nope, I'm not. But you should be."

Red. That's all I can see when I look at his smug face right now. "I swear to God, Cody, if anything happens to her while you're sitting there on your ass..."

"You'll what? Get up and kick it? I'd like to see you try."

"Yes, you motherfucker. If anything happens to my wife, I will make sure I walk again so I can kill you with my bare hands, after I kick your ass."

"Ah, so you do still have fight in you?"

"Excuse me?" I say through my teeth.

"Allie," he calls out, "I think it's safe for you to come in here now."

I look at him with my jaw dropped; then shift my eyes toward my door when he nods his head in that direction. In walks Allie, carrying the same cup Cody came in with.

"Allie?" I ask in disbelief.

With my attention on her, I didn't even see Cody stand or walk toward the door, not until he's behind her and kissing her head. "Thanks for letting me scare the piss out of him," he says to her, and then he looks at me. "I'll be in the waiting room. You two need to talk. Don't fuck it up this time, jackass."

We both watch Cody walk out, and then Allie steps to me hesitantly and stops at the foot of the bed. "I signed up for life together, Chase, in sickness and in health. Would you walk away if I were the one in that bed and you were the one out of it?"

"Of course not," I answer.

"Then why would you ever think I would?"

"You wouldn't. That's why I said what I did..."

223

"Never again, Cowboy. Or I swear I will walk away and I'll never look back. We are in this together. Just like we have been everything else. Do you hear me?"

"Loud and clear, Darlin'. Loud and fucking clear."

"Good." She exhales slowly and fidgets with the coffee cup in her hands, picking at the sleeve around it. Her eyes look heavy, and show the evidence of her crying in the puffiness around them. She's wearing the same clothes she had on yesterday. Her hair is in a messy, crazy ponytail. And she's never looked more beautiful. Or exhausted.

"Where did you go last night?"

"Against the wall about two and a half feet outside your door…"

There's no way. She couldn't have actually sat outside my room all night. "Where were you really?"

"I was on the floor outside your room. I wasn't going anywhere. There was no way I was leaving you. Even if you said you wanted me to."

"Jesus. I am so sorry. I didn't mean for you to sit on the floor all night. I wanted to protect you from hurt, not subject you to it."

"And pushing me away, hurting me with your words and your actions, was how you were going to accomplish that?"

"I've got a brain injury. I wasn't thinking clearly." My head isn't an excuse at all, but I'll use anything and everything I can to make what I did right. Even if it's throwing an injury at her.

Then she tilts her head back and laughs. It's a genuine laugh that makes my heart, and the air around us, lighter than they've been since I woke up last night.

"You would use your head injury as a defense to kicking me out. I bet you'll use it and your back to get anything and everything you want until you're better, won't you?"

"That depends," I say, smirking.

"On?"

"Whether or not it'll work."

"Maybe you should give it a try and find out."

"My head hurts, like a mother, honestly. And my legs don't work. My back is broken. And I really could use a kiss to feel better... And you're the only one I'll take it from. Would you mind?" I say, smiling at her.

"If I must, you demanding thing. Don't get used to being pampered, though," she says, smiling back at me and setting her drink down before she steps up to my side.

With my arms held out she leans in and lets me wrap her up tight. She smells like coconut and vanilla still, with hints of my favorite perfume lingering on her shirt. She's warm and unwavering, even as I begin to cry in her arms.

"Shhh," she says, tucking my head into the crook of her neck. "I've got you. I've got you."

She repeats the words over and over, holding me as my quiet tears turn into full sobs.

Now that I'm in her arms, the weight of everything has caved in on me. And I'm terrified. I don't know how I'm going to live with this. I don't know how I can be the man she, and our girls, need. I've never had to be dependent on anyone else. Not since I was a kid. I've never felt more helpless in my life, and I don't know if I have the strength to get past this. That scares me more than anything else. What if I'm not the man she believes I am?

Allie holds me until I've cried out every last tear in my body. She doesn't loosen her grip. She doesn't let go. She stands steady and bears the weight of our world changing on her shoulders, and in her arms, with a strength I can only admire and hope to have one day.

"I love you, Chase Aaron Canton. We are going to get through this, do you hear me?"

When she pulls back to look me in the eyes, I see it there—the determination and fight that will get us through everything life throws at us—even my stupidity.

"I love you, too," I reply, watching our first test walk through the door as a team of doctors and nurses come to deliver more news.

Twenty-Six

Chase

"Are you sure you don't mind going out to Colorado and staying with our girls?" I whisper to Cody across the room. The arrogant bastard is propped against the door, hip resting against the jamb, with a fresh, just fucked look on his face.

"Not at all. Allie said earlier that you guys will be getting an air ambulance transfer to Denver tomorrow early?"

I nod my head. "They want me to have surgery within a seventy-two-hour window or my chances for recovery diminish drastically."

"So home tomorrow then, that's good," he says, resting his head against the jamb now, too.

"No, Denver tomorrow. Home…" I let the words hang in the air. I don't know when I'll get to go home again.

"Don't go there, Chase," Cody warns, and steps closer, pulling a chair with him so he can sit beside my bed.

"I have to go there, especially while she sleeps. I have to be realistic. My back is broken and I can't fucking walk. They barely just pulled a wire out of my brain, and I've still got a hole in my skull, barely covered by my scalp being stitched over it."

He grimaces and then rises to look at the shaved patch on my head with stitches in the middle of it. "You make it sound so bleak. At least you're alive. When I called her…" He stops talking now and looks all around the room, but avoids me.

"When you called her… What?"

"You haven't seen it, neither has she. And I'm praying to God neither of your girls especially, have seen the footage of you getting caught up, tossed, and crushed. I didn't think you'd live through last night. I called her thinking she would get here in time to tell you goodbye. That was it."

I watch him closely, and when he finally does look at me, his eyes are red-rimmed and glossy. "It was that bad?"

"Worst I've ever seen," he answers quietly. "I don't know how you are alive right now, but I've never been more grateful. When I get to your house, and when I explain everything to the girls again, I'll make sure they know how strong you are."

I let out a frustrated groan when he brings up the girls. "We told them what's going on. But they aren't going to be prepared for all of this."

"Not even a little. I'm a grown-ass man, and I'm still coming to terms with you like this. You're their hero…"

"Some hero, right?"

"Nah, the best hero. But this is going to be hard for the girls…all three of them," he says, his voice lowered even more, then nods in Allie's direction. She's finally sleeping in the recliner in my room. Best I could tell, it had been around thirty, thirty-two hours at least since she'd last slept. She needed it. And I needed some time to think and talk to Cody.

"I know it is. That's why I need a favor. It's something I would never ask if I didn't think there was any other way…" I say to him.

"What's up?" he asks seriously.

"When you aren't at rodeos, make Colorado your home again until I get all my shit figured out?" I know he has his reasons for staying in Texas, but he's the only person I trust to help us wade through everything coming our way.

He sits back down beside my bed and thinks silently for a minute, then he starts, "I'll be there as long as you all need me. I wouldn't let you or your girls go through this alone."

I clear my throat a little. "Thank you."

"Just so you know, I'll be drinking all of your beer as my payment for my good deed," he grins at me then adds, "and for my celibacy. Unless you don't mind me bringing women back to your place?"

"Try it, and you die." I smile back at him.

"That's what I thought."

"Speaking of…she better not have been one of my nurses."

"Relax," he says, chuckling a little. "She was the X-ray tech, and it was during her lunch break."

"Christ, you really are a pig." I laugh at him and the sound and motion make my head hurt.

"You should try to get some rest while Allie is. You're going to have a ton to go through the next few days, you'll need the sleep when you can get it."

"You're right, and my head is starting to hurt again." I hate admitting it, but it's the truth.

"Hit the call button, then ask for the good stuff to help you sleep. I need to get back to the hotel, check out, and then catch my flight to Denver, so I can get to your munchkins anyway."

"Thanks again. I really appreciate it."

"That's what family does, right?" he says easily.

"Yeah, the family that gives a shit and that chose you. Says nothing about my parents."

"Fuck them. You have me and Allie."

He's right. I do have them. And I'm lucky for it. My parents bailed years ago and I don't really need nor want them here. "I don't need anyone else anyway."

"Damn straight. Tell her the girls and I will call tonight." He stands from his chair again and reaches for my hand, squeezing it where it lays on the bed.

"I will. We'll see you and our girls tomorrow?" I ask, making sure I'll see them before they cut me open; because there's a risk something could go wrong.

"We'll be there waiting for you."

"Be safe, getting to them, and getting them to us."

Cody grins and gives a little salute, then turns to leave the room at the same time as Breeze walks in.

"You paged?" she asks with a smile.

Cody. He must've hit the button when he let go of my hand before he left.

"I'm in some pain…"

"Say no more, we'll take care of that. You just try to get some rest."

While she gets more meds in me, I close my eyes and try to sleep. Given everything on my mind, that's a lot easier said than done.

230

Allie

The distant sound of an alarm going off is playing over and over in my head, getting closer and louder with each new cycle. It's not until it's blaring loud do I wake up, panicked and jumping to my feet, remembering immediately we are in the hospital. I turn to Chase and let out a relieved breath.

He's okay. It wasn't his machine.

He's actually sleeping right now. His head is turned on his pillow facing me, thanks to the neck brace being off, as though he fell asleep watching me. I step up and very gently run my fingers through his hair, minding the spot where his stitches are, then lean down to kiss the top of his head.

His hair smells like antiseptic, sweat, and Chase. It's a little longer than he would usually let it be, but he planned to get it trimmed when he came home after this weekend's exhibition. Now…I don't know when he'll be able to get it cut. Or if it'll bother him he can't right now.

The alarms start to sound again so I step out of his room and look right, then left. There's a lot of commotion in the room beside Chase's. They must've filled it when I was asleep. I hope whoever is in there is okay, or they will be.

I look down the hall again, taking in the window in the small waiting area that's empty. Judging by the dim light coming through the window, the sun must be setting.

It's probably after eight already. Which means I was out for hours. I missed Cody leaving. I may have even missed tonight's rounds and word on when Chase and I will be transferred tomorrow. I need to find one of his nurses. I need to go back into his room and find my phone so I can call Cody. I need to get a bite of food before my stomach alerts everyone else to the fact it's hungry, too.

I need to do a lot of things. Before all of that, I need to make sure Chase is okay still. I've only been out of his room for a couple minutes, and I can already feel the anxiety creeping in that if I'm too far away, something will happen. I'll come back and find his room is the one full of medical staff, working hard to keep him alive.

That's my biggest fear. When I'm awake, and even in my dreams while I was asleep.

I walk back into his dimly lit room, and he's awake, looking around. As much as I wish he were resting still, I'm so relieved to see him that I cross the small room in as much of a hurry as I can and kiss his lips.

"What was that for?" he asks when I pull back.

"I was having a bad dream before I woke up. I'm just really happy to see you."

He raises his hand to my face and smiles sleepily at me. "I'm happy to see you, too. What were you doing?"

I shake my head, not wanting to tell him what it sounded like in the next room. "Nothing, really. Just stretching my legs. When did Cody leave?"

"Around two this afternoon. He said to tell you bye and that he and the girls would call tonight."

"I'm sorry I missed him, but I'm glad he'll be with the girls."

Chase brushes his thumb over my cheek and then slides his hand to the back of my head, pulling me closer so he can kiss me again. "Me, too. It'll be good having him home."

I kiss him four times, quickly, then kiss his nose. "He'll go crazy not getting any action in so long."

That makes Chase laugh loudly, and hearing it makes my heart so happy. "He got some this afternoon. He'll be fine."

"You're kidding me?" I look at him with my mouth slightly ajar. "Who? Where? When?"

"Some tech, during her lunch break…"

"He is such a pig," I respond, laughing. "At least we won't have to worry about him bringing anyone to the house. Right?"

"I threatened his life if he tried it. We're safe."

"Thank God." I rest my forehead against his and close my eyes. "Did I miss anything important?"

He moves his head back and forth, slowly, against mine. "We should know tonight sometime when we will be leaving tomorrow. We've been instructed to get as much rest as we can until then."

My stomach chooses now to be when it growls loudly, alerting Chase to my current needs. He chuckles and lets go of my head. "Go down and get some food, Darlin'. You haven't eaten all day. You need to."

"I'll go down in a bit, I think their Subway is open until nine."

"Okay, but don't forget."

"I promise," I say and lean down to kiss him again. It's got to be overkill, but when your husband dies in your dreams, and then you wake up hearing the alarms of another patient who may be dying next door, there really isn't such a thing as too many kisses. There never could be again.

Twenty-Seven

Chase

Allie squeezes my hand as we watch the surgeon walk out of my room. It's only nine thirty in the morning, but we've already had an incredibly long day with our flight from New Mexico here to Denver happening at around six o'clock.

"I like him," she says, taking a seat in the chair beside my bed. "He's very matter-of-fact, but he was kind. Direct but soft with his delivery."

"You're putting way too much thought into his personality," I say to her, smiling. "As long as he fixes me, he could be the biggest fucking asshole in the world and I wouldn't care."

"Daddy!" screams Aubrey, as she bursts through the door. "That's a bad word!"

Seeing her barreling toward the bed, like a Monkey on a mission to get to me, is the best thing I've seen in days. She runs right to Allie's arms and then climbs up into Allie's lap so she can see me better.

"I'm sorry, Monkey," I say to her. "I didn't know you were listening or I wouldn't have said any bad words."

"You has to put money in the curse jar. Just like Uncle Cody."

Allie and I both laugh, and then Cody and Ava walk into my room, too. Ava's hand is squeezing his tightly; even I can see the whiteness in her grip around his fingers.

"Hey, Pip," I say to her, first. "Thanks for bringing my girls," I add to Cody.

"Hi, Daddy," she whispers. Looking over everything attached to me and around the room closely.

"It was my pleasure," he replies, then guides her forward. She steps slowly toward me and the bed, careful not to touch anything.

"You won't hurt me, Ava, I promise. In fact, I think big hugs from both of you would help me so much."

Allie helps Aubrey onto my bed and tells her to be gentle, but to give me a big feel better hug. Ava lets go of Cody's hand and walks around to the other side of my bed, then pushes up to hug me at the same time as Aubrey.

With each of their arms wrapped around me, I hold them as tight as I can and say, "I love you both so much. I've missed you."

Aubrey, oblivious to just how bad everything is for me, pulls away and leans back on her heels beside my waist, grinning wide. "I missed you soooo much too! But we had fun with Tatum and Uncle Cody. They both let us stay up extra late."

Ava keeps a hold of me and doesn't say anything. She just buries her face in my neck and stills there.

"Is that so?" I ask Aubrey, raising my brows in Cody's direction.

"They were in bed by ten," he says, holding his hands up in innocence. "That's apparently really late for this one. Michelle told me you gave them special late nights sometimes when we switched shifts." He steps closer and taps Aubrey's right shoulder, then moves farther to the left, making her look at nothing and laugh.

"I suppose extra exceptions can be made for special nights," I respond. "Right, Mommy?"

"Absolutely," Allie adds, then guides Aubrey into her lap so I can focus on Ava.

I move my other arm over to her, too, and start to rub her back. With my chin tucked slightly, I whisper into her ear, "Are you okay?"

She shakes her head against me, telling me no.

"Are you worried about me?"

Now she nods.

"I'm okay. I'm right here." I kiss her head and hold her to me, glancing at Cody and Allie. We should've known Ava would take this hard. She's old enough to understand, and given her tendency to look things up, read, and generally just know more things than should be humanly possible at nine years old, she usually understands more than we'd like.

I can feel the coolness of her tears roll onto my neck and over the top of my hospital gown, leaving it damp against me.

"Hey," I try to soothe her, rubbing her back more. "I'm okay. Will you talk to me? Uncle Cody can come around and help you climb into bed with me.

He goes to come around when she pushes up on her own and lies beside me, not moving from my shoulder or neck even a little.

"Ava," Allie tries to get her to budge, but she still doesn't.

"It's okay, she can stay there as long as she wants." I turn my head in and kiss Ava's again. "Will you listen if I talk to you and your sister, Pipsqueak?"

Ava nods again and I smile. "That's my girl."

"I'm your girl, too!" Aubrey shrieks, making Allie shush her, reminding her we're in a hospital and need to use our indoor voices.

"Yes, you are. You're both my girls. Did Uncle Cody tell you what's going on?"

Ava nods against me, and Aubrey nods in Allie's lap.

"Good. I'm going to tell you a little bit now, too. Okay?" I take a deep breath and rub Ava's back again, needing to do it more for my own comfort than for hers right now. "I got hurt getting off a bull the other day. And right now that means I get really bad headaches sometimes, just like Ava did. But my back is hurt too."

Aubrey looks up at Allie with wide eyes, causing her to nod her head and confirm what I'm saying.

"I hit my back pretty hard, and I can't walk right now. And I have to have surgery today so they can try to fix it."

"Does it hurt?" Aubrey asks.

"Only a little, but I don't feel too much, so I'm okay."

"Are you paralyzed?" Ava asks me against my throat, but it's loud enough for everyone in the room to hear.

Cody shakes his head, indicating he didn't use that word with them, and Allie just covers her mouth with her hand.

"How do you know about that word?" I ask her.

That finally gets Ava to sit up, tears streaking down her little cheeks. "One of the mommies from my school is paralyzed. She can't move her arms or her legs. And she has a special chair that moves with her mouth. She did show and tell in our class last year."

"Oh, baby girl," Allie says, looking between us with wide, sad eyes.

"We are always honest with each other, right?" I ask Ava.

"Right," she agrees quietly.

"So I'll be honest now. I might not be able to walk again." I pause to clear my throat and swallow back the lump forming there, thanks to having to explain this to my little girl. "But the doctors are going to do the surgery today so they can try to help me walk again. But even if

237

I don't, I won't be the same as your classmate's mom. I can still use my arms, and I have a little bit of feeling in my legs. It's not a lot, but it's something."

"So you won't be like her mommy?"

"No, he'll still be your same Daddy, Ava," Allie pipes in. "He may be in a wheelchair, and he may get out of it and be able to walk and play like normal again. We just have to stay strong for him, and hope and pray for the best. And we are good at that, right?"

Ava looks toward Allie and Aubrey and nods her head. Her cheeks are red, there are dried streaks of tears down it; in this moment, it makes Ava look younger than she is. More innocent. In need of protecting from the world; something I can't do for her right now.

"I'll be okay, Ava. I will. No matter what happens today."

"Okay," she says, unconvinced.

"Do you know what would make me feel better?"

"What?"

"Maybe you, your sister, and your mom could go get me a Rice Krispies Treat and a water from the vending machine? Do you think you could do that for me?"

"We can definitely do that for Daddy, right, girls?" Allie says, setting Aubrey back on the ground and standing. "Come on, Ava, let's go get him, and us, a yummy treat to feel better."

Ava leans forward to kiss my cheek and then slips off the bed. "We'll be back."

Allie takes each of the girls' hands and they walk out, allowing Cody to step over and take Allie's seat beside me.

"Fuck," he says, pulling his ball cap off and rubbing his head. "She didn't say that word to me even once, or I would've tried to do some damage control. I didn't even let her near a phone, tablet, or computer."

"I'm not mad, nor was I going to blame you. She's smart. Too damn smart for our good."

"You aren't kidding. She had me doubled over laughing at times last night, and then downright terrified to speak and say the wrong thing other times."

That makes me laugh. "She is her mother's daughter."

"No shit. Aubrey seems to be rolling with all of this pretty well. So that's good."

"Yeah, I'm glad she's only six and not really with the medical picture. Seeing Ava so upset is hard enough."

"You've still got a chance to walk again though?" he asks me, turning his hat in his hand.

"I have some sensation and feeling in my legs, and the cord injury is incomplete. The docs won't give me a guarantee, but they said it's a possibility."

"Another way to set you apart from the paralyzed school mom."

"I hope so. But I don't want to guarantee the girls anything. It'll be hard enough for Allie and me if this surgery and recovery don't work. And you saw how Ava took everything else."

He nods his head. "You handled that well, though, both of you did. You didn't dash her hopes, but you didn't guarantee anything, either."

"We're a team when it comes to parenting them, Allie and I are always on the same page. What's best for them is what matters, and what we do. It was unspoken, but we both know to tread lightly with how much hope we give."

"Good. But the girls will be fine, Allie will make sure of it. So will I." He looks around the room I'm in and then up at the powerless TV. "How are you doing?"

"I'm fucking terrified," I tell him, looking down toward my lap. "How can I be the man they need if I can't walk, or leave a chair?"

"I don't know how you adjust, make life work for you when you're an up and get the work done early type. But your legs don't make you the man they need. How you are as a father and husband does."

"I guess, I'm just afraid. This wasn't in the plans. None of it was. You know what my plans were. How do I achieve those now?"

"We were going to partner up, right?" he asks, resting his elbows on his legs and watching me expectantly.

"You know that's what I wanted." He's the only person I wanted to bring in on my plans, that's why he came to the meeting with me. He's my best friend, my brother, and one hell of a business partner and cowboy.

"Then we will make it work." He shrugs and leans back again, as though we can just keep moving forward like I'm not looking at a life in a wheelchair.

"Just like that?" I say incredulously.

"Just like, Chase. We will make that shit work. We can still do everything you planned to. It'll just take a little more time and patience. But we'll figure it out."

"I hope you're right." I drop my head back on the pillow behind me and look up to the ceiling. Every little thing I planned to have happen between now and the end of the year has been shot to hell. Though I appreciate his enthusiasm, I don't see how we can make it all work.

Allie

The girls and I take the long way around the floor to the vending machines, and we make a pit stop in the bathroom for Aubrey. I know Chase doesn't actually want those things, he can't eat them until he's out of surgery, but I suspect he needed a break, and to talk to Cody.

But I'm not going to stay gone for long, he's going into surgery very soon, and I want every minute in his presence I can get.

"Do you think he'd want a Dr. Pepper, too?" Ava asks, standing in front of the pop machine and evaluating every option.

"No, baby, just his water. You can have one, if you want it."

"I can?" she asks in a tone that would indicate I just offered her a miracle.

"Just this once, for your daddy, yes. You can get a Dr. Pepper." I hand her the bills and let her get Chase's water, and her soda, then I get me a water and Aubrey a Sierra Mist.

"Ava, get Krispies for all of us, please." She takes another handful of dollar bills from me and dispenses five Rice Krispies Treats from the vending machine.

"I got one for Uncle Cody, too." She tries to hold onto all five treats carefully, but with her and Chase's drinks, she starts to drop them.

"Aubrey, why don't you take a couple treats for Ava, and your drink, and we can head back."

Both kids do as I suggested, evening out the load so we don't drop anything, and we make our way back to Chase's room.

241

"We come bearing snacks for everyone," I announce as we walk in, giving them warning to stop talking about whatever it was they were discussing, so the girls don't hear anything they shouldn't.

"Thank you," Chase says with an unconvincing smile.

"Yeah, thanks," Cody says, standing up. "I've got to make a call and some arrangements, so I'll let you all spend some time together before…"

"Thank you, Cody," I say, giving him a small smile.

He bends down over Chase and gives him a hug, whispering something in his ear that I can't make out. Chase nods and Cody pulls back with the slightest hint of moisture along the crease of his eye.

"See you on the flip side," Cody says so we can all hear. "Ask them to make you more attractive while they're in there, too. It's really not fair to stick Allie with that mug for life, if it can be helped."

That simple statement draws a real laugh from Chase, and me, and lightens the heaviness surrounding us so much that the air feels thinner and easier to breathe.

"Fuck you," Chase mutters, still chuckling. "You know what we talked about?" he asks Cody, waiting for Cody to nod yes before he continues, "I'm counting on you. Thank you."

"Stop getting all sappy on me," Cody says, "besides, that's what brothers are for. But, I'll see you on the flip side, so it doesn't matter." With that, Cody walks out, putting his ball cap on backward as he crosses the threshold of the door.

Cody leaving has let us spend the last hour with Chase, talking, laughing, and trying to forget about the procedure we're waiting for him to have. Aubrey has been showing us bits of her floor routine and Ava has been looking up funny jokes to share with us on my phone. We've made good memories together in this small, sterile room. Memories I know I'll cherish for life, regardless of the outcome of his surgery.

I glance at the clock over the whiteboard hanging on the wall and notice it's getting to be that time. "Girls, why don't you give Daddy hugs and tell him you love him, his doctors and nurses will be ready for him soon."

Chase looks up at the clock, and then at me, and his stress flashes behind his eyes before he puts that smiley mask back in place for the girls.

"I need big hugs when we say goodbye."

I smile at him and watch Aubrey turn toward him in his bed, with her sticky fingers spread out so she doesn't get marshmallow on him.

"Bye, Daddy," Aubrey says, yawning wide. "I love you."

"I love you, too, Monkey. So much." He draws her tiny frame into his chest, from where she's perched on the bed beside him, and hugs her tight. She wraps her arms around him and hugs him back, then scoots off the bed, giving Ava room to climb up in her place.

"You're going to be okay?" Ava asks as soon as she's seated at his side.

"Of course," he replies with a grin that may fool our daughter, but not me. "I'm going to be just fine. I would never let a little accident keep me down. Right?"

"Right," she says, nodding once. "And we can ride together again soon? You can help me practice?"

Chase glances at me over her head, giving me that look, and then focuses back on Ava. "It will take me a while, Pipsqueak. I've got a lot of healing to do before I can ride again. Okay?"

Her face falls, but she answers him anyway, "Okay, Daddy. I just want you better."

"That's what I want, too. And I'm going to fight hard to get better as fast as I can."

"You can do it, I know you can."

Before Chase can respond, his nurse pokes her head in. "It's time, Mr. Canton, are you all set?"

"I am," he responds, then pulls Ava into his chest, just like he did Aubrey, hugging her tight. "I love you, too, Ava. You look after your sister while I'm getting better."

"I will, Daddy. I love you, too." Ava sits up and holds her hand for Chase to press his to, and their fingers link together. "Good luck," she whispers, then climbs off the bed so I can move in.

I step up beside him and slide my fingers through his hair. "You better come out and back to me, Cowboy. Or else..."

He grins and nods beneath my hand. "You aren't getting rid of me that easily."

"I don't want to get rid of you ever," I say, as I lean down to kiss his lips. "I love you, Chase. We will get through this and come out stronger. We just have to hold on tight until this crazy ride ends."

"I won't let go if you won't."

I take his hand just like Ava did, but I don't let it go. Instead I bring our hands higher and kiss over his knuckles, where his wedding ring would be if it weren't around the chain on my neck. "I'll hold on for all eternity."

His nurse comes back in with the aide and I take a step back so they can prep his bed to be moved.

"You can walk with us down the hall," the aide says, "but then you'll have to go to the waiting room."

I nod and wink at Chase. "We'll be waiting for you."

"I can hardly wait to see my girls again. I love you all. Just remember that, okay."

He's not asking. He's telling us. He's afraid, and though it's rare, there is always room for complications and the unthinkable.

"We love you, too. You can tell us again when you're out."

We follow them out of the room and down the hall, where they pass through a set of doors and wheel Chase back for surgery. I take the girls' hands and we watch as the doors swing closed, then I turn them down the hall toward the waiting room. I nearly jump out of my skin when Cody is standing a few feet away, leaned against the wall, with his arms crossed and his eyes focused on the doors Chase disappeared behind.

"I thought you'd already left for, ya know..." I whisper honestly. I know he has a big ride this weekend he needs to leave and prepare for soon.

"Not a chance," he whispers, shaking his head. "I'm a scratch this weekend. My place is here with my family. Waiting to see if my brother is okay."

I nod my head with a slight smile. "Follow us then, Uncle Cody. We're heading to the waiting room so we can settle in for the duration."

He bends and scoops Aubrey into his arms. "Lead the way, ladies, we will be right behind you."

Aubrey wraps her arms around Cody's neck and lays her head on his shoulder.

"C'mon, Miss Ava, we'll show them where the comfiest seat is so your sister can relax. You both were up really early today.

Ava and I lead them to the waiting room, and I point out the bench seat that's cushion can be unfolded and laid out as a small couch bed. Cody carries Aubrey over and sits, helping her get laid out on it before he covers her with his coat.

"You'll be a good dad one day, you know that, right?" I ask him, handing Ava my phone to watch videos on.

"Eh, I don't know how true that is. But thanks. I've just watched Chase with these two, a lot." He shrugs his shoulder and looks down at Aubrey. She's already starting to nod off, tucked beneath his jacket.

"You will. You brought a jacket in the dead of summer, and haven't worn it once yet. So you brought it for them."

"Like I said, I've watched Chase with them a lot." He shrugs it off, very typical of Cody, and then takes his phone out, focusing on its screen.

We sit in a comfortable silence for what feels like an eternity, waiting for news on Chase's surgery. Both girls are asleep and passing the time until Chase is out in their dreams. I just hope they're good ones.

"I heard what Ava said to him," Cody whispers, getting my attention after a while.

"About?"

"Riding. We both know he won't be in any condition to help her reach her dreams anytime soon..."

"Don't start, Cody," I warn.

"I am going to start, Allie. I'm hopefully going to finish, too. Quit being a stubborn ass and tell your daughter about your past. You can teach her. You can give her, her dreams. So stop hiding behind some false, fucked-up excuse about you don't want to hurt Aubrey, and you hated that life and want to forget it. It's a crock of shit. That life gave you all of this."

The tone and punch of his words leaves no room for argument, yet I find myself wanting to argue, to defend my choices.

"Save the excuses," he says, reading me before I can speak them out loud. "You're being a coward and your family deserves better. Ava deserves better. She needs you."

"Cody, you don't know what you're asking."

"I do. I'm asking you to woman the hell up, teach your daughter everything there is to know, and let her become what she wants for as long as she wants to do it. You aren't forcing her. She chose this for herself. Don't punish her for having dreams, or for you being a chickenshit. Tell her. Teach her. Make her the champion it's in her blood to be."

He stands from the couch when he finishes and gives me a look. "Be the woman he knows you are. Do right by your girls, and take up the slack that he's going to need your help with."

He walks out of the waiting room and down the hall in the direction of the restrooms without another word.

Once he's gone, I think about his words. About the pointed remarks he made about me being afraid, and then I look at my girls. I don't want them to grow up ever feeling like they can't speak up, or like they shouldn't be proud of everything they accomplish. Yet, that's the example I'm setting. He's also right; Chase won't be able to teach her. There's a chance he'll never even walk again.

Ava is going to need help. I could hire someone else to teach her to ride competitively, but who knows how they'll push my daughter, how they'll make her feel. I owe her more. I owe Chase more, too.

I need to quit hiding behind my excuses and tell my kids who I am, who I was when I met their dad. Ava needs to know, and because I wouldn't have any of this life if I'd never ridden, too.

Twenty-Eight

Allie

"**M**rs. Canton," a nurse says, as she crosses the threshold into the waiting room. It's been just over five hours. Five long, torturous hours waiting for information on how the surgery is going.

"Yes?" I acknowledge, standing up and crossing my arms over my midsection defensively, preparing myself for anything she may be here to tell me.

Cody stands from where he's sitting with the girls, playing tic-tac-toe, and walks over to stand beside me.

"Your husband is out of surgery, and they are going to be taking him back to the ICU to go through the recovery process and be monitored. His surgeon will come out as soon as he can to update you, and after about an hour, hour and a half, someone will let you know you can get back into the ward and see him." She gives me a smile and goes to turn and walk away.

That's all? She isn't going to tell me how he is, if it was a success? What to expect?

"Wait," I say nervously.

She stops and turns back to us with a smile. "Yes, ma'am?"

"Is he okay? Did it go well?"

"He's got to come out of his sedation, and he will be groggy for a while, but he should be okay. As for the surgery, I'm afraid I can't give you any information.

You'll just have to wait for the doctor. He'll be along soon."

"Okay," I mumble, "Thank you."

She reaches out to give my arm a little squeeze, and then she leaves us standing, watching her back disappear, confused and not knowing much of anything at this point.

"He made it through," Cody says quietly, aware of the girls watching us. "Hurdle one is clear."

"Keep reminding me of that until we see him?"

"You got it." He wraps me in a one-armed hug and then goes back to sit with the girls, explaining to them what the nurse just told us.

Chase made it through his surgery. He's alive. That's all that matters. But...

I really, really hope they were able to get in fast enough, decompress and stabilize him enough, that he will be able to walk again someday. His rodeo career is over; that breaks my heart for him. He will never get to be a champion again. Everything we have gone through, all we have given up and missed out on as a family, and it's just over. That is going to hurt him deeply when it really sinks in. And there will be nothing I can do or say to make it any better.

I wanted him to end things on his terms. To call it quits when he wanted because he wanted to. I didn't want it ripped away from him so rapidly. He deserved better from life than he's been dealt over the last forty-eight hours.

"What are you thinking about over there?" Cody asks, tossing a bottle cap my direction and hitting me in the stomach with it.

"A little childish, isn't this?" I ask back, holding the cap up.

"It effectively got your attention." He smirks my way. "What's on your mind?"

"None of this is fair. Not a single bit of it. He will never get his dreams met now."

"Maybe not one, but he has others that can still come true," Cody responds, then takes his turn in the game he's playing with the girls.

"Cody, that dream, I don't think either of us will get it. Not now. I was reading up, there is a good chance that he won't be able to…"

That news makes Cody drop his head and shake it. "Really?"

"Unfortunately, yes. There is a chance, but it's incredibly small. Unless he heals enough."

"Damn, I'm so sorry. I didn't realize."

"Thanks. But he's alive, right? And we have enough," I say, looking between my daughters.

"He is. And you do. The rest you can sort out later."

Chase

Muffled voices, hands adjusting me, incessant beeping that needs to shut the fuck up. Seriously. What is that sound?

I open my eyes and blink a few times, adjusting to the light over my head, then glance around at the nurses beside my bed.

"Mr. Canton," one says, in an annoyingly high-pitched voice. "Are you with us?"

"I am," I croak out, my throat sore and burning. "How did it go?"

"Your doctor will be by in a while to discuss with you. First, we want to get you set up in here, let your anesthetic wear off a little, and monitor your pain."

"Can I have something for my throat?"

"Is it sore?"

I nod my head. "How long did the surgery take?"

"From the time we took you down to now, just over five hours. You actual surgery was probably around four, four and a half. You had a tube down your throat, that's why it's sore."

"That long?" I try to remember how long the doctor said it should take, but my head is still foggy, and the concussion can't be helping any.

"It doesn't mean anything was wrong, that I'm aware of, he just took his time."

"Right, okay." I agree. I wish I could remember exactly how long the doctor said it would take for each scenario, and whether long was good or bad. But I can't. And she clearly isn't going to tell me. "My throat…can I have something to drink?"

"I'll bring you some ice chips for now, and then we'll see about getting you some ginger ale brought up."

"Thank you. And my family?"

She smiles, revealing the slight gap between her teeth, her green eyes bright beneath the dark makeup around her lids. "Your wife, daughters, and your brother are all waiting to come back. I'll go out and get them."

"I appreciate that." She smiles again, then turns on a squeaky heel and walks out of my room, leaving me and my broken body to think about everything alone.

At least the beeping stopped. Around the time she stepped away from the machines, in fact. That's good. Now the constant clicks of the clock hands ticking by are reminding me of time, my surgery, and the fact I really want to see my girls, but they aren't here yet.

251

It's reminding me I still have no idea what my prognosis is or whether I'll be able to walk again. It's reminding me I have no answers at all. That frustrates me to no end.

A commotion outside my room draws my attention from the clock to the door, where both my girls are walking in carrying balloons and smiling wide, with Allie and Cody behind them.

"We heard you could use some company," Allie says, "and a drink. Your nurse passed this to me in the hall and instructed me to let you take sips until you're certain you won't lose it."

"And we brought balloons!" Aubrey says excitedly.

"I see that. I love them. Thank you, girls. They're perfect to make me feel better."

Aubrey and Ava exchange proud smiles with each other, and then set the balloons up in the corner of the room, out of the way where Cody pointed them.

"I won't lose it," I finally reply to Allie. I smile at all of them, feeling the tightness in my chest start to lighten up a little just from their presence. "Have you heard from the doc yet?"

"No, he was pulled into an emergency surgery right after yours, they said he'd come in here and update us when he's able."

"You know more than me."

Allie steps around the girls and sets my drink down on the small table, then leans over and gives me a kiss. Her lips are so soft against my dry, chapped lips. They are perfection, and I want more of them.

"How do you feel?" she asks, pulling away.

"Not yet," I whisper, reaching up for her neck and guiding her back to me. I kiss her again and smile genuinely when she exhales against me.

"I've missed those."

"Darlin', you have no clue how much *I've* missed them." This time I let her pull back and then look at our little audience. Cody is by the door, smirking and shaking his head. And the girls each have their faces scrunched up and they're giggling quietly between each other.

"We get it, you two haven't kissed or—" Cody trails off, glancing down at the girls before finishing, "in a long time. But the three of us don't want to see it."

Allie laughs and rolls her eyes, and I flip him the bird, garnering another loud laugh from Allie and one from him, too.

"You'll get it one day." I shrug and then look between all of them. "I'm feeling okay. Everything is still pretty numb and drugged up from the surgery, but I'm sure the pain will come soon. I'd like to know what's going on with me."

"Me, too," Allie agrees. "But I think it'll be a while. Cody said he could take the girls to the hotel for the night, grab some pizza for dinner, and then they'll come back in the morning."

I nod my agreement slightly. "I don't know if I want them here to hear all the doc has to say anyway."

"I didn't figure you would," Cody says. "Let me know what's up when you guys find out though?"

"You'll be my first call, I promise," Allie assures him.

Ava and Aubrey stop talking when they realize we're discussing them leaving, and Ava steps closer to my bed. "Do we really have to leave?"

"You do, Pip. But you can come back tomorrow."

"I'll be really good and quiet, if you let me stay."

"You'll have more fun with Uncle Cody, and you can't stay here tonight. The hospital won't let you," Allie answers her.

Ava's head drops and her shoulders slump forward.

"Hey, come here really quick. Both of you," I say to them.

Ava and Aubrey each step up to my bed, one on each side, and I reach down for their hands.

"You two need to go. You need to get good sleep tonight. And I need to talk to my doctors and spend some time making plans with your mom. But I promise you, I will be okay, and I'll be so excited to see you in the morning. I need to know you're taken care of and happy, so I can focus on getting better. You going with Uncle Cody will help me. That's all. I'll be okay overnight. I'm not going anywhere."

"Promise?" Aubrey asks.

"I promise."

Ava looks up at me. "I love you, Daddy."

"Oh, Ava, I love you, too. You go and have fun tonight. Then you can tell me all about it tomorrow."

She nods her head and steps closer, reaching around my chest as much as she can to hug me. Then Allie holds Aubrey up to do the same thing, since she's a little too short still.

" I love you, too, Aubrey."

"Love you too, Daddy."

The girls let go of me and give Allie hugs and love goodbye, before meeting Cody at the door.

"You two, behave in this wild room," Cody suggests, jokingly. "Try to get some sleep, both of you. The girls and I will be fine and we'll have fun."

"Thanks again." I know he doesn't need the thanks, but he's showing up and being here for us big-time. He's going above and beyond to make this as easy as it can be for all of us.

"You'd do it for me." He gives us a little wave and ushers the girls out the door, calling back, "See you tomorrow."

254

As soon as Cody and the girls leave, Allie climbs up into the oversized bed, sitting beside me and leaning back, careful not to jostle me, but staying close as she can.

"How are you really feeling, Cowboy?"

"Terrified, sore, anxious…"

"Wow," she says quietly.

"What?"

She reaches for my hand and links our fingers together, brushing her thumb along the top of mine. "I just didn't think you'd be honest, but you were. You never admit fear."

"I'm broken. My head is a mess and it still hurts. My memory of what happened is still shot. All I have right now is my honesty."

"And me. You have me, too. And I'm ready to fight with you."

I bring our hands up slowly, stopping when they're at my lips, and I kiss over her knuckles. "Thank you."

"Never thank me for loving you. That's just stupid." She lays her head on my shoulder and continues to rub my hand, soothing and calming me, until my eyes get heavy and I start to nod off.

Before I'm completely out I say, "Wake me when the doctor finally shows up."

Twenty-Nine

Allie

I step out of the bathroom and look around the hall, making sure nobody sees me before I wipe my mouth and put my hand to my head. This has been the longest seven days of my life. The longest seven of all of our lives. Chase's accident was one week ago today, his surgery five days ago, and the highs and lows that have come with all he's endured—the concussion, compressed spinal cord, vertebral fracture, fusion and decompression surgery, ultimately his cauda equina diagnosis, and subsequent paralysis from it—have put me in a tailspin.

I've never been more stressed, or worried, in my life. My stomach is in knots, my heart races constantly, and food holds absolutely zero appeal to me these days. Nothing but sugar and sweets sound good. They're all I can hold down. And sleep? Well, who needs it anyway?

Now is not the time for anyone to realize my stress has me getting sick every morning or fighting back nausea every time I eat. Not with Chase's transfer to the rehab hospital next door happening in an hour. Not with my husband terrified, stressed, and upset about the fact that his prognosis means that unless, or until, he's got feeling back, can walk again, and has recovered immensely, we will likely never be able to conceive another child.

He was so brave, asking his doctor that question this morning. But I don't think either one of us was fully prepared for the answer we got. We certainly weren't ready to give up on that dream yet. We will overcome this. We can look into fostering and adopting. We can find another way...it may just take a while before we are there mentally, emotionally, or even monetarily.

Cody has the girls out at a park somewhere, playing and being kids, because they can't stay cooped up in these hospitals any longer.

The world needs to cut us a break. We've lived a very blessed life up to this point, and we are still so blessed that the bull didn't kill Chase, but we need a break. I need a break.

Thirty

Chase

How do you measure your worth as a man? Is it your ability to be a virile, reproducing individual? Is it being able to get up every day and do for your family? Is it how much you love your wife and children? Or is there some other way to measure it?

What happens when two of those three things are ripped away from you without rhyme or reason?

It's been nearly a month since my ride. It's been a month since I was the man I used to be. I'm struggling to figure out who I am, and can eventually be, again.

I work daily with a team of specialists determined to help my mind and body rehab and strengthen, with the hope that maybe, just maybe, I'll be able to walk again. I keep my fingers crossed and pray constantly that I'll at least be able to make love to my wife again, to show her in every way imaginable, when words fail, me how much she means to me. How much I love her.

Nobody can make any guarantees, though. The bull fucked me up, in more ways than my body can physically show.

"Hey, Cowboy," Allie says, interrupting my thoughts, as she walks into my room. My room, in this rehab hospital. My room, as though this is home and I'll be here forever.

"Hi, Darlin'."

"How are you doing this morning?"

We go through this every day when she gets here. I'm not sure if she's hoping one day I'll say I'm great and can walk again, or if she's just asking because she doesn't know what else to say. Because, really, what is there to say?

My life wasn't the only one changed and affected by all of this. So was hers. So were the lives of our two little girls.

"Same ol', same ol'."

"I'll take the same rather than worse," she responds cheerily, walking over and bending over my chair to kiss me.

I kiss her back then wrap my arm around her and pull her toward me, forcing her to turn her body and drop into my lap before she stumbles.

"Chase!" She giggles. "What are you doing? I don't want to hurt you."

"You aren't going to hurt me, you couldn't, and I'm having a moment and just need you close. As close as you can get."

I never would've admitted that to her before all of this, but along with a team of skilled nurses, doctors, and physical and occupational therapists, Craig also assigns a psychologist to every patient. I was opposed to talking to mine, at first. However, the thoughts I had in the first week here, how down and hopeless I got, the idea that death would've been better than all of this—I agreed to participate with mine.

Part of our process is me sharing those feelings with Allie when I have them. I can't keep it all in. The only way any of this will work is if I'm open, determined, and hopeful. According to my therapist, I can't be hopeful if I'm harboring dark and hopeless thoughts.

They've also provided resources for her, and our girls, too. Ava has struggled the most with this. She's old enough to understand how serious everything is, but still too young to fully understand the ins and outs of what we are dealing with. Aubrey, on the other hand, has adjusted fairly well so far. She gives me extra hugs, and her new favorite place to sit is on my lap, here in my chair. I can't even put a number on how many episodes I've seen of *Mia and Me* and *Sofia the First* at this point.

"I'm right here," Allie responds to me after a few moments of silence. "And I'm not going anywhere. So what's on your mind?" She wraps her arm around my neck.

"All of this," I say, indicating the room around us. "This." I grab my chair. "Who am I, Allie? How do I find purpose in all of this when everything I've ever known about myself, about being the man you and the girls need, is gone?"

"Oh, Chase," she says quietly, starting to run her fingers through my hair, playing with it because it's gotten too long and she can. "You're still the same man you've always been."

"But how? I can't provide for you three. I can't take care of you in ways a man should be able to take care of his wife. I can't give you a baby…that's the one thing I did all of this for. It's what I was working hardest for."

"I want you to listen to me, and you listen hard, okay?"

I nod my head.

"You still provide for us. You have been providing for us in more ways than just financially and physically. You set up our property, our ranch, our hands, and our business to be sustaining. You love, support, and encourage me and the girls. You don't have to be the breadwinner to provide, Chase. What if I made more than you? Huh?"

"Then you'd make more than me, it would be ours. Right? We'd combine what we each brought to the table for the better of our family?"

"Exactly. I will focus on the advertising for our business. I will make sure our animals get seen, contracted for events when you can't."

"Will you also help me and Cody run the school Cody and I want to open?"

"What school?" She stills her fingers in my hair and looks at me curiously.

"The morning all of this happened, Cody and I met with Rex, the guy we stayed with in Texas that week…"

"Okay?"

"I was thinking about calling it quits on full-time rodeo after this season, I wanted to open up a school at home. Train kids, rising riders, how to get good, be safe and smart. Then I'd rodeo some weekends, stay more local. We met with Rex to see how he started his school, what it would take."

"I—I don't even know what to say, baby." Her fingers start moving again, and I can feel her tugging on the ends of my hair.

"Tell me it's not stupid, that even with everything, we can make it work?"

"Is that really what you wanted? To stop riding full time and to start a school?"

I nod my head and hold my breath, waiting for her answer.

"We will make it work. I promise." She presses her lips to mine again, and this time neither of us pulls back.

I kiss her hard, pouring everything I possibly can into it, hoping she can feel exactly what she means to me, what her belief in me means.

Allie

His lips are firm, insistent. It's like because we can't be together in other ways, he's turned up the strength and abilities of his mouth—the unyielding power of his lips, the touch and temptation of his tongue brushing and rolling against mine—so I can feel it from my head, down to my toes, with the most feeling pooling in my core, causing a low moan to rumble from my diaphragm and up my throat, reverberating in our connected mouths.

"Chase," I whisper to him, not wanting this feeling to pass, but needing him to know one thing, "You can still take care of me, we can still be intimate, in other ways. We'll figure them out together."

"I miss being with you—touching you—taking care of you."

"I'm right here, Chase. You don't need to ask for permission, not with me. Not when it comes to touching me. That hasn't changed." I kiss him again, angling my chest toward his, holding my hands to his cheeks and swiping my tongue over his lips. "We are still us."

He exhales slowly against my lips, then I feel his hand move down my side and chest, following the path from my ribs and the side of my stomach, over my hip, and along my leg, leaving goosebumps in the wake of his touch.

"How long has it been?" he asks me, his voice a little huskier, lower than before.

"Since?"

"We…you…"

"Almost six weeks," I stutter out when his hand moves over the top of my leg to the inside, then slowly creeps up.

"You haven't since we were last together?"

I shake my head no, unable to speak now that his fingers have found their way under my shorts and stolen my voice.

"Haven't you wanted to?"

I shake my head again, managing to reply with a shaky voice, "Not without you."

"You're too good for me, Allie." He grazes the soft skin going up my leg until he reaches my panties, then he traces along the line curving around my thigh. "Kiss me again."

I do as he commands and start out with a featherlight touch of my lips to his, just like the feel of his fingers moving over me right now.

"Harder."

"I will if you will," I tease him, smiling against his upturned lips.

"There's my Darlin'."

He moves his fingers from the outer edge of my panties in, circling over my clit with a firmer pressure than before. It makes me groan against his lips, and I kiss him a little harder, doing my best to maintain the same feeling and intensity as him.

With each increase in his movements, I add a little more to the kiss.

When his fingers slip beneath my panties, my tongue seeks access to his. When he grazes over my needy clit and sends a shockwave of pleasure through me, my tongue brushes over his. With everything he gives me, I return the favor in the only way I can, until I can't anymore because he's worked me into such a frenzy that I can't keep up.

"Oh God, Chase…" I moan, dropping my head to his shoulder and speaking into his neck to muffle it a little. "That feels…"

"Feels?" he says, still moving expertly over me. I'm so wet that his touch glides along my folds and over my swollen, hypersensitive bundle with such ease they may as well be coated in oil.

"Good, so good."

"Widen your legs just a little, let me make it feel even better."

I do as he says, panting against his neck, eyes closed, just waiting to see what he's going to do for me next. With the added room, he's able to sink two fingers inside of me, stroking in and out at a steady pace, curling them in to make sure he's hitting exactly where I need him to.

It's all too much. Between the consistent rhythm of his fingers inside me, and his thumb still circling and teasing me outside, my body winds tighter and tighter, the tension building and building, until it snaps, and releases a strong, body shaking orgasm from me.

"Oh. My. God," I pant out, finally opening my eyes again, and finding him staring at me with the biggest smile he's had in the last month firmly on his lips.

"Was that as good as it looked?"

"Better, it was better. The best." I slide my hand up his neck and along his jaw, then tilt it down so I can kiss him without lifting my head from his shoulder.

"Thank you."

I blink rapidly a few times, then laugh. "You're thanking me? I'm pretty sure it should be the other way around. I was the one that got off…"

"Yeah, you did," he responds, then adds in his cocky voice, "I've always been able to get you off. I know your body. I know what you need."

"Ah, there he is."

"Who?"

"The cocky, amazing, *man* I married." I emphasize the word so he knows, no matter what has changed for him physically, he really still is every bit the man I fell in love with all those years ago.

That makes him laugh. "And that, right there, is why I'm thanking you. You gave me back something I didn't know I'd ever have again. And it means more than you can imagine."

I place another kiss on his lips. "We'll have fun exploring new things. And you know the doctor said after time and recovery, you may regain full function and feeling there. You've already come so far in just a month."

"I know. But I don't want to get my hopes up too much, the fall may be worse than the one I took a month ago if I do."

"Don't sell yourself or your strength short either, though."

He pulls his hand out from beneath my clothes, and I instantly feel the loss. It's not until I realize I haven't felt the slightest bit sick since we started fooling around does the nausea I had all morning come back with a vengeance.

"Allie?" Chase says, the playful tone in his voice moments ago gone and replaced by worry now.

"What?"

"What's wrong? You just went pale and got a weird look on your face."

"I just don't feel well. I'm okay."

Before he can answer, a knock sounds against his door, and then his nurse comes in. "Are we ready for therapy?" she asks, smiling when she sees us together. "Hi, Allie."

"Hey, Kasey."

"I think we're all set," Chase responds next, then looks at me. "Right? Or do you want to wait?"

"No, we're all set. Let's get you down there and see what you amaze us with today."

I slip off his lap and step aside, letting him wheel himself all the way to the therapy room.

Thirty-One

Chase

Another week has come and gone. Though, this past week has been the best of the last five total, yet. It's early September now, so the days aren't as brutally hot. I've gotten to spend more time outside the hospital comfortably with Allie, and the girls, when they're able to come down now that school has started again. Allie and I have found other creative ways for us to share an intimate connection together. Some of the teenage, don't get caught, element of fun and danger has helped make things even better.

In the last week, I've also regained some feeling below my waist. It's more of a prickly, pins and needles feeling that comes and goes, but my team of providers say it's a very good sign. Complete recovery can take years—if it happens at all—but to be showing this progress after just over a month is an incredible start.

I've allowed myself to get more hopeful, and I'm pushing myself as hard as I safely can to continue making progress. For myself. And for my girls.

Allie has been so worn out and tired lately. She continues to not feel well. The stress of all of this is getting to her. I know she wants to be here, but not being with the girls back home, being a normal part of their everyday lives, is hard on her.

When she walks back into my room, after walking Tatum and the girls out, she's got a can of Sprite and a sleeve of crackers in her hand.

"Tatum said she would text when they make it back to the Springs," she says tiredly. "And Cody texted and said he'll be flying in tomorrow night, and he'll be here on Monday to see you and push you."

"Good, then you should go home tomorrow for a couple of days. Get some rest, pick up the girls from school, live life as you would have last year or any other year."

"I'm not leaving you, Chase," she responds with an annoyed tone. "Now let me enjoy these crackers and Sprite before they threaten to come back up."

I watch her sip slowly and nibble carefully, taking the moments of silence to really look her over where she stands. She's lost weight, probably from all the times she's thrown up this week. She looks smaller in every way, but her chest has gotten bigger. Not just in looks, but there's definitely been more for me to fondle and play with over the last week than before. That's one memory a man could never lose, even with a head injury.

"How do those taste?" I ask her.

"They taste good, but my stomach is—" She sets her can down on the countertop and rushes into the bathroom. I follow behind her, wheeling through the door just as she bends over the porcelain and empties her stomach of everything she just put into it.

"I'm here," I say, wheeling up behind her and reaching out to pull her hair behind her neck. "I've got you, just let it out." I rub her back in lazy, soothing circles until she finishes, then I scoot back just a little so she can stand and get to the sink.

She rinses her mouth out and turns to look at me; her eyes red-rimmed and bloodshot from straining. "That was awful."

"Come here," I say, patting my lap.

She moves to my lap immediately and sits down, resting her head on my shoulder, and lifting her legs just enough so I can wheel us back into my main room.

"Allie, I need you to see a doctor. This isn't normal and I'm worried about you. You can't let your body get run down and sick just because I'm here. Please."

"I'm fine, I promise. I'm just run down. Stressed. I'll be better when we get you home."

I press a kiss to her head and wrap my arms around her. "Please?"

"Chase, I'm really fine."

I don't believe her for even a second. Not one. This isn't normal. She finally came clean about being sick every day right after my injury, but that stopped. My therapist said she was likely having an extreme reaction to the anxiety and fear over my surgery and prognosis. But that all stopped for a few weeks. Things have only gotten better for me. This feels different. I see so many differences in her.

"No, you aren't. It's been five weeks since I got hurt. I'm doing better. You were doing better. And now you aren't."

"It's been a long five—oh my God. It's been five weeks since you got hurt?"

"Five to the day."

"No... it can't have been that long, there's no way. Right? It can't be." She pushes off my lap and walks to her purse, grabbing her phone out of it.

"What can't be?" I watch her fingers move over the screen, flicking sideways with purpose. "Allie?"

"I'm late, Chase."

"For?" I ask, completely and utterly confused.

"My period..." she raises her eyes from her phone to look at me.

"How late?" I try to recall the dates, but they don't come to me. It's probably due to stress and everything she's been going through with me.

"Three weeks. I should've started just over three weeks ago." Her voice is soft, contemplative, hopeful, and yet her eyes show how hesitant she is to get excited.

"You've never been this late. Ever. Right?"

"Only when I was pregnant with the girls, and..."

I let her words sink in, and then my mind wanders back to just before she was sick. To every time we have been together over the last week.

Larger breasts.

Nausea.

Her exhaustion.

"I... You need to take a test," I say, trying to maintain some level of calmness, even as the excitement over the prospect of her being pregnant, of things working out how they should have for us for once, starts to overtake me.

"This could just be from stress, Chase. That can have such an adverse effect on a woman's cycle and hormones. You need to know that, okay?"

I nod my head, grinning wide, and wheeling across the room to her. "I get it. But you're pregnant. I know it. I'm certain of it."

"Don't... Don't say that. Not yet. Please. I couldn't take the letdown again. Not right now. We are going to act as though this is only a byproduct of stress until we know for sure. I can't go through that loss again right now. I just can't."

I wheel right up to her and lock my chair into place, then lean forward and wrap my arms around her legs, resting my head over her belly. "We won't get our hopes up," I lie. "But you need to take a test soon. I bet one of my nurses could provide one."

"No, don't say anything to anyone," she rushes out, fear lacing her every word. "Let me sip my Sprite and settle my tummy, then I'll run to the store down the street and get us a test. But I don't want to tell anyone. Not yet."

"I won't say a word then." I kiss her stomach again, then pull her back into my lap. "Drink your Sprite, and when you feel up to it, you go. We will do everything else together, okay? Positive or negative, this time you won't be alone to deal with it.

Allie

Fear. Hope. Nervousness. Excitement. And nausea, always nauseated anymore. That's what I'm feeling walking back into the hospital and heading up to Chase's room.

My stomach settled enough about an hour ago for me to be ready to leave and buy a test. So I waited until the end of day rounds with Chase's team were over—getting to hear that his latest scans are looking good, the fusion and decompression seem to be healing perfectly, and given the return of sensation to his lower half, he may get to go home within the month—before I left.

Walking out the doors, knowing how he's healing, made the weight on my shoulders lighter than they've been in a long time, but the hope and fear that I may be pregnant, or I may not be, added a different heaviness on my heart.

This time, no matter what happens, I'll have my husband by my side.

I enter his room quietly, then close the door with an audible click, making sure it's secure. "I got it," I say to him, not caring how obvious that is. My hands are shaking, my heart is racing again. I don't care that he knew where I was, it was just something to say.

"Let's do this then," he says back easily. "Do you have to pee yet?"

"I do."

"Then do your thing, and I'll be right here waiting for you."

I take my purse, and the test into the bathroom, and fumble the box opened, taking out the sticks so I can use them.

Please, God. Let this be it. Let us be getting our dreams. Please.

I send up the same silent prayer, over and over while I do what I need to, then I set the tests on a paper towel beside the sink, and walk out of the bathroom.

"Three minutes and we'll know…" I swipe my hand beneath the sanitizer dispenser and rub them together, much longer than I need to, while Chase watches me with a smirk.

"I love you."

"Why?"

He drops his head back and laughs hard. "Why do I love you? Well, because you're my best friend—don't tell Cody—for one. You are my wife. My soul mate. The mother of my children. And you're incredible, too. In every way. Are those good enough reasons?"

"They are, but why did you say it just then?"

"Because you're freaking out. You needed to hear it now, before we look at those tests and see what they say. You need to know, regardless of what they say, I love you more now than I did yesterday, and I'll love you even more tomorrow."

His words, determined and full of love and support, are my undoing. I've fought off the emotions that hit me every time I take one of these tests, every time I get my hopes up, so hard. I was determined not to go there this time. But with everything he just said to me, I can't fight them off anymore. His words were the dynamite needed to break the dam of tears I'd built up.

"Hey," he murmurs, wheeling over to me and taking my hands. "It's okay. It's going to be okay. I promise."

He turns each of my hands palms up and raises them to his mouth one at a time, kissing over them, then he glances up at the clock on the wall.

"It's time," I guess, sniffling back more tears.

"It's time."

I walk into the bathroom and grab the tests off the counter, too afraid to look at them by myself, then carry them out to him.

"And?"

"I can't…not alone…together?"

"Together," he agrees. "Let's go over to the chair so you can sit, too. Then we'll look together."

I follow behind him, hand quivering around the tests in it, then take a seat in the recliner in the corner of his room, right beside his window.

"I'll look at one, you look at the other?"

"Whatever you want us to do, we'll do it." He smiles at me and locks his chair into place right in front of me.

I hand him one test, keeping the other for myself. "On the count of three?"

"You count," he encourages me.

I nod my head and swallow hard, overwhelming nervousness forcing my nausea to ramp up again.

"One…"

"Two…"

"Three…"

We each look down at the tests in our hands, and I see it… Two bright pink lines.

I'm pregnant.

"Holy shit!" he exclaims. "We did it, baby! We really did it. We're going to have another baby!"

Relief, happiness, and even more love flood my system, forcing out a loud, happy sob from deep in my chest. "We did it," I repeat, over and over after him.

He pulls the test from my hand and sets it down, then he pulls me into his chest and holds me tight while I sob the happiest tears of my life.

After a few moments, it dawns on me that I'm shaking too hard to be the sole cause of it, and that's when I feel the wet drops of his tears on top of my head. He's crying too. The strongest, most resilient, determined man I know has been moved to tears because we have finally made another little life together.

Thirty-Two

Allie

Somehow, throwing up every day and being constantly nauseated is more than worth it now. I feel terrible. I've spent every day for the last five weeks sicker than can be. Borderline Hyperemesis Gravidarum—the pretty, scientific name—for extreme morning sickness.

I never would've imagined, walking back into Chase's room four weeks ago, that the reason I'd been so sick was because I was growing our baby. I never would've imagined when I walked into Chase's room four weeks ago that he'd be back up on his feet, moving slowly and with assistive devices for short distances on his own.

He's a miracle, according to his doctors. There is no rhyme or reason for him to be progressing this much yet. That's what they maintain, even as he breaks more and more barriers, anyway.

But I know the reason. It's this baby. He wants to be everything he can be, do everything he got to do with the girls, with Baby Canton.

He's pushed his PT and OT even harder since we found out we are expecting. He's regained muscle tone and strength, feeling has continued to return, albeit very slowly, to his feet, his legs, and at times to his saddle region. My husband has done everything in his power to become a living Superman.

He gets to come home today. After nine weeks in the hospital, our family will finally be under the same roof when we go to bed tonight.

"Mommy," Aubrey walks into the kitchen, carrying a white poster board, "when will Daddy be here?"

"Uncle Cody texted me about fifty minutes ago, saying they're on their way, so he should be here in about fifty more minutes, give or take a little. Why?"

"I want to make him a sign. Will you help me?"

"I will help you a little bit, but then I have to get out there with Ava for a while, help her with her riding. I can draw letters for you to color, is that fair?"

She grins wide and nods her head. "Very fair!"

"Let me see your poster, I'll write 'I missed you Daddy' on it. Is that okay?"

"Yes, that's perfect. Thank you, Mommy."

"You're welcome."

I spend some time drawing out bubble letters for Aubrey and then make my way out to the riding pen, where Ava and Lightning are waiting for me.

"You ready, Ava?" I rub my stomach slightly and exhale slowly, breathing through this attack of nausea until it passes.

"Yep," she says, climbing up onto Lightning's back. "Thank you for helping me learn to barrel race, even though you don't feel good."

"Well. Feel well," I correct, smirking. "You're welcome, baby. I should have offered to help you sooner, and I'm sorry I didn't."

"It's okay. I forgive you. Do you think Daddy will be surprised?"

"I think he will be so surprised. And so proud."

That sets a beaming smile on her face as she sets off to do the drills I had her start working on a few weeks ago. I can't teach her as much as I wish I could right now, given the baby and morning sickness, but we are working on things still.

While Chase knows she's been riding again, and that it was a firm shove in the right direction from Cody that made me decide to be honest and help her, Chase doesn't know how much progress she's made. He will be more than proud of the determination and dedication she's had to get here.

When we finish with the few drills she was working on, we get Lightning back into his stall and Ava inside to shower. Chase will be here anytime now, and we all want to be ready and waiting for him when he arrives.

Chase

A ride home—up our property line, overlooking our lands and the bulls out grazing—has never felt so good, ever. In just a few short minutes, I'll be arriving home from a rodeo for the very last time—at least as a participant. It's about nine weeks overdue. I'm not going to be walking through the door on my own two feet—yet. But I'll be home.

Home. For a while I didn't know if I'd ever make it back here. But here we are.

I get to be with my girls, and my baby. Nobody knows about the baby yet, not even Aubrey and Ava. After the last child we lost, we didn't want to risk pain or loss again—or split ourselves wide open with it—by telling other people so they could ask and try to find the right words for the worst possible scenario a parent can endure. So, for the last four weeks, it's been my and Allie's secret. The biggest and best secret I've ever had.

"You ready for this?" Cody asks, guiding his rental car over the road that takes us right up our drive.

"I've never been readier to be home."

"I bet. We got a ramp set up to get you in the door. I know you won't need it long, given all the progress you've made with walking, but no need to risk an accident if you're having a rough day."

"Thank you, I appreciate that. Everything you've done here and for the girls between rodeos."

"That's what family's for," he says, shrugging like it's no big deal.

"You've gone above and beyond, Cody." I look over at him. "I watched your rides from last weekend. You're getting caught leaning too much."

He laughs. "You can take the cowboy out of the rodeo…"

That draws a chuckle out of me, too. "Right? But really, you're going to win it all this year with me out of the picture now, don't risk that by getting lazy with your form."

"Yes, Coach…" he mocks. "Speaking of, Allie's really on board with the school plan?"

"She is, she said it'll bring in good money for us, and it'll keep me involved more, and she knows I need that."

"Good, because I bought a place about twenty minutes down the road, so I could be here to run shit with you, and I'd hate to have to put it back on the market before I even get settled in."

"You bought a place here?"

"I did. I'll bring you all over once I get moved. It's a good portion of land, nothing like your spread, but it'll do me just fine. Since I'll be spending most of my free time here, I didn't need all you have."

"You finally came home."

"Yea... My family needed me. And I need them, too."

"Does Allie know?"

"Nah, she'll figure it out eventually. I'm not stealing your homecoming thunder by sharing now."

"You just don't want her coming over and trying to take over decorating and unpacking."

"There is that too, yes." He looks over at me and we both laugh. This is what we needed. It's what we've always needed, our family to be together, whole. And that includes Cody.

"There it is," he says quietly.

My home is in sight, and just in front of the door I can make out three beautiful girls, waiting, our daughters holding what appear to be signs in front of them.

As we get closer and closer, I can't help but take in everything: the wraparound porch, white swing hanging off to the side of the front door, the navy house with gray window trims. This is the home Allie and I had built together. It's the place I may have taken most for granted out of every other place I've ever had before.

Rodeo was such a huge part of my identity. Rodeo was where I put my focus to give us everything we could ever want. But everything I could've ever needed was already right here. That didn't become obvious to me until I was laid up in a hospital bed, facing the prospect of losing everything but my girls and this home.

I'm not sure how I've come this far, but I won't fuck up my second shot at life. Not now. Not ever.

Cody pulls to a stop, right in front of our house, and I look out my window, smiling at Ava and Aubrey, who are both bouncing up and down on their toes. Allie takes the steps beside the new ramp down to me slowly and walks right up to my door, pulling it open and leaning in with a rushed, hard tug.

"Hey, Darlin'."

"Cowboy," she sighs, "You're home."

"And I won't leave without you again."

She smiles and steps back a little when Cody brings my chair over, before they each help me out of the car, letting me stand and shuffle with their assistance to sit in it. I can't wait for PT to start up here so I can gain more strength, so I won't need their help to shuffle or sit anymore. It starts next week, and I'm going to hit it hard. I want to be fully mobile by the time our new addition gets here.

And I will be.

I've never been more determined to rehab an injury in my life.

Once I'm seated, Allie steps between my legs, slides her fingers though my hair, and leans in to kiss me.

"Welcome home," she says, smiling against my lips.

"Thank you." I kiss her a second time then look up to the porch where the girls are waiting. "I think I'd like to say hello to my two best daughters now. Come down here, girls."

Each of their eyes light up and Ava drops her sign, bolting down the steps in a hurry, waiting just long enough for Allie to step back before she throws herself into my arms.

"I missed you so much, Daddy!" She wraps her arms around my neck and hugs me tight.

"I missed you, too. You just saw me two days ago."

"But you haven't been home in forever."

"No, I haven't."

Aubrey carries her sign down the steps with a little more caution and stops in front of us. "I made you a sign. Look!"

I turn my head to read her sign, 'I missed you Daddy', then grin. "I missed you too, Monkey."

"You aren't going to leave us again, are you?" she asks.

"No, I'm home to stay," I assure her, then open my arms to her once Ava is done hugging me. "Come here, Aubrey."

Not one to drop a sign she made on the ground to risk getting it dirty, she thrusts the sign at Cody then bounds into my arms.

"I love you so much, Daddy."

"I love you, too."

After a few moments Allie speaks up, "Shall we get Daddy inside?"

"That's a good idea," I answer.

"Need help up the ramp, or do you just want me to carry your sh—tuff in?" Cody asks.

"Good save," Allie says.

"I can make it up the ramp myself, can you and the girls take my stuff in though?"

Cody gives a little salute and guides the girls to the trunk, where they grab all my stuff and carry it up and into the house. As soon as they're gone, I pull Allie back between my legs and lean forward to press a kiss over her belly. "How do you feel today?"

"I got sick earlier, and I'm still nauseated, but okay."

"Take it easy for the rest of the day, the girls and I can take care of things." I kiss her belly again and move my hands over it, whispering, "Hello in there. I'm going to need you to take it easy on your mommy. She needs a little break. Could you do me that solid?"

Allie laughs and bends forward, pressing a kiss to the top of my head. "I don't think it works that way, Daddy."

"Sure it does. This little one and I are going to have a tight bond."

"Yeah?"

"Definitely."

"If you two are finished," Cody calls from the front door, "The girls and I are ready to dig into your welcome home cake."

Allie laughs softly against my head and mumbles, "Let's get inside before they dig in. Baby Canton and I will be okay. You can take care of us tonight."

I nod my head in agreement and start my roll up the ramp.

Cody pops his head back out, grinning wide, and adds, "Oh, and, congratulations. I can't wait to meet your newest addition. I'm happy for both of you."

He disappears back into the house, the sound of laughter from our girls following almost immediately, and I just smile at Allie. "The cat's out of the bag now."

"He won't say anything."

"No, he won't."

Once we reach the top of the porch, Allie steps behind my chair and takes hold of it. "Let me."

"I suppose you can get me over the threshold this time. But after today, when I'm back on my feet, the honor will forever be mine again."

"Deal."

She pushes me through the front door and into the living room with our family.

We've had one hell of a ride over the last nine weeks, over the last two and a half, three years. But we held on tight, and now everything has finally fallen into place. We've got our family here. We've got a baby on the way. And I've got a second chance at doing this life right with all of them.

Epilogue

Chase

"You did it, Darlin'. I am so damn proud of you." I lean over the bed and press a kiss to Allie's head as a nurse places our son on her chest. He's a seven and a half pound, brown-haired, brown-eyed little man with a set of lungs on him unlike anything I've ever heard. He's perfect.

"What should we call him?" she asks, looking down at him with tears in her eyes.

"What about Chance?" I move my hand over hers on top of his back, staring at them both in awe.

"Like a second chance?"

"Like a second chance. Like new possibilities. That's what he is for us."

"I love it. Chance…Joseph Canton," she adds, looking up at me. "After his uncle."

"We wouldn't be here without Cody, all his help, would we?"

"Not at all."

"Chance Joseph Canton," I say out loud. "I love it."

" I love you. Both of you." She kisses his fuzzy head and then lifts him off her chest, holding him up to me. "Hold your son, Daddy."

I take Chance into my arms and bring him to my chest, laying my own kisses on top of his head, and swaying side to side. "Hi, Little Man," I whisper to him. "I told your mom this months ago, but I'm going to tell you now, too. You and I are going to be best buds. I'll teach you everything there is to know about being a good man, a good husband, and most importantly, a good dad. I'll support you in whatever you want to do. And I will love you forever."

He just looks up at me, mellow and relaxed in my arms. His eyes are wide, his skin still pink, and his head a little misshapen, and I know. I can feel it with everything I have in me, he and I will be close in a way I never was with my own dad. I know, without a doubt, he will be the greatest man I will ever know when he grows up.

I've been on cloud nine for the past twenty-four hours with Allie going into labor and Chance's arrival, but the excitement I have waiting for Ava and Aubrey to get here and meet their little brother is an entirely different level of excitement.

I watch my wife feed our little boy, falling in love with her more and more by the second, until that tiny rap against the door finally comes.

"I'll let them in," I say, basically jumping up from my seat to get the door.

"Thank you," Allie says, chuckling a little. "He's about done here, so I will wrap it up for now, so they can meet him."

I nod my head and walk to the door, opening it for our girls, with Cody standing behind them. "I won't stay," he says, grinning. "You all need this time, I just didn't want them by themselves. I'll head out to the waiting room until you're ready for visitors."

"Thanks, brother," I respond, sticking my hand out to meet his, shaking it firmly.

"Congratulations! To you, too, Allie!" he calls around me, then steps back. "I'll be around." He turns down the hall and saunters off, whistling as he goes.

I turn my attention to our girls, each wearing their big sister shirts, and squat down.

"Are you two ready to meet your baby brother?"

"Yes!" they answer, in unison.

"We even washed our hands already, Uncle Cody said we should so we could hold him.

"Come with me then," I say, smiling proudly and taking their hands. I lead them into the room and toward the bed, where Allie is sitting up, holding Chance in her arms.

"Hi, my babies," Allie says to them.

"Hi, Mommy," Aubrey says, letting go of my hand to move closer to Allie.

Ava keeps her hand in mine and watches them closely, her smile growing impossibly wide. "Is that him?" she whispers.

"It is. Why don't you hop up on the bed with your mommy and Aubrey, and we'll introduce you to him?"

Ava finally lets go of my hand and moves up onto the bed next to Allie's legs, and Aubrey climbs up on the other side.

"Girls," Allie says, "This is your baby brother, Chance."

She angles Chance so the girls can see him, and Aubrey's eyes light up. "He's so cute!' she squeals excitedly.

"He's so tiny," Ava says in wonder, moving closer and reaching out for his hand.

She takes it slowly, carefully, then smiles wide. "We're going to be the best big sisters. I promise."

"We know you will," Allie responds, wiping a tear from her eyes. "Do you both want to hold him?"

Ava and Aubrey nod, and I take that as my cue to help them get situated so they get their turns with Chance. Ava gets him first, and then Aubrey, and they couldn't be more elated or in love with their little brother. Seeing all three of my kids together makes my heart burst with pride. This is everything.

Life has given us some pretty unexpected ups and downs, but today is the first day of the rest of our lives as a family of five, and we've got everything we could've ever possibly dreamed of having.

The End

Thank you, readers, for taking the time to read my very first book baby, and for taking a chance on me. I hope you loved Chase, Allie, and their girls as much as I do. They took hold of my heart, and soul, and I couldn't have dreamed of a better couple to start my writing journey off with. If you enjoyed them, and their story, I hope you might leave a review to share your thoughts. You can do so here on Amazon, and also on Goodreads. I would greatly appreciate *any* thoughts you may have about "Hold on Tight".

And, if you enjoyed their story and you want to read more from me, I hope you will also add book 2 in the Cowboys & Angels series to your Goodreads TBR today. Book 2 will feature Cody, and the woman that may just change his mind, and his ways, when it comes to one-night stands and his aversion to commitment.

Other Works

More than Winning (A Cowboys & Angels Short Prequel) — Available Now

Never Let Go (Cowboys & Angels, #2) — Coming Fall 2019

Acknowledgements

I don't even know where to start with my acknowledgements. The list of people that have helped and encouraged me along the way is endless and words will never be enough to express my gratitude to each and every person that has helped me. But I'll do my best.

First and foremost, I have to thank my parents. Since I was a little girl, all three of you have done everything in your power to give me everything I could ever need, or want, in life. You have supported, defended, and encouraged me with a fierceness that nobody could ever possibly match. You've held my hand, held me, and been there through every single high, every single low, and all the tears shed over everything good and bad, no matter what. The second I told you all that I wanted to write this book, that I was really going to do it, you made sure I knew that no matter what you were all in my corner. You've read my words, you've listened to me talk about plotting, characters, and writers block with an understanding and love that has meant the world to me. I wouldn't be me, or have the courage to follow this dream through, if it weren't for you. I love you all so much. Thank you.

And my grandparents—thank you. Thank you for taking an interest in my book. Thank you for asking questions and being as excited for me as I am. Thank you for praying for me endlessly and loving me always.

Anjelica Grace

The words in this may not be your cup of tea, I'm sorry. But even with that, you have been my cheerleaders every step of the way. I love you more than you could ever possibly imagine. And I'll see what I can do about fading some of those pesky inappropriate scenes to black, just for you, so that you can read and enjoy what you have so enthusiastically supported from day one, too.

Next, I have to thank my beta readers, because if it weren't for you all agreeing in the start to take a chance on my story, I wouldn't have been able to finish the process. Your support and advice, and your love for Chase and Allie, meant everything. And it made all the difference. So; Bailey, Rachel, Karlyn, Stacie, Brooke, and Joanne thank you all SO MUCH! I hope you're all ready for Cody's story, because I'm going to need you all again soon!

Where my Betas were absolutely crucial to making sure the story was worth sharing with the world, my editor, Karen Hrdlicka, was the absolute best and most important part of the writing process. If not for you, Karen, my story would be full of repetitive words, missing punctuation, and wouldn't be even a quarter as pretty and polished as it is. And as a bonus, I'm grateful to have you as a great friend and someone I've come to absolutely adore and value. Thank you for helping me. Thank you for being my Editor Extraordinaire. And thank you for making me a better writer.

To all of you, my readers, again, thank you. I wrote this with hopes that even a handful of you would be taken in by this story. I wrote this hoping that maybe, just maybe, my words could provide an escape for you like so many incredible authors have done for me. Your reading and supporting me and these characters is what makes me want to keep on writing. You are the best!

Sami, Sami, Sami... My Bestie of over fifteen years now. I wouldn't have been able to accomplish this, or so many things in my life, if not for you. You have been there on my best, and very worst days, and you've never failed to take on my joys and sorrows as your own. Thank you for being my rock, and my best friend always. You seem to know just when I need a text, a visit, or a random snap of my Sweet Pea and Little One to cheer up. Thank you for always being there. Thank you for believing in me. I love you.

And last, but certainly not least, my best friend part two... My HB... My inspiration... Em. You're the person I look up to most with writing, who has led the way for me, and given me so much help and advice. YOU are the reason that this book ever got written to begin with. My writing story starts with you, and your asking me to write a Christmas short for an anthology you were putting together. I never would've imagined one short story would turn into all of this, and it wouldn't have happened without you. So, thank you. Thank you for giving me the push I needed. Thank you for all the work you put into making *Hold on Tight* what it is, too; from teasers, to being my Hulk Beta, to formatting all of this, and reminding me to breathe when I freak out because holy shit, I wrote a book, you have been there every step of the way. I couldn't have done it without you. Chase and Allie are because of you. And words couldn't possibly convey what your friendship—first and foremost—or your encouragement and help mean to me. I read/write/smile you always. You're stuck with me.

Stalk Anjelica

You can find her on Facebook, Goodreads, Instagram, Bookbub, and Twitter.

www.anjelicagraceautho.wixsite.com/authoranjelicagrace

About Anjelica

Growing up, writing was always a passion, and I always dabbled in words—be them in my journal, writing short stories, or even starting my first (unfinished) novel in college—but I never shared them. Now, I'm doing what I love, and I'm ready to share my words with anyone kind enough to read them.

I was born and raised about twenty minutes north of Denver, Colorado. School and soccer were always my primary focus growing up, but I read as many books as I could, and wrote short stories as often as humanly possible outside of those obligations. I stayed local for college and majored in Biology, with every intention of going to medical school. That never panned out. I realized what I want most out of life is to one day have a family and children of my own, and to be able to write a book. Multiple books, if I'm honest. And becoming a doctor wouldn't have left much time for either of those things. Now, I'm working on finishing more school to follow my new career dream, and writing books in my spare time.

Manufactured by Amazon.ca
Bolton, ON

39729206R00173